Summit's Shadow

Heather Werner

Launch Point Press
Portland, Oregon

A Launch Point Press Trade Paperback Original

Summit's Shadow is a work of fiction. Names, characters, places, and incidents are either the product of the author's imagination or are used in a fictitious manner. Any resemblance to actual persons living or dead, business establishments, events, or locales is entirely coincidental. Internet references contained in this work are current at the time of publication, but Launch Point Press cannot guarantee that a specific reference will continue or be maintained in any respect.

All rights reserved. Launch Point Press supports copyright which enables creativity, free speech, and fairness. Thank you for buying the authorized version of this book and for following copyright laws by not using or reproducing any part of this book in any manner whatsoever, including Internet usage, without written permission from Launch Point Press, except in the form of brief quotations embodied in critical reviews and articles. Your cooperation and respect support authors and allow Launch Point Press to continue publishing the books you want to read.

Copyright © 2024 Heather Werner

ISBN: 978-1-63304-067-0
Ebook: 978-1-63304-066-3

First Printing: 2024

Editing: Jane Cuthbertson, Anne Battis
Cover: KLR Covers

www.LaunchPointPress.com

Praise for Summit's Shadow

2025 GCLS Goldie winner for Paranormal/Occult/Horror

2024 Lesfic Bard Award winner for Action-Adventure

"I loved this fast-paced, nail-biting thriller!" -Kara at Goodreads

"I'm always up for a girls trip! This was a fun and immersive read, I read it in one fell swoop on a 4 hour flight. The descriptive writing makes you feel like you are climbing the mountain with the ladies. And the message at the end will make any nature lover nod in enthusiastic agreement. I'm looking forward to more novels by Heather Werner!" -Kay Jay at Amazon

"This is one of those stories you start reading, become intrigued by, and by the end realise it is going to be one that you'll never forget." -LESBIReviewed

About Summit's Shadow

Tana Walker has only ever felt at home in the mountains. So when her college roommates plan to reunite for a girls' trip, she suggests an Alaskan expedition to attempt the treacherous Mount Torket. At over eighteen thousand feet tall and crisscrossed with crevasses, avalanche zones, and dangerous pitches, Mount Torket is a climber's dream—or nightmare. Unbeknownst to her teammates, Tana has summited Torket once before, nearly two decades ago. The day her entire family vanished from its icy peak without a trace.

The higher they climb, the more the women suspect they're not alone. Footsteps and shadows stalk their every move, growing bolder and more vicious as the days wear on. When a slew of near-death accidents befall their journey, Tana realizes that Torket is no typical mountain—and her parents' disappearance was anything but ordinary.

As Tana's quest for closure morphs into a fight for survival, she and her friends must band together, even as Torket threatens to rip them apart. Otherwise, they'll end up as one more batch of souls lost to the dark and hungry mountain.

Acknowledgments

No book is a solitary endeavor, and I am beyond grateful to all those who helped bring this one to life.

First and foremost, thank you to the team at Launch Point Press for believing in this story, especially Jodi Zeramby, for managing every detail of this lengthy process, from initial contracts to the final pass of a proofreader. Jane Cuthbertson's edits were invaluable, and her gift for coaxing depth and love from the characters has made this a richer story.

My fellow Dark Scribblers, Katie, Kara, Glen, and Chris, thank you once again for your kind words, sharp critiques, and, above all, your friendship throughout this journey. This past decade of writing alongside you all has been a great joy.

Nickel and Lara, thank you for your camaraderie on the trails and your notes on how best to portray the technical details of our beloved sport. Thanks to the many climbers with whom I've shared a rope, a tent, or a summit. There is nothing in life that compares to staring down a storm beside you. Your strengths, your flaws, and your hearts are written into these characters.

Chris, climbing and writing may be foreign worlds to you, but you embrace the unknown with aplomb. Thank you for your steady love and support through every adventure.

And finally, thank you to all the women who broke trail before me: my mother and my Girl Scout leaders, who pushed me to my first summits, my Capen Hill camp counselors, who taught me to care deeply for our planet, and the many teachers who opened my eyes to a beautiful, exciting world far beyond my small town.

As we climb, may we continue to build cairns for our younger sisters to follow.

Dedication

To Juanita, for teaching us to never pick the lycopodium.

Chapter One

A few miles beyond the swell of Anchorage, Alaska, a small Toyota wound its way north, the three women inside gazing at the surrounding splendor.

Tana Walker sat behind the wheel, her wide eyes swallowing up the landscape of her earliest memories, searching for any shred of familiarity—the lakes where her father had taken her fishing or the rounded hills her mother had encouraged her to climb, even when her skinny legs trembled with fatigue.

Alaska had changed in the twenty years since she'd left. The buildings were taller than she remembered, the suburbs stretching into what was previously untouched land. Even the natural landmarks seemed foreign, the hills and valleys she'd traversed with her parents unfamiliar to her adult eyes.

As the last traces of suburbia faded into the rearview mirror, the world around them unfolded into lush greens and radiant blues. Pristine, snow-fed lakes sparkled in the late April sunshine, their glittering surfaces nearly blinding. Mounds of unmelted snow dotted the landscape, growing in size as they spread up the surrounding hillsides. In the distance, snowcapped peaks rose above the valley like knife blades. Hidden just beyond their view, the deadly Mount Torket awaited their arrival.

"Not too shabby, Tana." In the passenger seat, Tana's college roommate, Misty Coleman, was gazing at the crystal clear river rushing alongside the highway. "If I lived up here, you'd never be able to kick me out. How could your parents leave this all behind?"

It was a question that had plagued Tana ever since her adoptive parents began showing her photos of their first home together, memories that had grown foggy since they'd moved. To her childhood eyes, the landscapes seemed impossibly fairy-tale-like, mystical worlds with breathtaking views and magic around every corner. She begged them to consider moving back until they finally caved and told her the truth.

She was the reason they had left Alaska.

"It was because of me," Tana replied, her gut twisting with guilt. "This was their dream, but they couldn't make it happen with a kid. One too many things to worry about."

Misty nodded sagely. "Oh, I get it, trust me. Being a stay-at-home mom, they drive me to drink. Homesteading on top of that? I'd have a complete meltdown within a week."

Though Tana couldn't have been more than six or seven at the time, her memory of the day was clear. The Subaru was full-to-bursting with clothes and household supplies, one door ajar for her to climb inside and make a nest among the chaos. She'd been unable to force herself into the car, sensing that if she left, she'd never be able to return. That a door would be closed to her forever.

"Look out!"

Tana snapped out of her reverie, gasping at the sight of a young moose trundling across the road. She slammed on the brakes, the car's back end fishtailing on the frosty blacktop. She winced at the oncoming collision as the car careened closer and closer to the animal—letting out an abrupt exhale as the Toyota screeched to a halt mere inches from the moose's flank. The young bull gave a yelp of surprise, then leaped into the surrounding brush.

"Everyone okay?" Tana turned to Misty, who nodded her assent. She spun around to the back seat. "Brynn, you good?"

Misty's younger sister, Brynn Lansing, was doing her best to mop splashes of coffee from her lap. "Fine," she grumbled, dabbing at her skinny jeans with a napkin. "Hope you all like the smell of Irish Cream because that's my perfume for the rest of the day."

"It'll pair nicely with the aroma of French fries," Tana joked. She'd offered her car for the five-day road trip from Seattle to Alaska, a generosity now tinged with regret. The amount of fast food wrappers, stray pickles, and loose fries that had worked their way into crevices was disconcerting. She'd be lucky if she ever got the stench out.

"The moose really come out of nowhere, huh?" Misty asked, pulling her spilled purse from the floor. A lock of wavy red hair had flopped over her forehead, and she impatiently swiped it back behind her ears. "I kind of thought that was a joke, like saying how the dingoes will get your baby in Australia. Now that we're off the highway, let's slow down a bit, okay?"

Though her tone was friendly, Tana sensed the rebuke in it. Misty had always been the mother figure of their group. Even back in college, when Tana and Calla drank themselves silly, it was Misty who led them back to the dorm, forced them to swallow some Tylenol and water, and tucked them into bed. It was no wonder that out of the three of them, she was the only one who'd married and had children. She was practically born for the role.

Brynn reached between the front seats, dropping a wad of coffee-stained napkins into her sister's lap. Misty sighed but dutifully added them to the trash pile.

"Wish I'd had my phone out," Brynn said. "I've never seen a moose in real life. Even when I climbed Denali—nothing. The guide company had all these pics of wildlife. Moose, bears, wolves, you name it. We didn't see a damn thing."

"Oh, that reminds me"—Misty turned to her sister—"unless you want a long, drawn-out lecture from Calla, try not to mention your guided trips. She has certain...*feelings* on those."

Tana laughed. Calla Tetreault was an extremist in every sense of the word. If a climb didn't leave her in fear for her life, then it hardly counted as a real adventure. Guided climbs, especially those that catered to rich, pampered tourists, offended her down to her core. When Tana had briefly considered climbing Kilimanjaro, an excursion known for its over-enthusiastic use of guides and porters, the weeks-long ranting lecture from Calla had finally convinced her to give it up as a lost cause.

With an agitated huff, Brynn flipped her blond hair back over her shoulders. "It's not like Denali is a cakewalk, even with a guide. And with Everest in a couple years, I'll have the Seven Summits done by the time I'm twenty-five. How many people can say that? The guides are only there to make sure we don't kill ourselves."

Misty and Tana exchanged a glance, their grins widening identically. The Seven Summits, a popular mountaineering challenge to climb the highest peak on every continent, was a topic Calla never grew tired of ridiculing.

"You want to take this one?" Misty asked.

As Tana found Brynn's eyes in the rearview mirror, she recognized the look on the younger woman's face as her own upon first meeting Calla. Calla was headstrong, brave, and assertive, everything Tana wished she could have been back in college, or hell, even now. When the three of them discovered they all shared a love of the mountains, Tana had trotted out her list of accomplishments—peak bagging in Colorado, backpacking in the Whites, rock climbing in the canyons of Utah. Her pride deflated like a balloon when Calla laughed, her smile brightening up an already beautiful face, and she promised to take Tana on a real adventure, none of that kiddie stuff. Though Calla hadn't meant to hurt her feelings, Tana couldn't help but feel like all of her accomplishments, and by extension, herself, were a joke.

Her cheeks flushed at the humiliating memory. She'd always felt a tad dull, a bit listless. She tended to blame it on being adopted, as though being disconnected from her roots had dampened her glow like a transplanted tree with yellowing leaves. Staring at her reflection in the mirror left Tana with the impression of a photograph faded by time. Mousy, mid-length locks framed a pale, drab face. Her eyes were a grayish brown, her lips only a hint pinker than the skin surrounding them. Teachers, boys, and even her parents occasionally seemed to look right through her, her bland features rendering her invisible. By now, she'd mostly gotten used to being overlooked, but the sensation was amplified when standing next to someone as vibrant as Calla.

"Don't take it personally," she told Brynn. "Some of these hardcore climbers like Calla think the popular peaks are nothing but tourist traps. It's snobbery, plain and simple. But if you ask them, they think they're fighting the good fight, that it's some righteous cause, keeping mountain climbing pure." She rolled her eyes. "And to them, the Seven Summits is the worst possible offense because not only is it a tourist trap, it's reserved for rich tourists."

"I worked my ass off to save up—"

"I know you did," Tana interrupted. "Misty told me you've been working double shifts for years. It's impressive as hell, and I give you all the credit in the world. But when Calla gets an idea in her head, it's hard to shake it loose. She decided a long time ago that those people weren't her crowd. The whole thing's a joke to her."

"Even Everest?" Brynn asked.

It pained Tana to see the young woman's features deflating, but she nodded. "*Especially* Everest." At the sound of a snicker, she turned to see Misty fighting back laughter.

"Remember what she used to call it?" Misty asked.

In unison, the two women recited, "A shit-covered monument to frail egos," before dissolving into laughter.

In the back seat, Brynn slumped against the window, a scowl plastered across her face.

They pulled onto a dirt road, the loose pebbles clunking against the underside of Tana's car. The Toyota had been a practical choice, reliable, and a good bargain. Even the color, a plain, grayish tan, was chosen for its function, as the dirt and dust weren't as noticeable on the neutral hue. But as they drew closer to Calla's home nestled in the woods, Tana felt a deepening sense of inadequacy. Everything about her was painfully basic, from her flat, lifeless hair to her nondescript sedan. Misty had a loving family—a husband and twin boys, recently out of diapers. Only a few years out of college, Brynn was crushing impressive peaks around the globe, and corporate sponsorships were surely only a matter of time. And Calla was...well, Calla. Surviving in the wilds of Alaska with only her wits and grit, much like Tana's parents had once attempted. Except Calla made it look easy. Closing the gap to thirty, what the hell did Tana have to show for herself?

"Looks like this is the place," Misty said, glancing from her GPS to the log cabin before them. "I thought we were still on a road, but I guess she's got her own private driveway."

"Dug it out herself," Tana replied, unable to keep the note of envy from her voice. "She sent me photos a while back. Said she wanted this place to be completely hers. Every detail, even down to the driveway."

"Of course she did. Once an overachiever, always an overachiever."

The cabin was like something out of a home and garden magazine, all gabled peaks and intricate wood-laying. Even as a college student, Calla had waxed poetic about her dream house, focusing on self-sufficiency and solitude. And sure enough, the roof was a tightly-knit pattern of solar panels. Raised planters surrounded the house, waiting for the last frost to recede. To combat the unforgiving climate, a massive greenhouse stood adjacent to the cabin, and rows of dormant apple trees lined the walkway to the front porch.

Tana slowed the car to a crawl, parking alongside the house. The three women had only begun to disembark when a figure came barreling out the door to greet them.

"Tana! Misty! You made it!" Before Tana could even turn, she was engulfed in a bear hug, Calla's thin yet ironlike arms embracing her fully. Calla pulled back and flashed one of her megawatt smiles. Lithe and tan, with high cheekbones and nearly coal-black eyes, she could have been a model in another life. One where danger hadn't beckoned to her with its siren song.

"And you must be Brynn. Misty's told me all about you. Hell of a climber, eh? I saw the pics of you on Aconcagua. Still smiling at twenty-three thousand feet. Our little eighteen thousander will be a piece of cake. Once we get our bags sorted, you'll have to tell me all about your trips."

Brynn looked to Misty for support before eliciting a jerky half nod, half shrug. With a laugh, Calla threw an arm around her and led her toward the stairs. "Shy, huh? Don't worry, we'll get a little liquor in you, and the stories will flow."

"Cal, this place is amazing," Misty gushed, grabbing her duffel and following their lead. "How much of this is yours?" She gestured at the surrounding land.

"Thirty acres," Calla called back. "Tons of wildlife as you head out back. If there's time after the climb, I'll take you deer hunting. They're a little lean this time of year, but you haven't lived until you've had my famous venison sausage. I've been selling them to the local diner for about a year now."

Misty caught Tana's eye, shaking her head in bemusement. Tana played along, rolling her eyes, but secretly, she couldn't quell the jealousy that churned through her. Though her lineage was a mystery, she took some pride in presumably originating from Alaska, and it was unsettling to see someone take to her home state much more naturally than she ever could. Or, certainly, her parents ever had.

Jogging up the front steps, Misty gazed at the intricate placing of logs in the entryway. They formed a geometric arc, shading visitors from the elements. Tana could barely hear her ask, "Did you really design all this..." before she disappeared across the threshold, leaving Tana alone beside the car.

The sudden quiet was a relief after days spent cooped up in the car with her friends, and Tana closed her eyes, relishing the moment. The cold Alaskan breeze kissed her lungs, filling them with the air she'd last breathed as a child, and yet, somehow, it still felt like home. Scent is the longest-lasting memory, and standing among the pines and hemlock, breathing in their sharp spice, she believed it.

Her parents had been wrong to say there was nothing left to find. Even if all physical traces of her biological family were gone—a thought she tried not to entertain—returning to her roots might be enough to jog her memories. She'd give anything to learn how they had disappeared. Even something as simple as remembering their faces would be worth the entire journey.

At the sound of footsteps, she spun around, startled out of her daydream. She opened her eyes to see...nothing. Twilight was falling, and the surrounding woods were a patchwork of shadows. She held her breath, listening for the sound, wondering if she'd imagined it. She heard her friends' voices drifting out of the cabin, jabbering away about the inner architecture.

The crunch of someone—or something—on gravel cut through the air, closer now.

"Hello?" she called. "Who's out there?" This far into the woods, a lost hiker was unlikely. The thought of a bear moving in for the kill spurred her into action. "Scat. Shoo," she yelled, stomping the ground for emphasis. "Get out of here."

Wait...was it brown or black bears that you could scare off with loud noises? It'd been years since she'd attended a survival course. Her heart hammered against her ribs. She grabbed her duffel from the car and slammed the trunk shut.

The steps were louder now, moving quickly. The shadows seemed to flutter and dance, obscuring whatever was rushing toward her. With a yelp of fear, she ran from the car, charging up the front steps—and straight into Calla.

"Hey, are you all ri—"

"Bear! Get inside!" Tana grabbed Calla's arm and dragged her through the entryway.

"Oh shit, you sure?" At Tana's panicked nod, Calla ran to the coat closet, yanked out a shotgun, and raced for the front door, her three guests trailing behind.

"Don't kill it," Brynn shouted.

"Only if I have to," Calla promised before charging out into the open air. "Turn on the lights," she yelled over her shoulder.

Tana fumbled for the switch in the entryway, her fingers playing over the knobs until the front yard was ablaze with light. Misty pushed past her, jumping to the ground beside Calla, a kitchen knife held aloft in one hand. The two women spun on the spot, searching for any sign of the beast.

"You see anything?" Brynn called, only to have Misty shush her with an impatient wave. They stood quietly, their eyes darting among the shadows.

"Nothing out here," Calla said, lowering her weapon. "You sure it was a bear? I don't see any tracks."

Unable to keep the defensive tone from her voice, Tana replied, "I definitely heard something big coming straight at me. I didn't imagine it."

"Maybe it was a moose or an elk or something," Misty offered, always the peacekeeper. "And it ran off when we started yelling."

"Maybe." Tana shoved her hands into her jeans pockets, attempting to hide their slight trembling from Calla's gaze. Only five minutes into her visit, and she'd already made a fool of herself. But she knew she hadn't imagined those footsteps. The sound of them circling closer was fresh in her mind.

Calla glanced at Misty's weapon and snickered. "What the hell were you gonna do with that?"

"I wasn't going to let you fight a bear by yourself!" Misty shot back. "You could've been killed."

"Misty, just to be very clear, if we're ever close enough to a grizzly to stab it, you can bet your ass we're already dead." She shouldered the shotgun, glancing at the two figures silhouetted in the doorway. "I think that's enough excitement for one night. Let's get you ladies settled in."

Chapter Two

Piles of gear littered the living room, and the neon-hued climbing ropes and jackets added a festive touch to the spartan, minimalist decor. Though Calla had an obvious knack for architecture, it appeared her talents didn't extend to furnishings. Either that or, like most mundane pursuits in life, she'd decided it simply wasn't worth her time.

The four women pawed through their duffels, comparing their ultralight stoves and mess kits, deciding which items would make the cut. Mount Torket required a hefty amount of gear, and any way to lighten their packs was an avenue worth exploring. Misty sorted through their medical supplies, compiling a single first aid kit without unnecessary duplicates, while Tana arranged their packets of freeze-dried food by calorie count. With a chuckle, she tossed aside a low-fat, low-calorie package of dehydrated peach cobbler, a waste of precious space.

Misty held up two bottles of pills, giving them a quick shake. "Diamox and Dex, just in case. I'll take a Diamox tonight before bed. Anyone want one? Or if you have your own, I can toss it in the kit for you."

Tana held out her hand. "Not a bad idea to get started now. I've had zero acclimatization, and the older I get, it feels like the altitude hits me lower and lower. I never used to feel anything, even on fourteeners. Now I get headaches at ten thousand if I don't pop a pill."

Misty tipped a pill into Tana's hand, then held out the bottle to Brynn, who shook her head.

"I never take those."

Misty rolled her eyes. "Of course not." She turned to Calla. "And you wouldn't take medicine if you were on top of Everest, succumbing to HACE, with your swollen brain oozing down your spinal column." She popped the two bottles into the first aid kit, shaking her head in mock disgust.

Calla let out a bark of laughter. "In that very specific case, I'd take the drugs. Only so I don't die on that trash heap."

"I don't think I've ever seen you get sick," Tana said. "Even in those videos you sent from Manaslu, you seemed totally fine. Frost nipped to hell but completely lucid, no trouble breathing."

"As much as I hate to ruin the illusion, I was definitely feeling it," Calla said. "We weren't quite in the Death Zone in that video I sent you, but pretty close. I think we switched to oxygen the next day. So maybe around twenty-four thousand feet? My head was killing me, I couldn't eat, felt like I was doing calculus when I tied up my boots."

"So even the great Calla Tetreault has her limits," Misty said. "Sometimes it's good to know you're still one of us mortals."

"I've been lucky," Calla said. "Never had any major issues, even in the Himalayas. Do you know there are actually cases of people getting hypoxia below ten thousand feet?" She smirked. "Can you imagine?"

Misty sighed. "You shouldn't laugh, Cal. We're all getting older. The altitude could start hitting us a lot harder. I'm actually a little nervous about this climb."

"Please. Chimborazo was only a couple years ago. The three of us handled twenty thousand without a problem. We'll be fine."

Tana held her tongue, remembering how sluggish and nauseous she felt standing on the summit, Misty in the same sorry state. If Calla hadn't been there to carry their backpacks and cheer them toward the finish line, they both would've likely turned back before the final push to the peak.

With the medical kit sorted, Misty redirected her attention to her rain layers, rolling them into a tight bundle and stuffing them into the front pocket of her backpack for easy access. "You all have no idea how much I needed this," she said, reaching for her wine glass and taking a swig. An empty bottle of Merlot lay among the debris, a gift from Misty that had been well-received despite the half-hearted objections about an early start tomorrow. "Being with people who don't rely on me for everything. I love my kids, but Christ, they're hopeless."

"They're toddlers," Tana replied.

Misty shrugged. "Hopeless toddlers."

"Wait 'til you and Todd start taking them backpacking," Tana said. "You haven't seen hopeless until you've pushed a kid past their limits, and you're ten miles from the car."

Misty raised an eyebrow. "You know from experience?"

"My parents love telling that story. Me, clinging to a rock, screaming bloody murder and refusing to take another step. Strangers intervening because they thought I was being kidnapped."

She chuckled, letting her gaze fall over her surroundings. The stone fireplace in the corner—no doubt Calla's own handiwork— glowed with cozy embers, casting an orange tint on the room.

The reflection glittered on the wine bottle, their own makeshift disco ball.

She breathed in the intoxicating smell of burning wood and earth-stained tents, allowing the familiar sense of contentedness to spread through her, a once-per-year treat reserved for these outings with the two women who knew her best. The one respite from her ordinary, lonely life back in Seattle. She struggled to remember the last time she'd done anything remotely social—drinks with coworkers, trivia nights, even getting suckered into an Herbalife party, and nothing came to mind. Had she really spent an entire year secluding herself? She knew instinctively that she ought to feel some emotional reaction to this revelation—sadness and shame came to mind—and yet, she felt nothing. Only a detached acceptance of the situation.

Misty's voice pulled her from her thoughts. "How are your parents? It feels like I haven't seen them in forever. Seven, eight years, at least."

Tana gave her head a little shake, bringing herself back to the present. "They're doing all right. I'd love to buy them a trip up here someday. Money's tight now, but I know how much they loved living in Alaska. My mom had a little greenhouse set up, and my dad built a meditation yurt."

Misty laughed. "Your parents were such crunchies."

"Still are. As crunchy as you can be in Seattle, anyway. They'd give anything to be back in the woods."

The thought of her parents drew a pained wince, their looks of hurt still fresh in her mind. They'd attempted to mask their emotions, although their tight smiles and somber eyes told Tana she'd struck a nerve with the announcement of her latest travel plans. With strained voices, they asked her why she wanted to return to Alaska when she could remember so little of it. There was nothing left to find, they reminded her.

Though she tried to deny it, their words rang true. The state had already combed through all missing persons reports and knocked on every door in the surrounding mountain communities. Every backpacker was harangued at the surrounding trailheads, hoping that someone, anyone, had a clue where Tana had stumbled in from. After months of fruitless searching and then another year of paperwork, the young couple who found her in the woods became her adoptive family—her mother and father.

Tana wished she could assuage their fears, the idea that she was searching for her biological family because they weren't enough. She'd certainly told them time and time again, making her wonder if this was something all adoptive parents felt. She'd hit the jackpot with her mother and father, two doting former hippies who had instilled a love of nature in their daughter. Her quest was one born of curiosity, a sense that there was still something in her birth state calling out to her. Certainly not an attempt to replace them.

Tana continued. "They were actually doing all right before I came along. My mom was apparently great at fishing, and my dad set up a barter network with the neighbors. Their own little cash-free libertarian commune. But with a kid, everything that used to be fun and romantic turns into a massive pain in the ass." She sighed. "They would've loved to do what Calla's doing. I'm pretty sure my mom wants to be Calla."

Misty snorted, gesturing across the room. "She can join the club."

In the far corner, Brynn had cozied up to Calla. Their tents rolled out in front of them. Though Brynn was only four years younger than their college trio, the blind hope on her face that she might be able to impress Calla skewed her appearance a decade younger. It was a hope that Tana painfully remembered as one of her own before realizing that impressing someone like Calla was nearly impossible. Calla ran a hand over the ultra-thin fabric of Brynn's tent, her lips curling into a grimace.

"It's only two pounds," Brynn said. "We're going to be out there for a week—why carry more weight than we absolutely need to? What's yours weigh?"

"Seven pounds," Calla answered.

"Seven? That's literally insane. You and Tana can take what you want, but Misty and I should really take mine."

"Can yours stand up to a blizzard?" Calla's voice had dropped low, a tactic she used to convey seriousness, which had the added effect of making her all the more intimidating. "How about gale force winds? Hell, how about a pebble?" She ran her fingers across the flimsy floor of Brynn's tent. "One slice, and you're sitting in snow for a week. Take my extra one, all right? If you can't carry it, I already factored it into my pack weight. I'm sitting pretty at sixty pounds."

At this, Brynn's face dropped so comically that Tana nearly choked on a sip of Merlot. "Sixty pounds? That's gotta be, like, half your weight!"

Tana and Misty exchanged a glance. Brynn had unwittingly walked into one of Calla's favorite talking points. Her dark eyes glittered as she asked, "How'd you ever manage to get up Aconcagua without hauling that much? Or Vinson? You're one of those Seven Summiters, right? You need serious amounts of gear for some of those peaks."

"I...uh...I mean...we had...."

Misty cut in. "The guides help her out, and she hires porters, Calla. Don't be an ass, you know that."

"Porters," Calla repeated, pausing to let the point drag out. "Let me get this straight. You travel around the world, bagging all these trophy peaks so you can post your summit photo online. Meanwhile, some poor SOB makes five dollars a day to haul your junk up the mountain?"

She leaned in close, her face inches from Brynn's, which was now burning bright red. "Don't you want to sink or swim based on your own merit? Stand on a summit that you earned yourself? What kind of victory is it if someone else does all the hard work for you? That's what this trip up Torket is all about—proving ourselves. Denali'll have a thousand climbers this year, with guides, porters, med tents, you name it. And why?"

Tana mouthed, "Because it's famous," to Misty.

"Only because it's famous," Calla said. "When there's a more beautiful, more challenging, more remote peak only an hour away. One that would require some actual guts. Because where we're going, no one will find us if we disappear."

Tana muttered, "Actually, we have a satellite phone and tracker."

Calla ignored her. "And if you fall, forget it, you're toast."

"Hardly. I'm a trained nurse," Misty said. "Plus, we've all had rescue training."

Calla continued, unfazed. "Even the locals are scared of this mountain. They avoid it like the plague."

At this, Misty perked up. "Wait a sec, this isn't some sacred place like Uluru, is it? We can't go up there if it's against some Native religious beliefs or something."

Tana shook her head. Mount Torket had been her idea. She knew the mountain wasn't unpopular for spiritual reasons but for safety concerns. Torket was technically demanding, a mishmash of crevasses and avalanche zones with steep pitches that could easily lead to a climber's death.

Few climbers attempted it, and even fewer returned to civilization. The rate of climbers who simply vanished while attempting the summit was staggering. While the National Park Service hadn't closed off the mountain to the public, any visitors to the Mount Torket information page were hit with an onslaught of warnings, the message clear: Torket wasn't a challenge to be taken lightly.

While the adventure alone was enough of a draw for the other three, Tana had more personal reasons to venture off the beaten path: Mount Torket was where her parents had found her twenty years ago, a ghost in the swirling snowy mists. Her memories of life before that day had disappeared, just like her family. Her adoptive parents, seeking to retain some of her presumed heritage, had named her Tanaraq, an Inuit name meaning granddaughter of the tundra. While she appreciated the gesture, it only served to remind her that she had no real ancestral line. She'd been born of the snow and ice.

Her biological parents were nowhere to be found, no matter how many threadbare leads she followed. The years stretched into decades, and it was only now, as she was drifting into solid adulthood without a firm footing on anything, career, family, or otherwise, that she felt the need to return. Surely, there was nothing left to find, and yet the urge to see the place where they'd been separated was overwhelming. What if there was some clue of their existence buried in the snow? A jacket with their names handwritten on the collar. A locket with a photo of her smiling face. It was foolish to hope for such childish dreams, but she couldn't help herself.

Though Calla and Misty knew she was adopted, she'd never confided the full extent of her past. Somehow, it felt too sacred to share, even with them. She had nothing left of her family save for the mystery of their disappearance. No names, no recollection of their faces. She didn't even know if they were actually from Alaska.

Had she wandered away from a camping trip? Gotten lost on the trails? Or—her stomach twisted—had they abandoned her intentionally? A silly thought, surely, but how could two people simply vanish into thin air, taking all of her memories with them? As though they'd placed a spell on her.

The need for answers, for closure, was an obsession. And not one she thought her friends would ever understand.

Tana turned to Brynn with a sad smile. "Torket's not sacred, it's deadly. The locals know better than to test her."

Chapter Three

A high-pitched screech cut through the air, and Tana fumbled in the darkness for her phone, lost in the jungle of clothing and gear piled in Calla's guest bedroom. Finally, her fingers curled around the familiar weight, and she tapped the glass, silencing the alarm. Wincing against the bright glow of the screen, which screamed 2:30 a.m. at her, she rolled out of bed, nearly stumbling from the after-effects of the wine that had yet to vacate her system.

A full coffee pot gurgled in the kitchen, where Misty was already pulling mugs from one of the cupboards. At the sight of Tana shuffling into the kitchen, she laughed.

"Looks like that Merlot was a mistake."

"You'd think we'd know better by now." Tana's smirk melted off her face as the first dull pounding radiated from behind her eyeballs. She hastily poured her own cup of coffee, nursing it as though it were the elixir of life.

Misty took a sip of her own, wincing as the hot liquid touched her tongue. "I took an Ambien last night. I'm sure that's not helping. Feels like I could sleep another ten hours."

"Thought you weren't supposed to mix that with alcohol?"

Misty snorted. "Tana, pop out twins and see how quickly the rules no longer apply. I've been using it since they started teething, trying to hold onto my sanity." At Tana's raised eyebrow, Misty clarified, "It was half a pill. I'm weaning myself off of them."

At the piercing sound of Brynn's voice, Tana turned to see both her and Calla entering the kitchen, neither looking worse for wear. Brynn's relative youth and Calla's imperviousness to any form of weakness appeared to have rendered them immune to hangovers. Brynn was already chattering away as she made a beeline for the coffeepot.

"It's in Kazakhstan," she explained. "The border is disputed, so nobody has been able to climb it without risking an arrest from one—or both—countries. It's one of the tallest unclimbed peaks in the world, waiting for someone to come along and scale her."

"Mmhmm," Calla replied, her eyes never leaving her mug. Though she was playing it cool and aloof, Tana suspected she was secretly loving Brynn's attention.

With their start time of three a.m. looming, Tana grabbed her mug and retreated to the guest bedroom, away from the lights and noise of the kitchen that were, frankly, too painful at the moment. At the sound of howling gusts outside her window, she pulled on her layers—long underwear, softshell, and finally, her wind layer. She looked longingly at her cozy down coat and pants, almost sleeping bag-like in their fluffy proportions, but decided against them, remembering the climbers' creed: be bold, start cold. As lovely as they'd feel now, she'd be regretting the extra warmth about five minutes into the ascent.

Calla's yell echoed down the hall. "Everyone ready?"

Tana slipped her feet into her mountaineering boots, thick with insulating layers to keep out the cold and a stiff, rigid sole to act as a base for her steel crampons. Laces tied, she stood and, with a grunt of effort, shouldered her backpack. The oppressive weight made her immediately want to unpack and search for more non-essentials to eliminate, but at the sight of Calla's irritated face in her doorway, she sighed and kept moving. Her boots clomped along the hardwood floors, following Calla's lead out to the truck where Misty and Brynn stood waiting.

They loaded their packs into the truck bed, helping each other boost the massive bags. Gear loaded, Brynn yelled, "Shotgun," and raced for the front seat beside Calla.

Misty sniffed at the childish move, her eyes finding Tana's. "Looks like someone's got a crush." She led the way into the truck's back seat, where the vents were blasting heat, a welcome respite from the bitterly cold wind outside.

"And we're off," Calla announced, guiding the truck onto the snow-dusted, pothole-ridden road. The headlights cut a swath through the inky blackness, illuminating their tiny strip of civilization through the untamed wilderness. "A little late for my liking. That's life, I suppose."

Tana caught the rebuke in her voice and glanced at the dashboard clock. It read 3:08.

The first prickles of sweat were already forming in Tana's armpits as they neared the trailhead. Overdressed for the warmth of Calla's truck, her extra layers were stifling, and she stared longingly at the icy landscape outside her window. The weather report for the following week promised plenty of wind and snow, news that Calla—always eager for an extra challenge—had welcomed with open arms but left Tana double-checking her backpack to make sure she'd packed her extra-warm base layers.

Crunched in the back seat with Misty, Tana could only cringe in secondhand embarrassment as she listened to Brynn reciting a list of climbs she'd completed without any sort of guide, no doubt highlighting her own strengths and bravery in the face of danger. Memories of Tana's own pathetic attempts to impress her college roommates flooded back, and she winced at the lengths she'd gone to show that she wasn't a basic, "outdoorsy" Colorado girl, that her heart truly belonged to the mountains.

Brynn continued to drone on. "And then I added my boyfriend's pack to my own. Such a lazy ass. He never could handle more than three days on the trail. I had to carry both bags fifteen miles—"

"We're here," Calla interrupted, pulling into the small snow-covered lot and effectively cutting off the conversation. The parking area was empty except for a lone SUV parked in the corner spot, the light dusting of snow on its hood suggesting its owner had started their journey a day or two ago. "I'll fill out the registry. You guys get ready." She secured the e-brake before slipping out of the cab, ducking against the wind on her way to the ranger's lockbox.

Misty leaned between the front seats and gave her sister a reassuring squeeze on the shoulder. "You're a writer, Brynn. Don't they always say, 'Show, don't tell'? With Calla, that's the way to go. Don't tell her how great you are. Words mean nothing if you can't back them up. Be tough, know your shit, have a good attitude, and she'll respect you." She paused. "And whatever you do, don't fuck up."

Brynn scowled, her eyes following Calla's figure in the darkness. "Great pep talk, coach."

They exited the truck, making their way to the bed to pull their gear free. Misty distributed their harnesses, and each woman slid them up her legs and around her waist before clipping their steel, spiked crampons to their boots. With a grunt, Tana hauled her backpack to her shoulders and cinched the waist belt. She welcomed the familiar sensation of the weight settling over her body, feeling her muscles shift into gear to support it.

Although Torket was invisible in the predawn hours, she sensed its presence, a monster lying in wait, daring them to come closer and test their luck. The wind whispered as it rushed past, sending a chill up Tana's spine that had nothing to do with the cold. She was no stranger to the pre-climb jitters. Every expedition made her stomach drop at the thought of not being strong or capable enough to reach her goal. But Torket was different. She couldn't quite put her finger on it, but something about this mountain felt darker, more sinister, like it was actively awaiting them.

Calla returned to the car, rubbing her gloved hands together against the chill. Her headlamp bathed them in a blue-white glow. "We're registered, and wilderness permits are paid for. You all owe me ten dollars or a decent beer when this is over." She scanned the near-empty parking lot. "Honestly, I bet we could've been up and down before a ranger ever swung by to check the cash box."

"Someone's got to pay to maintain these trails. May as well do our part," Misty said.

Calla grunted in response. She unslung a length of rope from her massive pack and held one end out to Brynn. "Since it's your first time climbing with the group, you want to take the lead? Show us old crones what you've got?"

A smile split Brynn's face. "For real? Yeah, definitely!" She grabbed the end of the rope and tied a quick figure-eight knot, attaching herself with a carabiner linked to her harness.

Calla wasn't one to give up the lead position without a fight, and at Tana and Misty's raised eyebrows, she whispered, "This way, I'll have an eye on her when she falls off a cliff." With a wink, she turned to her own length of rope and tied a quick knot.

"You really think we need to rope up this low?" Misty asked. "Feels like overkill."

With a quick glance at Calla to ensure she was listening, Brynn asked, "Did you not read the trail reports I sent you? Even with how bad global warming's been, the glaciers drop super low on Torket. Less than a mile in, the trail crosses right over some major crevasses. With the warm weather this spring, that ice is going to be paper-thin." Though Tana didn't have any experience with siblings, she guessed Misty was bristling at her younger sister's superior tone.

A mischievous grin flitted across Brynn's lips. "We're playing Russian Roulette. If you want to play without a safety line, be my guest."

Misty snatched the rope from Brynn's outstretched hand. "Ok, smart ass. When you have kids, you let me know how much free time you have to read the damn trail reports." She unrolled the coil of rope, handing a center section to Tana. "Mind if I take the end?" she asked. "Not to get too gross, but I haven't drunk that much wine in a while, and my stomach isn't loving life right now, if you catch my drift. You'll be safer upwind."

Calla laughed as she strapped on her crampons, clamping the steel spikes tightly to her boots. "Don't lie, Misty. We've been climbing together too long for that. We all know you tend to trip over the rope. No shame in liking the back."

Tana clipped onto the rope between Calla and Misty, smiling at the sound of Misty grumbling under her breath. Almost a decade after they'd first met, the group dynamics were still the same as their college days. The addition of Brynn had only given Calla a new ally.

"Everyone good?" Brynn called back.

At the chorus of affirmation, Brynn turned on her headlamp and then started into the trees. The trail was visible, but only just. Overgrowth threatened to revert the thin strip of civilization back to wilderness, and Tana guessed that the brush was only trimmed once a year, if that. She had to admit that Calla had a point. For such an impressive peak, it was all but forgotten. Nobody wanted to climb a mountain without name recognition, and Denali stole the thunder from all of Alaska's other peaks.

As they marched through the darkness, Tana turned her gaze skyward, hoping to catch a glimpse of familiar constellations, but the clouds shrouded them in a gray haze. Even the moon struggled to penetrate the mist. Beyond the light of their headlamps, the edges of the trail were a mass of black shadows. Trees and boulders morphed into behemoth creatures of the imagination, all waiting to pounce on unsuspecting visitors. She knew it was silly to let her thoughts wander to such dark corners. She'd spent most of her youth hiking in the woods, even at nighttime. But the idea that something was lurking in the shadows was tough to shake.

The cold air coursed through her lungs—a welcome distraction—and she reminded herself to focus on her breathing. Already over ten thousand feet, the difference in altitude was palpable. Her steps were heavier, her breathing more labored. A dull pounding echoed between her temples, though whether the result of altitude or too much wine was debatable. And Brynn, no doubt in an effort to prove herself, was marching along at top speed.

As if reading her mind, Calla called out, "Ease up, speed demon. We've got a long way to go. Pace yourself." She turned back to Tana and shook her head. "Kids these days," she whispered.

"Thank God," Misty muttered, and Tana was relieved to hear she wasn't the only one panting. "I didn't want to be the one who said it. She's so competitive, she'd never let me live it down."

Their pace slowed to a steady walk, giving Tana's breathing a chance to stabilize. Her headlight followed Calla's boots as they moved confidently through the snow. Though she'd often join

Misty in teasing Calla about her compulsive need to lead the team, secretly, she'd always enjoyed walking behind her. There was something soothing about her steady footfalls, how she never faltered or slipped. Walking the trails, surrounded by nature, with her eyes trained on Calla's steps, had become a meditative experience, where nothing was asked of her but to continue putting one foot in front of the other. It was the one place where she didn't feel pressure to perform or pretend to be greater than she really was. Here, she could accept her own mediocrity. In the mountains, she could simply be. She'd lost track of how many climbs she'd completed in this way, following Calla's self-assured lead to the top. Hundreds, probably. And that suited her fine.

No longer listening to her own labored breathing, the sounds of the forest became more pronounced. Tree branches creaked under their own weight. Small nocturnal creatures scurried among the underbrush, making one last dash for food before the sun rose. The wind slipped through the trees, the rustling leaves whispering as they brushed against one another.

Except...Tana strained to hear over the sound of their footsteps. It wasn't the wind. Someone really was whispering. It was soft but undeniably human.

"Hold up," she said. Misty stopped short, but Brynn and Calla, oblivious, kept walking until the rope pulled taut, jerking Tana forward. "Stop," she cried, spinning in place to determine where the voice was coming from. "You hear that?"

Misty nodded. "I heard it too, a second ago. Someone's out there."

"Someone's following us?" Brynn's voice came out higher pitched than normal.

"Shh, listen," Tana said.

The wind was louder now, and there was no mistaking the human voice carried along with it. It broke in and out, indecipherable words snatched at by the breeze.

"Who's there?" Calla demanded, her hands reaching for one of the dozen pockets she'd sewn onto her waist belt. She pulled out a can of mace and held it in front of her, poised and ready.

A quiet descended over them, their pursuer pausing, perhaps to assess this new threat. In the sudden silence, Tana opened her mouth to suggest they keep moving when the air around them exploded with voices, all speaking the same unfamiliar language.

Tana gasped and swiveled on the spot, her headlamp illuminating nothing but trees and snow. Her head filled with what sounded like hundreds of people all speaking over each other, fighting to be heard. Her teammates' eyes were wide and alert, and even Calla seemed unsure of what to do, turning on the spot with her can of mace, looking for a target.

"Leave us alone," Brynn screamed, but if anything, the voices grew louder, hollering back their response.

"Run," Calla yelled. When Brynn refused to move, she gave her a rough shove up the trail. "Move your ass—now!"

Brynn took off running, the others close behind. The screams, mournful and pleading, followed them, piercing the air and making the hairs on Tana's arms stand at attention. Their pursuers sounded close, like they could reach out a hand and drag her into the woods, never to be seen again. Unable to stop herself, she glanced back over her shoulder, peering against Misty's headlamp at the trees beyond.

A tug on her foot made her gasp, and in that split second, she was sure that whatever was chasing them had finally pounced from the shadows. But as gravity pulled her to the ground, she realized that her left crampon had snagged her right pant leg, effectively tying her legs together. Her arms flailed as she toppled forward, slamming into the rocks and snow that lined the trail.

"Stop," she cried, but Brynn and Calla were singularly focused in their panic. They continued to run at top speed, pulling the rope taut so that it smacked Tana in the face. She had a split second to register the burn it left across her cheek before she was yanked, midsection first, down the trail. She heard Misty screaming at them to stop, to no avail. Tana slammed along the ground for a few yards before her weight forced them to a halt. Calla's face suddenly appeared in her line of sight.

"Can you get up? Are you hurt?" She reached a hand under Tana's armpit and hoisted her to her feet. Her ice ax was in hand, the pick pointed toward the trail. She felt along the back of Tana's pack until her fingers clamped around the ax strapped to the side. "Here." She yanked it free and pressed it into Tana's hands.

Beside them, Misty was holding her own ax aloft, ready to strike. She shot Tana a quick glance. "You okay?"

Tana nodded. The pain in her face barely registered, no doubt a side-effect from the adrenaline surging through her veins. Her hands trembled, the ax shivering in the glow from her headlamp. From the corner of her eye, she could make out Brynn's light farther down the trail.

Scanning the ground for footprints or any sign of their pursuers, Tana was shocked to see the tree cover had been replaced by mounds of snow and craggy boulders, evidence of how far they'd managed to climb in their panic-stricken bolt for safety. Here, above the tree line, the truck was surely miles behind them.

The four women stood in silence, straining to hear their pursuers, but the wind had lost all of its former human touch. The voices had quieted, a thought that should have filled them with relief, but Tana couldn't help but wonder if they were waiting in the shadows like a mountain lion going still right before it pounced.

"Are they gone?" Tana whispered.

Calla swept the area with her light, taking in their immediate surroundings, devoid of all traces of other people. "I think so—"

Brynn's scream cut through the air, making her teammates jump in shock. They turned in unison, watching as she dropped to the ground, her headlamp sweeping over them like one final, desperate plea for rescue. Then she vanished from sight.

Chapter Four

In the half-second it took for Tana to register what had happened, her stomach turned to liquid. Brynn was gone, swallowed whole by whatever nightmarish creature had been chasing them. An instant later, she and Calla were yanked off their feet, Misty close behind, their climbing rope dragging them toward the same terrible fate that had claimed Brynn.

Instinct immediately took over. Tana crossed her ax over her chest, rolling onto her stomach and burying her pick in the snow and ice. Even with all of her weight pressed onto the ax, she was dragged along the ground. She dropped her toes, jamming her crampon spikes into the snow for extra purchase. "Dig in," she screamed, praying Misty and Calla would have the presence of mind to self-arrest.

Finally, the tug on her harness lessened. She glanced over her shoulder to see Calla splayed on the ground, toes dug into the ice, and ax beneath her chest.

"Brynn!" Misty gasped, and Tana turned to see her struggling to untangle herself from the rope. Her ax was nowhere in sight, and Tana guessed that when they'd been knocked over, Misty had gotten caught in the rope and dropped it.

Calla craned her neck to look behind her, careful not to release her grip on solid ground. "She fell in a crevasse," she yelled back.

Tana almost laughed with relief. Of course, an unseen monster hadn't swallowed Brynn. The idea seemed preposterous and, frankly, embarrassing when faced with the reality of the situation. But the abashed smile dropped off her face at the thought of Brynn still in danger. Crevasses were the final resting place of far too many unlucky climbers who'd fallen into these deep fissures in the glaciers.

For all they knew, Brynn could have been knocked unconscious, her bones could have been broken, or hypothermia could have set in faster than they could retrieve her. She may not have been eaten alive, but if they didn't act quickly, the outcome would be equally devastating.

Calla yelled down the line, "Misty, unclip and get up here. Tana and I will hold her steady. Check and see if she's okay."

Misty did as instructed, hustling along the trail to where Brynn had dropped out of sight.

"Careful," Calla warned. "There might be patches of thin ice."

Dropping to her hands and knees, Misty crawled the last few feet, her gloved hands pawing at the snow, feeling for loose ground. She reached the edge of the crack and peered inside, the light from her headlamp disappearing below the ground. "Brynn?" she called. "You okay?"

Brynn's pained groan floated up to where Calla and Tana lay on the ground. "Hit my head, but I'm fine. My arm's kind of stuck behind me."

"I'll come down to you. Sit tight. I need to set up an anchor real quick." Misty pushed herself away from the crevasse edge and unclipped her backpack, tossing it to the side. She turned toward Calla, her hands reaching for the angled aluminum shafts she kept strapped to the side of her pack. When hammered into the ice, they'd make an anchor strong enough to hold Misty and Brynn's combined weight.

"Wait!" A hint of panic had crept into Brynn's voice, and Tana wondered if the voices that had chased them into this predicament made her wary of being left alone, even for a couple of minutes. "I think I can climb out. Just give me a hand, okay? Calla, Tana, you're holding the rope, right?"

"We've got you," Calla called back.

A series of grunts rose from the crevasse as Brynn fought to gain purchase with one arm out of commission. Metal scraped against ice, and Tana pictured Brynn's feet scrabbling for any kind of hold in the narrow chute.

"A little higher. A couple feet, tops," Misty coached, "and then I can grab you." She pointed down into the crack. "Solid ice above your right foot. Dig in there."

Tana saw Misty's unsecured torso dip below ground, a reckless move Misty would make only for her sister, emerging a moment later with Brynn's arm in hand. She dug her crampons into the snow and yanked hard, pulling her sister from the crevasse. The two collapsed onto the trail, gasping in the frigid air. Brynn cradled her twisted arm, rubbing it to bring back the circulation.

"Oh, thank God," Misty whispered.

No longer holding Brynn's weight, both Tana and Calla relaxed, lifting their stiff bodies from the frozen ground to join their teammates.

"Nice work," Calla remarked when Tana caught up to her. "If you hadn't been so quick on the draw with your self-arrest, I might've gone in with her." They peered into the deep crack, the ice walls darkening from white to blue before descending into shadow. Calla whistled in appreciation. "And Brynn would've had a hell of a way to keep falling." The compliment was unexpected, so humble and un-Calla-like, that Tana couldn't stop the grin that stretched across her face.

Misty was examining Brynn's head, pressing a bandana against the bloody scrape where she'd made contact with the ice. "We should've had our helmets on," she said, her accusatory gaze finding Calla. "She could've been killed."

Calla held up her hands in defense. "I had no idea we were already on the glacier. We must've really been flying up the trail."

The reminder of why they'd been running in the first place made all four women involuntarily turn toward the trail they had just sprinted up. The sky was brightening with the rising sun, illuminating the trail with a soft, pink glow. In the light, the idea that they had been running from voices in the woods seemed comically childish. The scattered boot prints and drag marks along the trail were a testament to their nighttime madness.

"Was it...real?" Tana asked. "It had to be, right? Either that or a group hallucination."

"I've never heard anything like that before," Misty said. "It had to be some weird Alaskan animal. We probably scared the hell out of it, and then it scared the hell out of us right back."

Tana shook her head. "It was definitely people. I didn't understand the language, but those were human voices. No animal sounds like that."

"Torket." Beneath the fresh bruise on her forehead, Brynn's eyes were wide with new understanding. "It's Inuit for *home of the spirits*." At their blank stares, she threw up her hands in exasperation. "Does nobody read up on a mountain before climbing it?"

Calla shrugged. "I assumed it was some guy's last name."

"Those things chasing us must've been the spirits," Brynn exclaimed. "That's why nobody climbs this thing. Not because Denali is next door. It's because the damn thing is haunted." Her voice dropped to an excited whisper. "That's why so many people disappear here. The spirits get them."

It was an insane theory, and yet, Tana couldn't help but be intrigued by it. Her entire family had disappeared into thin air on a mountain named for its spirit presence. Was it really that wild of a leap to make? A horrible thought popped into her head—was this what had happened to her parents? Had this been their last moment? A final, terrified chase through the wilderness?

Calla's groan cut through Brynn's excitement like a knife through butter. "Are you fucking kidding me?" she spat, wiping the look of wonder off the young woman's face. "We heard some weird wind, maybe some animals, and we panicked, plain and simple. Herd mentality—as soon as one of us loses our mind, it becomes contagious." At the sight of their accusatory stares, she relented. "And okay, I admit, I didn't react as well as I could have. I shouldn't have yelled at Brynn to run. But seriously, guys, we're talking about being chased by ghosts."

"Spirits," Brynn corrected.

Calla shot her a look, then continued. "We got spooked, and I'm not proud of it. But let's not make it worse by pretending it was something out of a horror movie. Hell, for all we know, it could've been some kids playing a joke on us. The family down the road from my place has teenage boys that are always messing around in the woods."

"Really?" Brynn asked, the contempt in her voice clear. "Spirits are too much of a stretch, but a bunch of teenagers, miles from civilization, running through the woods before the sun's even up, that sounds plausible to you?"

Inserting herself between the two glaring women, Misty held up her hands in a sign of surrender. "Whatever it was," she said, her eyes darting between them, "it scared the bejeezus out of us, and now we have two injuries."

"Two?" Tana asked.

Misty pulled out her phone and snapped a quick shot of Tana's face. "Take a look at yourself," she said, handing over the phone.

Tana gaped at the sight of a slash mark from her cheek up to her temple, where the rope had worn her skin clean off. Against her fire-engine red jacket, the blood appeared grayish and dingy, as if the muted plainness of her face was more than skin deep.

Softened by adrenaline, the pain now returned full force, a hot, pulsing burn. She traced the line with her finger, feeling the strip of tacky blood. She vaguely remembered falling onto the rope, but amidst the chaos, it had barely registered.

"I think we should turn back," Misty said. "We can clean up, recalibrate, and try again later. This is no way to start a trip. We're rattled, and that's when mistakes happen."

"No." Tana hadn't meant for it to come out so forcefully, but the idea of leaving empty-handed wasn't something she could stomach. She wasn't sure what exactly she was looking for, whether it was a sign of her parents' lives or reaching the summit as a way to honor them. All she knew was that turning back wasn't an option.

"We can come back tomorrow," Misty argued. "We'll go to Calla's, get a decent night's sleep, and be back on the trail at the crack of dawn."

Tana pursed her lips, trying to keep her frustrations from spilling out. The firm deadline for her return to the office was like a glaring neon sign urging her forward. Cutting a full day's worth of climbing would drastically lessen their chances of reaching the peak, especially if they needed to take a rest day or shelter from the elements during the climb. And though she wouldn't dare say it to Misty's face, she'd noticed over the years that Misty tended to grow a tad too comfortable with a bottle of wine and a cozy fireplace. If they turned back now, there was a chance Misty would try to call the whole thing off.

"I'm fine," Tana said, forcing a sense of calm resolve into her voice. She grabbed Misty's pack from the ground and pulled the first-aid kit from inside. "A little antiseptic, and I'll be good to go."

"Same," Brynn said. With an impatient wave of her hand, she brushed away the bandana that Misty was still trying to dab against her head and reached for a disinfecting wipe. She glanced at Calla, but no longer with the open admiration of a lovesick puppy. Her eyes blazed from Calla's rebuke, and a new defiance smoldered in their depths. "I'm not afraid of a little bruise. Or some angry spirits."

A dimple appeared beside Calla's lips, a sign that Tana had long ago learned meant she was biting the inside of her cheek, though whether to keep from laughing or verbally tearing into Brynn was unclear. After a few seconds, she did neither. With her lips pulled into a fake smile, she turned to Misty.

"Well, Mist, looks like the troops have spoken. Onward to glory."

Chapter Five

Sunlight poured over the mountain, and with the tree line now far below, the four climbers were bathed in a golden glow. The sunshine sparkled off their climbing axes and carabiners, reflecting flashes of light onto the surrounding snow. Yet the mood was anything but sunny as they trudged up the steep terrain toward Camp One.

After insisting that everyone strap on a helmet, Misty had taken her place at the back of the line, muttering under her breath about the stupidity of pressing on. Every half hour or so, Tana was jerked backward by the waist, the line pulled taut. She suspected Misty was doing it intentionally as a way to burn off excess anxiety, so she let it slide. But each tug of the rope made her grind her teeth in frustration.

Calla had once again ceded the lead position to Brynn, though with far less enthusiasm this time around.

"Watch out for crevasses," Calla warned before clipping into the second figure-eight knot. "A couple miles in, there's a crossing where we'll need to lay down the ladder." She tilted her head backward, indicating the telescoping ladder strapped to the back of her bag.

Brynn, still bristling from her embarrassing fall into the crevasse, clipped in without a glance in Calla's direction. "Yeah, I'm aware," she huffed. "I'm the one that read the trail reports, remember?"

"Mhm," Calla replied. "And you're the one who almost broke her neck this morning..."

Brynn spun on the spot. "Running from—"

"Ghosts?" Calla asked, a patronizing smirk on her face. "Oh, right, my bad. Spirits."

Eyes narrowed, Brynn turned back without a word and marched down the trail, her boots stamping the frozen ground.

Calla glanced over her shoulder at Tana and flashed her a grin, but Tana couldn't find the joy to return it, not when it came at the cost of their team's camaraderie.

She'd lost track over the years of how many sniping comments Calla had leveled at undeserving targets, a habit that went all the way back to their college days, when they'd spend rainy afternoons holed up in the local climbing gym, bemoaning the long lines to finally nab a spot on the wall. To pass the time, they'd size up the other climbers, dissolving into giggles when shirtless men would hold a difficult pose a few seconds too long, scanning the crowd to see who was admiring their flexed muscles, or when a new climber would freeze on the bouldering wall, too unskilled to reach the top, too scared to let go and fall to the mats below. But as usual, Calla tended to take things too far.

A young couple—their shy smiles and stiff posture marking them as new love—was next in line for the bouldering wall. The man, a chubby, bespectacled twenty-something, was explaining the route to his date, tracing the path for her with his finger.

"This route's one of my favorites," he told her, a nervous grin alighting on his face. "I'll give you some beta—that's what we call directions, basically—once you get to the top. There's one really tough section up there. It always trips me up."

At this, Calla snorted, intentionally loud enough for them to hear. Misty smacked her on the arm.

"Getting beta from a beta," Calla laughed, ignoring Misty's whispered pleas for her to shut up. She winked at Tana, then stood and sauntered over to the wall, pointing at the colored tape attached to the lowest handhold.

"See this? V-zero. It means this is as easy as it gets. We use these routes to teach kids the basics. It's about as hard as climbing a ladder."

At this, the young man's face flamed red.

Calla smiled at the woman, sizing her up. "A week of training, and you'd leave these routes in the dust." She dipped her hands into her chalk bag, spreading the white powder over her palms. "And in a year, if you're good, you could be doing this."

She gripped one of the rounded handholds, nodding at the V7 rating to make sure the woman appreciated the difficulty. Then, in a burst of rocket-like speed, she flung herself from hold to hold, an aerial acrobat. At the top of the wall, arms flexed, she held the pose a moment too long, like the peacocking men she cackled at. Her dark eyes searched out the young woman's, making sure she fully appreciated the sight before clambering over the top of the wall.

A few seconds later, Calla bounded back to where they stood, her cheeks flushed with color. Ignoring the man entirely, she focused her radiant smile on the woman. "Piece of cake. Let me know if you get bored with the easy stuff. I'd be happy to show you something a little more...interesting."

The woman's date looked like he wanted to sink into the mats and die.

When confronted, Calla would always argue innocence. After those two climbers had left the gym—less than twenty minutes after arriving—Misty had rounded on her, demanding to know why she always had to be such an ass.

Caught up in her own ego, Calla insisted she was only trying to help. With a mentor still climbing V0s, what hope did that woman possibly have?

Now, over a decade later, that childish arrogance still had a habit of rearing its ugly head. Tana hated seeing it fuel the tension in their team. This climb was their only reunion for the year, and not even twenty-four hours in, they were already sniping at one another. Not only was it bad for morale, but in such a dangerous environment, they needed to be fully invested in each other's well-being. Small cracks in their unity had the potential to tear the team apart.

They lapsed into silence, each woman lost in her own thoughts. Rising up the west face of Torket, their pace slowed considerably. Approaching an altitude of twelve thousand feet, their overloaded packs were a vampiric drain on their energy. Once again, Tana wished she'd done one last paring down of non-essential gear. Those extra packets of hot cocoa and the fuel canisters to boil water for them would have been an easy thing to discard. And why had she brought her solar charger when Calla already had one? Though it was easy to blame her lack of foresight while packing, in reality, she knew she should have trained harder. The carefree days of her twenties, when she could bound up a mountain with little preparation, were quickly fading into her past. With a new decade came new hurdles and the responsibility to take better care of her body.

She focused on her steps, kicking into the snow for purchase, then stopping for a breath. Kicking in again, and stopping to breath. The pattern lulled her into a state of meditation, where all that mattered was her steady breathing and keeping pace with Calla's boots ten feet ahead. The sense of exhaustion and the burning in her lungs melted away, her thoughts turning simple and serene.

Kick, rest, breathe, kick, rest, breathe—

Another tug on the rope startled her from her trance. She turned to glare back at Misty and, against her better judgment, opened her mouth to tell her that enough was enough—it was time to grow up and get over it. Then came Brynn's voice, pulling her attention ahead.

"Looks like that climber from the parking lot was here."

Up ahead lay a six-foot chasm in the trail. To its left, a steep drop-off plunged hundreds of feet to a mess of boulders below.

To the right, an icy granite slab dared climbers to try their luck on its slick, glass-smooth holds. The penalty for failure was a terrifying drop into the chasm. It was too far of a span to jump, which left only one option: climbing over the crevasse itself.

Another mountaineer, presumably the one who owned the SUV in the lot, had already placed a ladder across the gap, securing both ends with ice screws and copious amounts of rope. A safety line had been bolted to the ground on both sides, its loose midsection flapping in the breeze channeled upward by the chasm.

"Aw, too bad. Looks like you carried that thing for nothing," Brynn said, unable or unwilling to keep the sneering tone from her words. She gestured at Calla's ladder.

Calla shook her head. "Oh yeah, genius? And what happens when they come back down and take their ladder home with them?" she asked.

"Oh...right."

Misty walked to the edge of the chasm and peered down inside. "At least the wind's died down a bit. Who wants to go first?"

At the sight of Calla and Brynn sizing each other up, Tana shook her head in disgust. Their high-school bullshit was going to get someone killed. "I'll go." She pulled a nylon sling from her pack and hooked two carabiners onto it, clipping one to her harness before gingerly reaching onto the ladder to grasp the safety line.

"Easy," Calla warned. "Remember, we're still tied to you. As much as I'd hate for you to fall, I'd hate for me to fall even more." Though her tone was joking, Tana didn't doubt the note of truth to it.

"How noble of you," Tana said, attaching her second carabiner to the safety line, then unhooking from the group rope, tossing it at Calla's feet with a grin. "Now, if this line fails"—she gestured at the safety line stretching across the gap—"I can die without you beside me to ruin my last moment."

Calla laughed. "Smart ass. Go on then, show us how tough you are."

Stepping up to the edge of the ladder, the good-natured smile melted from Tana's face. She had no idea how long the drop was. She'd always been lousy with distances. But however far down those craggy boulders were, they were a great enough drop to surely kill on impact. She stepped onto the first rung of the ladder, carefully positioning it between the rows of spikes on her crampons. She pressed down, testing the sturdiness of the setup. The ladder shifted slightly under her weight, but the anchors held firm. Behind her, Calla dropped to her knees and positioned a gloved hand on either side of the ladder.

"I'll try to steady it," she said.

Tana nodded, took a deep breath, then stepped forward, both feet now on the rungs. She pulled the safety line to her body so that it was taut, helping to keep her balanced.

"Nice and easy, Tana," Misty said.

She lifted a foot, then stepped to the next rung, trying unsuccessfully to avoid looking past her boots at the open expanse below. The chasm swam into her periphery, making her wobble with a quick burst of dizziness. She paused, closing her eyes against the view, inhaling a steadying breath before continuing on. Another short step, then another, and she was halfway across the ladder.

"Almost there," Brynn called out. "Doing great."

A burst of wind howled up, blasting Tana with a frigid gust from below. She grasped the safety line and pulled it tight to her body, spreading her feet as wide as possible on the rungs in an effort to stay upright.

"Hold tight," Calla yelled over the gust.

Tana squinted against the vicious wind, her teeth clenched in frustration, and that's when she heard them, unmistakable in their clarity—a chorus of human voices. Her eyes burst open, and she swiveled her head, searching for the source and finding only snow and ice.

She vaguely heard one of her teammates call out to her, maybe to ask what was wrong, maybe to tell her to hold still, but their words were lost to the wind before they had a chance to register. She was transfixed by the voices. The...spirits? Could Brynn possibly have been right? Because there was definitely something, no, someone out there. In the light of day, there was no mistaking it for a terrifying group delusion.

Another gust of wind tore through her, bringing with it the aroma of a campfire and charred meat, then something earthy, like sage. A wave of nostalgia crashed over her, inexplicable in her current circumstances, yet unmistakable. A piece of her wanted to jump into the wind currents and let it wash over her, this small shred of her past. The voices were stronger now, their words still an unintelligible language, but their rhythm, rather than invoking terror, was a comfort.

Her eyesight flickered as the snow around her became soft and fuzzy, like television static. Black shadows danced around her vision, solidifying for a moment before dissolving into static once again. Though they were no more than silhouettes, taking shape only for a second, Tana was positive they were living, breathing creatures. She could almost feel the life emanating from them. The desire to see these shadows for what they were, to be a part of them, overwhelmed her. She stretched out her hand, her fingers tracing the air, hoping to stir the flickers into solid shapes.

A sudden scream cut through the air as Tana was slammed to the ground, the breath pushed from her lungs. The world snapped back to its original state, quiet and coherent. She struggled to push her face from the snow.

"Are you insane?" Calla bellowed. Her nose was inches from Tana's, and her pupils dilated with fear. As she slid to Tana's side, Tana realized that the oppressive weight on her back had been Calla, still wearing her gigantic backpack.

Calla leaned back onto the snow, covering her face with trembling hands. "Holy shit," she groaned. "You could've died. Fuck. You should've died, pulling a stunt like that."

"Did you see what happened? You saw the shadows, right?" Tana asked. She had no idea what Calla was ranting about and hoped that whatever she'd witnessed wasn't all in her head. A group hallucination was strange enough. To be alone with these visions was far more terrifying.

"We heard the voices again and saw...something. Not really sure what. Shapes? Shadows? What the hell were you thinking? Were you going to jump?"

Completely bewildered, Tana could only shake her head in confusion. "Jump? Like off the ladder?"

Misty and Brynn were making their way across the ladder now, and Calla went to help them disembark safely.

As soon as Misty had both feet on solid ground, she dropped down beside Tana, her face pale and taut with worry. "Are you crazy?" she hissed. "Why would you unhook from the safety line?"

"I did what?" Tana looked between the three women, dumbfounded. How long had she been standing on the ladder? From her recollection, she'd only been out there a few seconds and never even touched her carabiners.

Brynn was staring at her with a look Tana didn't much care for. A mixture of fear and pity. "You stopped for a little while," she said. "We thought you were waiting for the wind to die down. Then you turned to the side and unhooked your harness from the line. We were all yelling at you to stop, but it was like you couldn't hear us. We thought you were going to jump." She glanced at Calla, all traces of her former anger gone. "Calla saved your life. She ran out there and—fuck, I thought she was going to topple off the edge—she grabbed you around the waist and tackled you onto the other side." Her face shone with open admiration. "It was the coolest thing I've ever seen."

Tana was at a loss for words. The whole series of events felt distant, as if it had happened to another person. She had no recollection beyond an intense feeling of longing. A sense of nostalgia, as though a long-forgotten piece of her past was hiding just beyond reach. She certainly hadn't planned on jumping to her death. If what they were saying was true...

She pushed herself up from the ground, grabbing Calla and wrapping her in a tight hug, trying to convey even an ounce of her gratitude. Calla could be an obnoxious, egotistical blowhard, but she'd risked her life to save Tana from self-inflicted danger. As far as Tana was concerned, all was forgiven.

"Thanks, Cal. I honestly have no idea what happened. It's like those voices put me into a trance or something. I know it sounds stupid, but it was like being under a spell." Calla hugged her back, her embrace almost painfully tight. Though she'd never let it show on her face, Tana imagined how terrified she must have been, watching a friend almost plunge over the edge.

Calla pulled free from Tana's embrace, her eyes slightly bloodshot as she gave her friend one last wan smile before turning back to the chasm. Staring down into the abyss, which could have easily claimed their lives, she let out a long, weary sigh. She bounced nervously on her toes, giving her arms a quick shake, as if she could dislodge the excess adrenaline shooting through her veins.

Brynn walked up beside her, her line of sight following Calla's to the boulders far below. This far away, their gray, rounded tops looked like a row of tombstones. At Calla's wearied gaze, she asked, "Well? You believe in spirits now?"

Chapter Six

After securing her ladder off the trail, Calla led the team over the last half mile to Camp One, a small basin protected from the wind by steep, rocky ridges on three sides. Here, they set up camp: Misty and Brynn in one tent, Tana and Calla in the other. Tana took it upon herself to set up the kitchen and start boiling a pot of water, both as a way to redeem herself for causing panic and to take her mind off how close she'd come to an unwitting suicide.

The sharp hiss of the stove pierced the air as Tana stared in thoughtful silence at the pot of water boiling above it. After the ladder crossing, they had consulted the map and determined that even if they did want to head back to the cabin, a suggestion Misty had pushed for, it would be tough to reach the truck before sunset. They were now several crevasse-laden miles from the parking lot, and after Tana's near-swan dive into the abyss, no one had the stomach for another ladder crossing so soon. Pushing on, at least for the moment, was the only reasonable course of action.

With the tents erected and a bathroom wall constructed out of snow, her teammates gathered around the stove, the warmth and promise of food attracting them like moths to a flame. Calla opened up her backpack and dug out their massive bear canister, a heavy plastic drum to protect their food from roaming critters. In the wild, unsecured food could prove a fatal mistake. While bears tended to stay below ten thousand feet, it wasn't unheard of to spot them at higher elevations in the mountains.

Calla unscrewed the lid and held up two packets. "Mac and cheese or ramen, ladies. What'll it be?"

A growl rumbled out of Brynn's stomach, and she gave Calla a pained look. "Ramen, I need the salt. You got any meat in there? I'm seriously starving."

Calla threw them each a stick of jerky, then tossed four ramen packets at Tana's side. "Here you go, chef. Make something magical out of that." She screwed the cap back onto the canister, positioning it beneath her like a stool. Pulling apart the wrapper for her own jerky, she sat munching thoughtfully, her eyes darting to Tana and then back down to the stove.

Tana sensed Calla's gaze and wished she'd say what was on her mind. Yes, she'd apparently blacked out from reality. Yes, she'd almost jumped to her death. No, she wasn't insane, and no, she wasn't going to cause any more problems. She hoped. That wasn't exactly a promise she could keep since she hadn't known she was breaking it the first time.

Instead, Calla directed her attention to Brynn, no doubt to steer the conversation into safe waters. "So you write, huh? Anything I've heard of?"

Brynn's cheeks flamed at the mention of her writing. "It's nothing special," she said.

"She's being modest," Misty interjected. "She should be writing novels. She's that good."

"I write travel articles for a small lifestyle magazine," Brynn said. "They do a lot of super touristy travel spots: Machu Picchu, Reykjavík, Venice, all the trendy places. I was brought on to show the more adventurous side of travel. More backpacking, trekking, rock climbing, that sort of stuff. I was hoping this could be another article." She shrugged. "I'd love to write a book instead. A true adventure story, like Bill Bryson's style. Touring new places, digging deep into what makes a place special, and having a few laughs along the way. But it's hard to turn your back on a steady paycheck, even a small one. Books are never a sure thing." She frowned, giving another listless shrug. "Maybe one day."

Calla chuckled. "You're a single woman, climbing mountains all over the world, and you chose writing as your profession. Somehow, I don't think relying on a 'sure thing' is your style."

"At least try," Misty urged. "The worst that happens is you fail miserably, can't make your rent, and have to move in with me as a live-in babysitter."

Brynn stifled a laugh. "You'd like that, wouldn't you?"

Misty smirked. "The chance to momentarily pawn off my demon spawn? Obviously."

"Soup's on," Tana said, checking her watch. The water had boiled for a good ten minutes, ensuring the snow she'd melted was sanitary. She dumped each ramen packet into a separate bowl and poured a swig of water over them. The sour, tangy smell of cheap noodles wafted up to her with the steam. On any other day, the aroma would have been nauseating, but after such a terrifying start on the mountain, the culinary concoction of her college years was a warm comfort.

Three hands reached in and grabbed their bowls, greedily pulling them back to their owners. All chatter ceased as they dove into the hot meal—the only sound was their ravenous slurps.

"This is that ninety-nine-cent brand, isn't it?" Misty asked. "I could barely handle it in college. This stuff goes right through me now."

Calla grinned, her smile full of neon-yellow noodles. "And—" She gulped, swallowing the mess in her mouth. "Sorry. And you get to carry that around with you the entire trip. Enjoy!"

"Wait, what?" Misty's eyebrows shot up to her beanie. "We can't bury it? I knew you had to bag it at Denali, but I figured that's because it's so popular. I even packed my little trowel."

Calla nodded, clearly enjoying Misty's discomfort. "We're in a national park. Them's the breaks, sorry. Good thing I grabbed a couple extra wag bags for the group."

Brynn chuckled. "This sport is disgusting."

"Wait until you climb Everest. It's possible people are exaggerating, but I've heard that accidentally shitting in your Everest suit is par for the course. I have a couple buddies who are guides, and the number of clients they've had to help clean up the mess would blow your mind."

Misty dropped her spoon into her half-eaten bowl. "And there goes my appetite. Thanks a lot."

The buoyant mood was a welcome break from the day's trials, though the longer they went without discussing what had happened and what lay ahead, the more Tana fidgeted with pent-up energy. She assumed they were avoiding the topic for her benefit, and it made her feel weak.

As though reading her mood, Misty cut across their conversation. "Tana, how are you holding up? You had a hell of a day." She glanced at the others. "We all did."

At the sight of all their eyes on her—Calla's piercing black to Misty and Brynn's matching bluish green—the words caught in her throat. They all appeared so painfully concerned with her well-being, which she fought not to take as a personal affront. Though none of them liked to admit it, mountaineering was an ego sport. Those with nothing to prove often gave up before a tough summit, leaving those with a chip on their shoulder to continue onward, seeking glory. It was no surprise that Tana had taken to climbing so keenly, as she'd been unsuccessfully trying to prove herself since childhood.

She thought back to their sophomore year of college, when she, Misty, and Calla had all applied for waitress jobs at the same hole-in-the-wall diner, hoping to earn enough from the tipsy two a.m. crowd to cover spring break in Mexico. When all three were hired, Tana vowed to herself that after a year in her friend's shadows, she'd outwork them both, finally earning her place in the spotlight. Misty may have had the brains and Calla the brawn, but in the real world, where things actually mattered, maybe Tana would finally have the edge.

In three months, Tana never mixed up a single order or dropped a plate of food. Her tables were spotlessly clean and meals were delivered with a smile. And yet, it was Misty who was promoted to hostess, the owner delighting in her warmth and quick thinking. And it was Calla who walked away each night with wads of cash stuffed in her pockets, her mischievous grin a magnet for both the drunken frat boys and their sorority girlfriends.

Despite her efforts, the world seemed cruelly determined to remind Tana that she was less than.

Climbing was the only respite, as though conquering nature could erase those feelings of inadequacy and soothe her broken sense of self. The effect was fleeting, often fading after a few days back in civilization, but for those few moments, she could glimpse a different side of herself. The person she wished she could be.

Here in the mountains of Alaska, she should have felt strong, alive. And yet her friends' looks of pity humbled her, scaling her down to that scared little girl she once was, stumbling through the snowdrifts on this very peak.

"I'm fine," Tana said, "and I can't apologize enough, especially to you, Cal. I'm so sorry for what happened back there. I..." She trailed off at the sight of her friends' concerned expressions, realizing she was only making herself look more hopeless. "I can't explain what happened. I don't even remember unclipping. I remember feeling really...nice? Happy? It's like my mind split from reality. Everything around me disappeared. Nothing like that's ever happened to me before."

"Altitude, maybe?" Misty suggested. She lifted her watch and flipped through the data readout. "We're just under thirteen thousand and didn't give ourselves any time to really acclimatize. It'd make sense if you were feeling woozy."

Sensitive to any sort of coddling at the moment, the childish term made Tana inwardly cringe. She reminded herself that Misty spent most of her days with two toddlers, so her vocabulary had involuntarily softened. She shook her head. "I took Diamox, and I don't have any other symptoms. My stomach's fine. No headache. Maybe a little trouble breathing, but that's normal."

With an aggravated glare at her sister, Misty said, "Maybe we could try slowing the pace down."

Unabashed, Brynn piped up, "Or maybe, since this place is obviously haunted, you were temporarily possessed." At her sister's disapproving huff, she raised her voice. "Listen, it makes sense. Say you're a ghost or a demon living on Torket, and all of a sudden, these four chicks wake you up from a deep sleep. This is your turf, damn it, and you're not going to let some strangers walk all over it. So it possesses you and tries to get you to jump off a cliff."

At the mention of supernatural forces, both Tana and Misty involuntarily turned to Calla, expecting another flare-up of irritation. To their surprise, she'd managed to force a smile onto her face.

"You and your imagination," she said. "No wonder you went into writing. Forget travel books. You should be writing horror movies."

"Don't you think—"

"No," Calla interrupted. "I don't think we're being haunted by the spirit of the mountain or whatever you've cooked up inside your brain." When Brynn opened her mouth to protest, Calla held up a hand for silence. "You can believe whatever you want. If the thought of a ghost story gets your ass up to the summit, then it's fine by me."

"You can't be serious," Misty said. "We're not turning around tomorrow morning? I'm all for a challenge, but you have to admit, this is getting creepy. Plus, Tana almost threw herself into the damn abyss a few hours ago. I don't know if it was altitude, or ghosts, or her brain misfiring, but something happened today, and we can't ignore that!"

"Then why don't we ask her how she feels? If anyone's pulling the plug, it should be Tana," Calla shot back. All three turned in unison to Tana.

Her stomach dropped at the sight of their expectant faces. Forcing a shred of authority into her voice, she said, "Seriously, guys, I'm fine. This climb is important to me, and I'm getting to the top of this thing. So please stop asking me if I want to turn back."

"This is summit fever, plain and simple," Misty argued. "This is how people die! We're going to be the morons in the news who couldn't quit while we were ahead."

Calla lifted the pot of steaming water and swished some into her empty bowl. "Three against one, Misty. You're welcome to stay behind if you want. Nobody'd ever try forcing you to come. But leave the woman alone." She dumped the dirty water into the snow behind her, then addressed the others. "We've got a hell of a day tomorrow, ladies. The climb up to Camp Two is a bitch. I recommend we all get a little shut eye while we can. Set your watches for four, and we'll hit the trail at the crack of dawn."

She, Tana, and Brynn all lifted themselves from the ground and began prepping their packs for the following day. Misty made no move to follow them. Instead, she sat stone-faced, staring into the pot of water.

As Tana repacked her mess kit, she fought the urge to apologize, hating the idea that she was the cause of her friend's distress. But she let the moment pass, unwilling to show a moment's weakness, lest Misty use that as ammunition in her argument to turn back.

After a moment of silent brooding, Misty reached behind her and grabbed her backpack, pulling it close. She unzipped the front pocket and retrieved a small baggie of pills from inside. In one fluid motion, she popped a pill into her mouth, following it with a quick swig of water. Her tense shoulders relaxed a fraction of an inch.

Still, the hollow expression in her eyes left no question what she was thinking.

They were making a horrible mistake.

Chapter Seven

A screeching ringtone tore through their tent, jolting Tana awake and eliciting a groan from Calla. Next door, the sounds of Misty and Brynn rousing from sleep drifted through the thin tent walls. Tana tapped her watch, blinking her eyes until the numbers were no longer fuzzy. Four o'clock glared back up at her.

"Remind me why we do this again?"

Calla laughed. "Because we're insane, obviously."

Tana snuggled into her sleeping bag, dreading the moment her warm, cozy body would meet the frigid air of the tent. She felt around the inside of her bag, a mishmash of items she was trying to keep warm overnight: her phone, lest it lose all battery life; her sunscreen, lest it freeze and explode; and her coat. She pulled the parka over her body, wriggling to get her arms inside.

Beside her, Calla clicked on her headlamp, then slipped out of her bag. Pulling a roll of tape from her backpack, she began painstakingly wrapping her feet for protection. The most avid climber of their group, Calla's feet bore the brunt of her excursions, which showed themselves in bone spurs and bunions that undoubtedly ached to walk on. Staring at her beautiful friend as she tended her feet, Tana was reminded of a ballerina, breathtakingly elegant in their natural habitat, but beneath the public facade, they bore the deep scars of their chosen sport.

Tana pushed the bag down to her waist, shivering in the sudden cold. She fished around the bag for her buff, pulling it down over her nose and mouth, and her beanie, which had fallen off during the night.

"Ready for a terrible day?" Calla asked, placing a pad of moleskin on one heel.

"At least you ditched the ladder. Plus, we ate some of the food, so the pack'll be lighter."

Calla chuckled. "A whole four ramen packets. That'll save me half an ounce." She tugged on her socks, then unzipped the tent to grab her boots. "Speaking of, I'll handle breakfast. You want to start packing up the tent?"

"You got it."

As Calla slipped outside, Tana grabbed her friend's sleeping bag, unceremoniously shoving it into its space-saving stuff sack, grunting with the effort of forcing the fluffy down feathers to compress tightly. The sound of trickling liquid came from just outside the tent door.

Misty yelled from her tent, "You better not be peeing where we're about to sit for breakfast."

"Didn't want to go all the way to the bathroom," Calla replied. "Haven't you heard? There's a ghost on the loose."

Tana bit back laughter at the synchronized sighs from the other tent. She packed up her own belongings, rolling her sleeping bag and pad into their stuff sacks, then dragged their things out into the frigid air.

The pot of water gurgled with the first hint of bubbles. Calla had lined up all four bowls, a packet of instant oatmeal dumped into each. Squatting by the stove, she held her hands out for warmth.

"Look up," she whispered.

Above them, the Milky Way stretched across the sky, a cloud of stars so mind-numbingly expansive that it made Tana dizzy to look at them. She sought out the constellations she'd learned as a child: the Dippers, Orion, Cassiopeia. She took a step away from the stove and spun in a slow circle, watching as the dazzling light danced around her. In Seattle, the stars were never this bright. Even her college days in Denver had been a disappointment. The tech boom and resulting population jump created a haze of light pollution. Views like these, free from human disturbance, were one of the reasons she'd gotten hooked on climbing in the first place. What she was seeing now was nothing short of magical.

A flicker of unadulterated joy shot through her, so unexpected she nearly cried out. The burst of warmth in her chest lasted only a second before dissipating as quickly as it had arrived. Tana lifted her hand, her gloved fingers tracing the invisible hole around her heart, which now felt cold and empty in comparison. What the hell had just happened? She looked to Calla to assess whether she'd felt it too, but Calla's gaze was still focused on the constellations.

Tana was well aware of what people said behind her back. She'd heard the whispered snippets from her cubicle far too many times. Robotic, emotionless, apathetic. She never tried to dispute the labels because, frankly, they rang true. She'd long ago accepted that whatever genetic deficiency had muted her physical appearance also extended to her brain chemistry. Though she attempted to hide this inadequacy, she'd never quite mastered the art of empathizing with her coworkers' grief, or fear, or even happiness.

The ability to feel this spark of elation, even for a moment, was nothing short of miraculous. She chalked it up as a testament to the natural beauty surrounding them.

The screech of a tent zipper pulled her back to reality. Misty and Brynn emerged, fastening their coats against the chill. Calla pointed skyward, and they let out a series of oohs and aahs, no doubt experiencing the same childlike wonder that had etched a grin across Tana's face.

Tana allowed them their moment, turning her focus to the tent. She snapped on her headlamp and yanked the snow stakes from the ground, letting the poles and nylon collapse in a heap.

"Coffee and oatmeal when you're ready," Calla called out. "Don't let it get cold, not after I've been slaving away for you all."

Brynn poured herself a cup of coffee, then plopped onto her backpack, still staring at the stars above. "It's beautiful," she said. "This is the best part of climbing. Mist, remember we used to go stargazing in the Appalachians with the Scouts?"

Misty nodded. "I brought my telescope one year. Remember the massive one Mom and Dad got me? That thing was ridiculously heavy. Totally worth it though. Everyone went bananas when they realized you could actually see Saturn's rings."

"Some people go their whole lives without ever seeing something that amazing," Brynn said. She took a sip of coffee, considering. "And that's a damn shame. Think of politicians, CEOs, hell, even your asshole manager at work, people that need to be brought down a peg and shown that they're not the center of the universe. How can you possibly think you're hot shit when you see that our world—everything humans have ever worked for and accomplished—is a speck among all this splendor?" She threw her arm toward the open sky. "I can't think of anything more humbling than this."

Tana grasped her mug of coffee, letting the heat seep into her palms. "Do you think there's anything out there?" she asked.

"You mean like aliens?" Even in the dim light, Tana saw Calla's raised eyebrows.

Tana shrugged. "Maybe. It's billions of stars, with billions of planets. We can't be all there is, right? I mean, think of how terrible most of Earth is. Corrupt governments, disease, climate change, we're always blowing up something in the Middle East...we can't possibly be the best that the universe has to offer, right?"

"God, I hope not," Misty said, her eyes transfixed on the constellations. "We're pathetic."

Tana wished she could convey how strongly she wanted it to be true, for there to be something besides this gray, bleak world where she was just another gray, bleak drone among billions.

Even after her parents enrolled her in Anchorage grade school and she'd finally begun speaking again, she still had a difficult time making friends. The other children pretended to be doctors and cowboys and princesses, their imaginations overflowing with what this world had to offer.

All Tana had wanted was a different world, one where she didn't feel like a sad wisp of a person. Not for the first time, she wondered if perhaps she was clinically depressed.

"I wish there was more," she said quietly.

"Me too," Misty replied.

Brynn nodded, still staring at the stars above. "Same."

Calla cleared her throat. "Real cheerful, guys. C'mon, drink up. Let's go have our asses handed to us."

The climb was as painful as the map suggested, a steep incline out of the valley on a route littered with icy boulders. The trail above them was a minefield of talus and crumbling rock, ready to fall at the slightest provocation. On this stretch, there was enough snow cover to justify strapping crampons to their heavy, plastic climbing boots, and the women moved slowly—their progress stalled as they clambered over rocks half their height. They had to constantly adjust the rope, as it tended to wrap around rocks or catch on sharp outcroppings, slowing their pace. The ground beneath their feet was littered with scree, a mix of sand and rock that shifted under each footstep. Every so often, a low roar would build up, and all four of their heads would lift in alarm, assessing what direction the rockfall was coming from and if they needed to take shelter.

Calla insisted on taking the lead position on this treacherous section of trail, pushing Brynn into second place. Though a strong, steady climber, Brynn had fewer years of experience, and her footsteps were less confident and sure. Watching her feet stumbling over the rough terrain, Tana was unable to lull herself into her normal routine of walking meditation, which, in such an unforgiving environment, may have been a blessing.

Calla pointed to a set of footprints in the snow. "That's gotta be the person who put down the ladder. First tracks we've seen, so we must be catching up. They're still powdery. They haven't iced over yet."

"Pretty big," Tana said, leaning over to assess the prints before the rope tugged her forward. "Probably a guy."

"Pretty stupid to try climbing this thing alone," Misty said. "Definitely a guy."

Brynn chuckled. "Ooo, you getting spicy back there, Mist? What'd Todd do this time? Another rough night at the casino? God, that man doesn't know when to quit."

Misty sighed, absentmindedly smacking the rocks she passed with the tip of her ice ax. "I don't know what to think anymore. It's like he's going through a mid-life crisis. At thirty-five. Is that a thing people do?"

"I've heard of a quarter-life crisis," Tana said. "I think that's when you're drowning in debt and can't land your dream job, so you become a Starbucks barista and cry yourself to sleep at night."

"Isn't that every young person's life?" Brynn asked.

"It's not like that," Misty said. "It's hard to explain. You guys are all still young and living the single life, while I feel like I've been placed into the "mother" box. Todd comes home, and he's pleasant enough, but he's never flirty. He never compliments me or asks what's going on in my life. And frankly, I can't blame him because there's not much these days. All I have to talk about is what new words the kids learned or how much food they spilled on themselves that day. I'm boring, and I know it. I bore myself even talking about it."

Misty let out an aggravated sigh, and the rope tugged at Tana's waist as she paused to consider her words.

"Then he'll tell me about how he's going wine tasting with friends from work or how Bill got a new speedboat, and they're going to take it out into the ocean on weekends. Or that he wants to take up skydiving. Skydiving! Can you picture Todd jumping out of a plane?"

Calla cackled. "Yes, and it's hilarious."

"I feel like he's looking for something new, and I'm not part of the equation anymore. I'm only there to take care of the house and kids. He seems tired of our life. And honestly, I can't say I blame him. I'm tired of our life." She paused to pull the rope from where it had gotten looped around a small boulder. "Guys, how the hell did I turn into the boring housewife? I used to be cool." She glanced around at the terrain, the snow-covered obstacles like the landscape of a different planet. "I am cool, damn it."

"One of us had to pass on our genes," Calla said. "And you're probably the only one who's suited for the job. I'm reckless. Brynn believes in ghosts. And Tana..."

Tana knew what was floating through her head, the honest truth they never dared say to her face. Men looked right through her. She'd been asked on a date exactly twice and had a strong suspicion Misty had facilitated both occurrences. While both men had been perfectly fine, there was no hint of that magical spark people wrote love songs about. Both evenings had ended with a stiff hug, no lean-in for a passionate kiss or promise of a second date. The thought of ever being head-over-heels enough to sleep with someone and having them feel the same about her was absurd.

Tana accepted it as her lot in life, though she knew the others whispered when they thought she was out of earshot. To help Calla save face, she offered, "And I can't stand the little brats."

Misty snipped, "Real helpful, ladies. I know it's stupid to compare, but being with Todd makes me think back to old boyfriends and wonder what could have been. Brynn, you remember Ryan?"

Brynn laughed. "I remember his dumb haircut. He's pretty cute now though. I see him on Instagram every now and then."

"Writing posts about his amazing, beautiful wife," Misty groaned. "Like Todd would ever do something that romantic."

"Look, Mist, if Todd really wanted an adventure, he'd go climbing with you," Tana said. "It's not like you haven't asked him. Maybe he's trying to make himself feel better because he thinks he's the boring loser parent. He sees you going climbing with us and knows you're on a different level than him. Maybe you have the whole situation backward."

Calla nodded. "That's exactly what's happening. Todd's great at a lot of things, but let's be real, Mist. You married a dork. He knows how incredible you are. You popped out two kids, and you're still out here climbing. He's feeling insecure, and all these new hobbies are his way of trying to keep up with you."

"Huh." Misty paused to consider. "I hadn't thought of that. Thanks, guys, that actually makes me feel a little better."

These shared moments were what Tana loved most about their annual group climbs. After graduating from college, they had drifted to wherever their careers and ambitions had taken them: Calla to live off the land in Alaska, Misty to a biotech startup in Boston, where she'd eventually meet Todd, and Tana to Seattle, where she'd found herself a comfortable if mind-numbingly dull role as an insurance agent. The pay had been decent, the hours bearable, and, more importantly, Seattle gave her access to some of the country's most beautiful mountains, with Rainier as the crown jewel of the view from her kitchen window.

With Denver and its easy access to peaks in their rearview mirror, Tana assumed, like most college roommates, they'd eventually drift apart. Not only were they physically separated by vast swaths of land, but their chosen paths could hardly be more different. It had been an unexpected surprise when Calla called her out of the blue, about a year after graduation, to plan a reunion climb. The only rule was that it had to be someplace none of them had visited before.

Now, almost a decade later, it was an annual tradition and one that Tana looked forward to immensely, if only to catch up with the women who knew her best. Living on her own in Seattle had intensified her hermit tendencies, and her already pitiable social skills had nosedived. At home, alone, she often mused how she might as well give up and adopt four cats because that was clearly the path she was headed down. Calla and Misty were her one lifeline to normalcy.

Misty continued, her voice tinged with doubt. "What if Todd's looking for something more? I'm a little embarrassed to admit this, but I opened his laptop a few weeks ago—"

Calla's shout cut through the air like a knife. "Rock!"

Tana lifted her head, expecting another harmless release of scree, only to see a beachball-sized stone bouncing down the trail, smashing against the surrounding boulders as it barreled toward them, seconds away from impact. Up ahead, Calla grabbed Brynn's arm and tugged her to the right side of the trail, ducking behind a cluster of sturdy rocks.

"Tana, move!"

Tana spun on the spot, looking for anything remotely resembling cover. She could run to Calla's hiding spot, but the rock was too close, bearing down on her with blinding speed. Instead, she made the split-second decision to dive to the left, beneath a shallow overhang, leaving their climbing rope stretched across the trail. Misty charged in beside her and pressed their heads to the ground.

The stone pounded down the trail, careening off rocks as it smashed through the debris. Smatterings of scree tumbled down ahead of it, like flower petals preceding a bride. A sharp crack of rocks, followed by grunts of surprise, echoed down to Tana, along with the realization that Calla's rock barrier had been hit. A half second later, the boulder tumbled past, snagging on their taut rope. The tug on her harness yanked Tana sideways onto the trail, her hands smacking the ground, searching for any kind of purchase. She felt Misty's hand clamp onto her waist, her nails piercing even through her gloves. For a heartbeat, the rock was suspended in a tug of war with the women, threatening to drag them along the trail before it finally pulled loose and continued down the side of the mountain. The thuds of impact grew softer and softer until finally, with one last echoing crash, they stilled.

Holding her midsection where the harness had pulled, Tana hoisted herself to her feet, trying to ignore the tremors in her knees as she searched out her teammates. "You two okay?" she yelled.

Both Brynn and Calla were massaging the sides of their heads. Brynn pulled her hand away, inspecting the red smear across her fingertips. A trickle of blood dripped into her eyebrow.

"Never better," Calla deadpanned. She lifted Brynn's face to get a look at her injury. "I'm not sold on this whole haunting idea, but if there was ever a mountain that was trying to kill us, it's this one."

"It hit you?" Misty was already on her feet, hastily unclipping herself from the rope and running to inspect her sister.

"Not directly." Brynn held up her hands, trying to block Misty's coddling before it began. "It hit the rock we were hiding behind, which, yes, hit us."

"Two head injuries," Misty said, her accusatory gaze flitting between Tana and Calla. "We haven't even been out here forty-eight hours. What's next, a concussion?"

As Tana trudged up the hill to join her teammates, the neon green climbing rope caught her eye. She bent down to examine the spot where the rock had made impact. The outside nylon was shredded, leaving the core exposed. Tana lifted it, racking her brain for the steps in a butterfly knot, a handy workaround that would isolate the damaged section while keeping the rope intact. But as she twisted the rope, looking for weaknesses, the core split, exposing a gash that ran more than halfway through. Tana's heart sank. It was no longer safe to use as a single line. If one of them fell, the force might be enough to tear it, sending the fallen climber to her grave. Fishing her pocketknife from her back pocket, Tana flicked open the blade and sliced through the rope.

"Aw shit," Calla said as she caught sight of what Tana was up to. "It snagged the rope?"

Tana nodded, her lips pursed into a thin line. "Almost took us for a joyride in the process." She pulled out her lighter and burned the two new ends, melting them to prevent future fraying. The acrid smell of burning chemicals hit her nostrils. "Looks like we're two teams now."

"Divide and conquer," Brynn whispered. She looked toward the summit, her mouth open in awe. "Well played, mountain."

Chapter Eight

A quiet settled over the dormitories, refreshing in its stillness. Downstairs, thousands of students were clamoring for their first taste of a college meal plan, an enthusiasm that would surely dim within days.

Blessedly alone after the chaos of move-in day, Calla sat atop her bunk, her phone pressed to her ear.

After the second ring, a man's voice answered. "Hello?"

"Hey, Dad."

"Honey, hey, everything okay? Don't tell me. It's the truck, isn't it? A thousand miles in one shot was a lot for that old gal."

"The truck's fine—"

"I'm heading to the airport now. If you forgot something, this is your last chance. I can be there in twenty minutes."

She bit back a smile. College was a foreign experience to her father—hell, her whole family. Yet he was determined to make sure it went smoothly for her, even suffering through two full days of driving across the heartland to drop Calla off with her rust bucket of a truck.

"Everything's fine, Dad. Just wanted to hear your voice. Not gonna lie, I'm feeling a little lonely."

"Those roommates treating you okay?" His tone hardened. "I know we may look like country bumpkins to some of these city folks, but I'll be damned if they're going to make you feel lesser for it."

Calla laughed. "No, they're fine. They seem nice enough. One of them is freakishly pale. It's like she hasn't seen the sun in ten years. Maybe she's anemic or something. We're actually going to do a girls' trip this weekend. Stay in the mountains, go hiking, get to know each other. It'll be a nice break after orientation week." She hated lying to her father but knew he'd be calling over the weekend to check up on her first week at college. Without a plausible excuse as to why she wasn't answering, he'd undoubtedly assume the worst.

"Oh wow, look at you, making friends already. Your mom would've been proud of you. She was always such a social butterfly." He paused long enough for Calla to wonder if the line was dead. "I really miss your mom, kiddo."

"Me too."

"If anything ever happened to you—"

"Dad! C'mon, don't be like that. Everything's going to be fine. You taught me well."

"Keep that can of mace in your purse," he said. "You really should've taken the Glock. I know what boys that age are looking for."

Her stomach twisted. She knew all too well what boys—and men—were looking for. And it was something she had no interest in. Her looks, a gift from her mother, had become a curse over the last few years, attracting an onslaught of unwanted attention. While Calla built up walls of sarcasm and surliness against their advances, her father was all too happy to supply actual firepower. "I'd be expelled if I ever pulled a gun out."

"Better expelled than raped."

"Jesus Christ, Dad."

"At least let me buy you a taser," he urged. "Or do the liberals hate those too? Ah shit, I'm at the airport. I've got to run. You sure you'll be okay?"

"Yeah. I just needed to hear a familiar voice."

"Anytime. Love you, Cal. Please, take care of yourself."

"Love you too, Dad."

The tinny beep of an alarm clock cut through the silent dorm. Calla slapped her phone, silencing the noise, and listened for the sounds of her roommates stirring. Already dressed, she slipped from the bunk and pulled on her boots, blindly lacing them. She shouldered her backpack and opened the door a crack, trying to keep the dormitory nightlights from bleeding into the room.

"What's going on?" Misty's slurred voice called out. "Where're you going?"

Calla sighed. Only a week into their college experience, she was already feeling smothered by Misty's protectiveness, which was only a shade less intrusive than her father's.

"Going for a climb. I'll see you later."

"What? The weather's terrible. Go next week instead. Tana and I can—"

"It's fine, I'll be back tonight. Tomorrow morning at the latest." She slipped out the door, cutting off the conversation.

At this early hour, the campus spotlights were still shining, their glow falling upon the parade of flags lining the walkways. The American flag, the Colorado flag, the college crest, and— Calla sucked in a sharp breath—a rainbow flag. In her tiny, conservative hometown, she'd never seen one flown, except maybe that one time Danny Caravello had said he was going as "one of the gays" for Halloween. The bright stripes seemed to mock her as she passed below them, and she dropped her gaze to the sidewalk instead.

Her pickup truck was parked on a side street off campus. Though freshmen weren't allowed vehicles on campus due to limited space, Calla insisted on having the truck nearby, a symbol of freedom to soothe her anxieties about moving to a city. Inside the cab, the familiar smell of dirt and hiking gear greeted her, a welcome respite from the dorms.

Though normally she'd cherish a two-hour drive alone with her thoughts, this jaunt through the predawn darkness twisted her stomach into a knot. Gusts of frigid wind knocked against the truck, already reaching speeds of forty-five miles per hour, according to the radio. They'd only intensify as the day wore on. "You can do this," she whispered, her fingers nervously drumming the steering wheel.

Finally, as the eastern sky showed the first trace of light, Calla pulled into the Pikes Peak parking lot. The lack of other cars on what should have been a busy weekend morning gnawed at her, and she reminded herself that she'd chosen today specifically for the deadly weather.

She strapped her crampons and ice ax to her bag, knowing that snow, even in late August, wasn't out of the question. Fourteen miles separated her from the summit, a number that only seemed more daunting now that she was exposed to the elements. She turned up her collar against the wind and started along the trail.

As she walked, her thoughts turned to her father, all alone for the first time in decades. His wife—her mother—had long since passed, and his only daughter was off to college in a faraway state. He'd poured everything into Calla, teaching her how to hunt and fish, how to change her oil, and how to fix a leaky faucet. She knew how to stretch a dollar and save for a rainy day, all thanks to his tireless efforts to make sure she was as well-prepared as humanly possible for whatever lay ahead.

He'd even tried ushering her into a normal adolescence, enlisting the help of their elderly neighbor to explain the finer points of tampon application, and escorting Calla to a beauty salon when nature gifted her with a unibrow.

Despite his best efforts, Calla couldn't shake the nagging feeling that she was woefully lacking in the ability to connect with her peers. Tinkering on an engine with her father or canning their fall harvest with the neighbors didn't translate to sleepovers and lunchtime chitchat. The rainbow flags on campus were a nagging reminder of how far behind she'd fallen. Was she already supposed to know where she fell in the kaleidoscope of colors, if anywhere at all? What would she say if someone asked? She felt lost in this new culture, a fish out of water. None of the skills she'd learned back home translated into the language of these city kids, all of whom seemed more worldly, more adult, despite their lack of practical skills. So what if she could drive a tractor or build a game trap? Who here would even care?

Her preference for older company hadn't been an issue when she still lived at home, not with her dad by her side. But here...

She stopped short, bracing herself against a spindly tree as a gust of wind nearly bowled her over.

Here, she was alone, unprepared. And though she'd be loath to admit it, that terrified her.

A dusting of snowflakes fell before her eyes. "Shit." She slipped off her pack and rifled through the contents, extracting a puffy coat and goggles. She pulled the coat over her other layers, relishing the extra warmth, then tugged the goggles over her eyes, blocking out the icy gusts.

Retrieving her satellite weather tracker, she frowned at the readout. Wind gusts were approaching sixty miles per hour, and the summit temperature had dropped below twenty degrees. Her father's words—make good decisions, kid—gnawed at her.

She stowed the device, shouldered her pack, and continued up the trail, forcing his words from her mind. She needed this summit—an inexplicable desire to conquer it urged her forward. Up ahead, the trees were thinning, and the moment when they completely disappeared was growing closer. If the wind was this aggressive here, how would she possibly remain upright once she no longer had their protection?

She hesitated at the tree line, the natural barrier between a difficult climb and a suicide mission. One wrong step could send her careening down the slope, her final thoughts a wave of guilt for wasting her father's sacrifices on a foolhardy climb. Yet as the sharp talons of doubt twisted around her, she ducked her head and burst from the trees, her boots clomping over the gravel trail.

A gust tore over the bald landscape, nearly swiping her feet from beneath her. She stumbled, pushing herself from the ground before running full steam along the trail. Her arms pumped, propelling her forward, the sound of her boots smacking the ground lost to the wind.

The trail rose sharply before her, a steep incline covered in loose scree. She sprinted up its face, her breath coming out in ragged gasps. A coppery taste filled her mouth, a sign of overexertion.

A howl echoed down the mountainside, preceded by a blast of scree. Calla had only a second to cover her face before the gust of wind knocked her sideways. She landed flat on her stomach, the breath expelled from her lungs. Small stones bounced along the trail, ricocheting off her face and body.

To the left, the hillside dropped away, a two-hundred-foot drop before disappearing into the trees. She dug her fingers into the dirt and gravel. Her face screwed up against the wind.

"What the fuck are you doing?" she whispered. As the wind screamed past, she dug her toes into the gravel for extra purchase.

She glanced over her shoulder at the trail. She could turn back now, and nobody would ever need to know. Hell, neither her dad nor her roommates even knew where she was. She could lie and say she'd gone for a quick romp through the hills, and nobody would be any wiser.

Still, her fingers refused to relinquish their grip.

She turned back to the summit, its snowy plateau hidden in the white expanse above. She needed to reach it. This was no silly quest for ego. She was...

She swallowed as the realization hit her. She was afraid.

Untethered from her small town, her father, and her memories—alone in a strange, new world. She was a small boat adrift at sea, with no earthly clue how to navigate the stormy seas of roommates and dating and girl talk. Capsizing was far more likely than she cared to admit.

If she could reach the summit, she could prove to herself that she was still strong and capable, even in the terrifying world of sororities and mixers. But if she failed here, in the treacherous landscape she knew best, what hope could she possibly have back at college?

She dropped her head into the dirt. Now that the thought was out in the open, it was beyond ridiculous. She'd rather get herself killed than own up to her childish social insecurities.

A choked laugh escaped her throat, ripped apart by the wind as soon as it left her lips. She stared longingly toward the summit, aching for the strength and self-assurance it promised her if only she could reach it.

A flash of light pulled her attention to the right. She winced against the glare, her eyes slowly focusing on a white pickup truck with a park ranger emblem on its side. She knew the trail periodically touched the road, but in the disorienting storm, she hadn't realized how close she was to civilization.

The truck screeched to a halt, and Calla cursed her choice of a bright red jacket, turning her into a beacon against the gray landscape.

"Hey. Are you hurt?" a man's voice called from the open truck window.

Calla waved him on, trying to indicate that she intended to keep climbing.

"It's like a hurricane out here!" the man yelled. "Get in the damn truck."

Her gaze flickered to the trail ahead. She could possibly make a run for it. If he was too scared to leave the safety of his truck, what could he do to stop her?

As if he could read her thoughts, the ranger shouted, "Look, I'm not in the mood for this, all right? Don't make me drag you over here."

"God damn it," she whispered. The summit was no more than a Band-Aid, an attempt to assuage feelings she refused to face head-on. In an ironic twist, this dangerous stunt only highlighted her cowardice. With a sigh, she pushed herself to her hands and knees to crawl toward the ranger.

Every step closer to the truck and further from the summit opened the floodgates a little wider. Doubt and anxiety poured over her. She'd abandoned her father. Nobody was ever going to like her and certainly not date her. They smelled the redneck on her and wished she'd go back to the woods.

Lips set into a hard line, she surrendered herself to the onslaught, letting it fill her up like a balloon. The pressure pushed against her chest, but she continued to crawl, opening up to the one thing she'd spent her whole life trying to control and subdue: fear.

Within a foot of the truck, she stood and grabbed the door handle just as the wind threatened to knock her back down. She clambered inside, struggling to yank the door shut behind her. The ranger reached over and grabbed the handle with her, slamming it closed.

He stared at her, a bemused expression on his sun-lined face. "I ought to fine you for being so reckless," he said. "If you'd needed a rescue, you would've put my whole team in harm's way."

Calla sat silently, staring at her lap.

The ranger shook his head, then picked up a paper bag and tossed it into her lap. "Doughnuts. The restaurant at the top makes the best ones in the whole damn world. A peace offering if you promise to never do anything this stupid again."

Calla reached inside the bag, pulling out a hot doughnut, still steaming. The scent of nutmeg and cinnamon filled the cab. She sighed. "Deal."

Hours later, Calla shuffled into the dormitory on legs that ached from exertion. Fighting to stay upright in the wind had proven extremely taxing, and the long drive home had given her muscles time to stiffen.

Tana and Misty sat on one of the bunks, staring at the small, boxy television Misty had brought from home. While Misty appeared transfixed by the antics of the women onscreen, Tana— her pale features still unsettling even after a week together—only seemed bored.

How was your climb?" Tana asked.

Calla peeled off her jacket, ready with a lie she'd concocted on the drive home about a quick jaunt to the summit of one of the nearby peaks. Instead, she heard her father's words from her first day of middle school, reappearing like a ghost.

"Remember, kiddo. It's okay not to be the strongest or fastest or toughest. Actually, some people really like when you're not trying so hard. Don't feel like you need to put on a show. I'll always know you're the coolest kid, anyway."

The lie caught in her throat. "I, uh, I didn't make it. Tried to climb Pikes, but I um...I got rescued by one of the rangers."

Tana's eyebrows shot up. "Oh wow, that's crazy. I always thought it'd be so embarrassing to be one of those people you see on the news."

Misty smacked Tana's arm. "Was he at least cute?"

Calla laughed. "He was probably fifty." She held up the paper bag of doughnuts. "Pitied me enough to give me these though."

Misty's eyes lit up, and she patted the bunk between her and Tana. "Ooo, bring those over here. We're watching *Real Housewives*." At Tana's eye roll, she said, "I know it's ridiculous. I started watching out of curiosity. But it really sucks you in."

Calla obliged, forcing back her own eye roll in an effort to form some kind of bond, even if it meant suffering through such inanity.

"You know," Misty said, reaching into the bag of doughnuts, "Tana and I climb too. You should've asked us to come with you. Then we could've told you how crazy it was, and you wouldn't have needed a rescue."

Tana held up her doughnut. "But then we wouldn't have these."

"Wait..." Calla turned to look her in the eye. "You're both climbers? Like mountain climbers?" She couldn't picture overly fussy Misty and quiet, subdued Tana anywhere near a mountain.

Misty fixed her with an exasperated stare. "That's what I was trying to tell you this morning when you ran out of here at the crack of dawn. Why do you think we picked this dinky college?" She scoffed. "Certainly not for its academic merit."

Calla slumped against the wall, speechless. This whole time, she'd been fleeing from failure, the moment when everyone—this college, this city, these women—decided she wasn't their type and cast her aside. The moment she slunk back home, her tail between her legs. When really, acceptance had been one honest conversation away.

"How about the three of us go out next weekend?" Misty asked. "We can do one of the fourteeners. A proper introduction to Colorado."

"And check the weather beforehand so nobody needs a rescue." Tana smirked, elbowing Calla in the side.

At the playful jab, a warmth spread through Calla's chest, loosening the viselike grip of anxiety. She snuck a glance back at Tana, whose cheeks were puffed up with doughnuts. There was something odd about Tana's looks, for sure, but at that moment, Calla found her strangely adorable. The warmth in her chest morphed, a rush of butterflies swirling into her belly.

She hurriedly turned back to the television, shocked at the flutter in her stomach and horrified that Tana might have noticed. She was suddenly very aware of Tana's warm body, pressed tightly beside hers. Only for proximity to the doughnuts, she knew, but it was still surprisingly pleasant. Her eyes glazed over, the two women getting a manicure on-screen fading from sight. A tiny smile tugged at her lips.

"I'd really like that."

Chapter Nine

With their communal line severed, Brynn's initial proposal was to team up with Calla, leaving Tana and Misty on their own rope team, the unsaid implication that there was a clear A and B team, and she fully intended to be part of the former. Her hopes were extinguished by Misty's dismissive laughter, followed by Misty stepping between the two women to clip Brynn securely to her own rope.

"I think Calla's rubbed off on you quite enough."

Smirking, Calla offered the tail end of her rope to Tana. "Good thing Tana's not as easily corrupted."

With everyone clipped in, all four women turned as one to look at the ridgeline above them, another half mile of clambering over the mess of rockfall debris. Camp Two lay another thousand feet above that ridge, a steep final push over a glacier field. Tana couldn't remember ever feeling as battered, both physically and mentally, by one of their climbs. The closest she'd come to feeling so beaten raw was a climb up Mount Washington with Misty. They'd gone to New Hampshire laughing about how the White Mountains were child's play compared to their beloved Rockies, only to have Washington's notoriously vicious weather leave them doubting if they'd live out the hour.

"No sense in delaying the inevitable," Calla said, the morning's enthusiasm drained from her voice. "Onward, ladies."

Brynn scowled at the sight of Calla's rope team leading the way, no doubt smarting at being forced into third place, but she let them pass without a word.

Tana heard Brynn's boots clomping along behind her, and she was grateful to once again be following Calla's steady footing, especially over this difficult terrain.

The minutes stretched into an hour, and still, the ridgeline seemed distant as they crawled through the boulders, remnants of thousands of years of erosion and avalanches. *And climate change*, Tana told herself, as if she needed another reminder. The mountains, Torket included, were like a neon billboard, screaming to anyone who cared to listen that the end was nigh. Their glaciers and snowfields were rapidly receding, leaving the debris fields, moraines, as their new defining features.

"Look." As if reading her thoughts, Brynn pointed to an outcropping far above, the rock sheared in half. Her finger dropped down the side of the mountain, tracing the scar where the other half had tumbled to its new resting place. "When I read up on Torket, I found a bunch of photos from decades ago, and the glaciers were massive. You couldn't see any of those rocks. Give it another decade, and they'll be gone. Then all of this will really start crashing down."

"The plague of humans, destroying the world," Calla intoned. "When are people going to finally realize we should stop making new ones?" She paused. "No offense, Mist."

"None taken," Misty said quietly. "It's definitely getting scary. I'm worried about what kind of world we're leaving the boys."

With their expansive spectrum of political views, it was a testament to the glaringly obvious evidence that they could all agree on this one issue. Misty was a devout Republican, often griping about Brynn's liberal, "bleeding heart" politics when they spoke on the phone. Calla was a libertarian down to her core, and Tana, as with most things in her life, had no strong opinion. Yet thanks to their love of the mountains and their desire to preserve them, they all wore the title of environmentalist. She wondered how long Torket, though impressive at over eighteen thousand feet, could sustain its ice.

The thought of the mountains—the only place she truly loved—being destroyed put a swift damper on her mood. She trudged upward, her eyes unseeing as her thoughts sank to lower and lower depths. How many more rocks would fall as the glaciers receded? How many hikers would be buried under their crushing weight?

As they always did whenever she was climbing, Tana's thoughts turned to her parents. Were they entombed under a slab of fallen rock? Their meat long dissolved, with only their shattered bones and hiking clothes left behind?

A pang of sadness radiated through her, so sharp and sudden that she involuntarily grasped at her chest as if she could quell the sudden ache. Her eyes burned with the threat of tears, and her lips pulled back, readying the release of a sob. But as quickly as it arrived, the melancholy was extinguished, like a match burst of flame on a windy day.

"What the..." she whispered. She knew what grief was supposed to feel like. She'd seen it play out time and again in movies. But much like joy, she seemed unable to conjure up the emotions that came naturally for others. To be struck with a bolt of such palpable anguish was astounding. She thought back to the elation she'd felt at seeing the stars that morning. Were sudden mood swings a symptom of altitude? Unlikely, and certainly not this low.

She could picture Misty's concerned gaze if she dared to bring it up. Another entry on her growing list of reasons to head back to the cabin. Tana blinked away the wetness from her eyes, hiding the evidence. Best to chalk it up as a fluke, maybe a testament to the emotional pull of nature, nothing more.

"Hey, guys," Brynn called out, breaking their silence. "What's the laziest mountain?"

A few seconds ticked by, and the only sound was their labored breathing.

"What?" Calla asked.

"Ever-rest." Brynn burst into laughter, the sound reverberating across the basin walls. "Get it?"

Misty groaned. "That was such a Todd joke."

"Wait, there's more! What's the most dangerous mountain?"

Grateful for the distraction, Tana asked, "What?"

"Kill-a-man-jaro!"

Her childlike laugh was so infectious that the others began giggling as well. Calla first, then spreading down their lineup until even Misty was laughing through her gasping breaths.

"Brynn, you're too damn much sometimes," she said. "You should babysit more often. The kids would love to listen to your dumb jokes." She lifted her gaze to take in their surroundings. "Oh wow, are we finally at the ridgeline?"

Calla was pulling herself up the final incline, her crampons scrabbling for grip on the icy ground. With one last heave, she yanked herself onto the ridge, her ice ax raised in triumph. "Finally!" She reached down to offer a hand to Tana, who was more than grateful to grab on. "Not too bad, eh? Just a little farther to go."

Tana turned to survey the basin below them, a full day's worth of climbing, and her chest swelled with pride. This was what she'd been chasing, this feeling of pushing through the fatigue and pain until she emerged stronger and tougher than before. She lent a hand to Brynn, pulling her up the last foot.

"There's Camp One," Calla said as Misty emerged on the ridge.

Tana followed Calla's pointing finger to the very bottom of the basin, where, if she squinted hard enough, she could make out the spot where they'd cleared away snow for the tents.

"I wonder," Misty gasped, "what it feels like to take a relaxing vacation." She coughed a thick, wet sound that cut across the low hum of wind. "Please tell me we're almost at camp."

"Half a mile," Tana said, trying to soften the blow. Climbers generally spoke in vertical distances, rather than miles and kilometers, to paint a clearer picture of the climb ahead. Telling Misty that it was only half a mile was far kinder than letting her know they still had several hundred feet to gain before the day ended.

Unwilling to cut her sister any slack, Brynn smirked. "Steepest half mile of your life." She pointed at the snowy incline before them.

"Only half a mile," Misty whispered, a one-woman pep talk. She gave Brynn a nudge toward the steep hill, urging their duo into the lead position. "C'mon, you brat. No rest for the wicked. Let's get this shit over with."

Half an hour later, as Misty's wheezing breaths were developing a slightly alarming rattle, Brynn crested the top of the hill, issuing a strangled cry of triumph. "We made it. Calla, camp's right here." Her arms, raised in victory, were barely visible in the cloudy mist that was slowly enveloping the mountain.

A relieved smile stretched across Tana's face. She'd always hated being last in line. Even on a rope team, where it wasn't an indication of speed, it made her somehow feel inferior to be pulling up the rear. She couldn't understand how Misty loved this spot—being the last to see their camps and summits, her joy filtered by the cheers and whoops of everyone before her. Or maybe she was reading too much into it. Maybe, like so much in her life, the middle was simply where she felt most at home.

As she crested the hill, she came face-to-face with Brynn, who threw her gloved hands around her and pulled her onto flat land. "We did it," she crowed. "We're halfway to the summit."

The sound of crunching footsteps pulled them from their euphoria, and all four women spun on the spot, Calla's hand reaching for the can of mace she kept beneath her jacket.

"Hey there," a deep, husky voice called out. A figure emerged from the white haze, easily a head taller than them. His sunshine-hued parka made it a wonder they hadn't seen him sooner. Above the open neck of the parka, a wiry, copper-colored beard obscured half of the man's face. "Didn't think anyone else was climbing this goddamned thing. Especially in this weather."

"Just us, as far as we know. We've got the whole thing to ourselves." Brynn said, oblivious to the horrified stares of her teammates. In an area with no cell reception, where hikers went missing regularly, she'd unwittingly told a much larger, and likely much stronger, stranger that they were alone together. "There were no other cars in the parking—"

Calla deftly stepped in front of Brynn, arm outstretched to the man. "I'm Calla, team leader, doomsday prepper, and fifth-degree blackbelt." With her free hand, she casually lifted the bottom of her parka, exposing the mace can.

The man gripped her hand and gave it a firm shake, his eyes crinkling in amusement beneath bushy brows. "Hell, Calla, I like the sound of you. My type of woman." He dropped his gaze down her body, sizing her up. "I'm a bit of a prepper myself. Maybe we can talk apocalypse scenarios later. You from the city? I'm always looking for people to ride out the end times with."

Calla sneered. "I'm out of your league, buddy." She gestured at the rest of her team. "This is Tana, Misty, and Brynn, and no offense, but we're not really in the mood for company."

Tana inwardly flinched at the aggressive tone, knowing it was a necessary evil. How many times had they gone for drinks, only to have men swat aside their flimsy rejections and park themselves at their table? Well, not her, per se. But she'd certainly seen it happen to Calla and Misty plenty. The only rejection they seemed to understand was one they were beaten over the head with.

The man raised his hands in surrender. "I'm not intruding, don't get all worked up. Just saying hi since I haven't seen another person in days. I'm Wyatt, by the way. I'm taking a quick break before moving on to Camp Three."

"You're not staying the night?" Brynn asked. "It'll be dark before you make it. Hell, it'll be dark in a couple hours. You should at least wait until morning."

Wyatt nodded. "Maybe, but the weather's moving in fast, and I want to tap the summit before shit hits the fan. You gals might be wise to do the same."

"Noted." Calla gripped Brynn's arm and pulled her into camp, ignoring Wyatt's amused grin. Once they were out of earshot, she hissed, "What is wrong with you?"

Brynn's mouth dropped into an O. "I was—"

"What? Telling that seven-foot troll that he had free rein to murder us in our tents?"

"He's not going to—"

"We have no idea what he's going to do. That's the point! You've been out on your cozy, guided, National-Geographic-endorsed trips, where everyone is nice and friendly and kumbaya, but that's not the real world, okay? Alaska's bad enough, with every guy thinking women are put on earth for their amusement. And up in the mountains? Forget it. If you haven't been assaulted by every climber and his father, you must be new."

Tana and Misty, who were listening intently, exchanged a glance. Calla had never mentioned being attacked. What the hell had happened to her after moving here? And why hadn't she trusted them enough to confide in them?

At Brynn's crestfallen expression, Calla's tone softened. "Look, I know this is coming off as harsh. But I know these guys, all right? I've been putting up with this shit since I was a teenager. Please trust me on this."

Brynn glanced back at Wyatt, who, while safely out of earshot, was still eyeing them curiously. "I get what you're saying," she told Calla, "but not everyone's a bad guy. You can't go around thinking everyone's out to get you, even here."

Calla looked skyward, trying to summon her patience. "Stay away from him," she said, dropping her pack to the snow. Turning her back on Brynn, she yanked open the top of her bag and began tossing items at their feet. Though she was clearly trying to keep the edge out of her voice, her tone held a glint of steel. "Everyone help set up camp. Hurry up, the sun's going down."

While Misty and Brynn pulled out their own tent, Tana crouched beside Calla, tentatively placing a hand on her back. "You never told us," she said quietly. "We could've helped you through it."

Calla continued to paw through her belongings, keeping her face angled away from Tana. "I dealt with it in the only language they understand up here. Alaska has its issues, but the one nice thing is that when someone goes missing, they give up the hunt real quick. Better to let nature take its course."

Her words were like a splash of ice water to the face. "Wait a sec, are you saying you—"

"I did what I had to do," Calla interrupted. "A single woman, alone in the woods, thinking she can homestead as well as the boys? And refuse to sleep with them while she's at it?" She laughed, a dark, hollow sound. "Someone like that needs to be taught a lesson. Well, they taught me all right. And then I taught them what the end of a forty-five looks like."

She dropped the tent in front of Tana and stood, cutting off the conversation. "Can you handle this? I'll boil water." She turned on her heel, stove in hand.

Tana could only stare at her, dumbfounded.

As Calla dug out a kitchen, creating a flat surface for the stove, Misty unscrewed the bear canister and shuffled through the contents. "Mac and cheese?" she asked. "We can all use the extra calories."

"Sounds delicious," Brynn called back, her upper body hidden inside their newly erected tent as she rolled out the sleeping bags.

Misty tossed a couple of packets of macaroni toward Calla, the plastic baggies landing beside her in the snow. Calla ignored them, her eyes hollow and unseeing as she stared daggers at the pot of water.

The heavy crunch of footsteps pulled her out of her thoughts, and she lifted her gaze up to Wyatt's bearded, smiling face.

"Wasn't trying to eavesdrop," he apologized, "I've got a packet of weenies that'll cook up damn good with some mac and cheese. I'm willing to share since I'll be off the mountain a day earlier than expected. Plus, not gonna lie, mac and cheese is my favorite, and I accidentally left mine at home. It's sitting right on the kitchen counter. Sometimes I'm a real idiot." At Calla's glare, he held out the package of hot dogs, a wide, earnest grin behind his beard. His eyes darted to Brynn's rear end, still sticking out of the tent, before quickly returning to Calla. "Peace offering?"

Calla stared at him for a few seconds, her eyes seeming to bore through him, as though she could read his intentions. Finally, she reached out and snatched the packet from his hands. "Dinner's in twenty minutes."

"Yes, ma'am."

Five dishes of macaroni were spooned up, chunks of sliced hotdog folded into their cheesy depths. Tana passed them around, secretly holding the one with the most visible hotdog pieces for herself. It was a greedy move, and she wasn't proud of it. Just hungry.

Wyatt accepted his with a grateful smile, wrapping his ungloved hands around the bowl to absorb the warmth. "This beats the hell out of the cold hot dogs and tortillas I was going to whip up."

"No stove?" Tana asked.

He shook his head, plowing into the macaroni. "When you're traveling solo, every ounce matters. I had a buddy who was supposed to come along, but he bailed last minute. Said his aunt died." He laughed. "I know for a fact that his one and only aunt is alive and well in Orlando. He freaked out after reading how many people have gone missing up here."

Brynn plopped down next to him. Her lips pursed as she pondered how to word her question. She flipped a lock of blond hair over her shoulder, a flirtatious move that left Tana wondering if it was intentional. "I may have a theory about that. But first, have you been hearing voices? Like, people talking? Sometimes screaming?"

"Screaming? You think people are getting murdered up here?" He paused, face scrunching up in thought. "Actually, I saw on Reddit that's one of the theories about this place. All the disappearances. Back in the nineties, there was a guy who escaped from the local jail. They were holding him temporarily, and he was supposed to be shipped down to Anchorage the next day. Dude had gotten into a brawl that turned ugly. You know how it goes, a few too many drinks and people lose control. This guy ended up killing two people. The guy he was fighting and his girlfriend who was trying to break up the fight."

"And this maniac was running loose?" Misty asked.

Wyatt nodded. "Apparently. He was never caught, and Torket's not that far from where they were holding him, maybe twenty miles. Some people think he's been camped out on the mountain this whole time, knocking off anyone who catches sight of him." He shrugged. "Personally, I think anyone who goes missing here probably fell off the side or something. Or crushed by rockfall. The south face of this thing is crumbling like crazy with all the glacier melt. Though a serial killer does add a certain danger to the climb." He smirked at Calla, who refused to return his grin. "We may need your martial arts skills once night rolls around."

"Actually..." Brynn hesitated. "We weren't thinking serial killers. We think it might be a little more supernatural."

"Like spirits?" He shrugged. "That's what Torket means, you know. Home of the spirits."

At this, Brynn's face lit up, and she turned to her teammates with an "I told you so" look.

"That's what it's supposed to mean, anyway. They took the Inuit word, *torngait*, and either completely misheard it or mangled it for European consumption. On the East Coast, they have the Torngat Mountains, and out here, it became Mount Torket. Kind of like Denali. Everyone thinks that's the original Alaskan word for The Great One, but it's a simplified version of the Koyukon word *deenaalee*."

Misty nodded. "A lot of state names are like that too. Weird mish-mashes of Native words."

"I haven't seen or heard anything," he said. "Not that I doubt you. It makes sense with the name of this place. And there's so much in our world that can't be explained away with science. The best those eggheads can do is guess and hypothesize. I think only a fool would dismiss the idea of the paranormal entirely."

At the seething look on Calla's face, Tana choked on a piece of hotdog. She fought to cough it out while simultaneously hiding the fact that she was laughing. Misty slapped her on the back.

"And it gets even weirder," Brynn said, scooching closer to Wyatt. "Tana had a..." She looked to Tana for support. "A vision? A demonic possession? It's like she blacked out but was still conscious. While we were crossing your ladder—thanks, by the way—she unclipped from the rope and everything. We thought she might jump right off."

"Oh shit, you guys used my ladder?" he asked. "How are you gonna get back across once I pass back over? I can't leave it behind. I borrowed it from my friend. That idiot who didn't show."

Brynn waved a hand in dismissal. "It's fine. We cached ours beside the cliff, right off the trail—"

"Anyone want seconds?" Calla's voice, so shrill that it was almost a screech, cut across them. She held out the pot, her hand trembling slightly from suppressed rage. Though her lips were curled into a smile, her eyes blazed like coals at Brynn.

Catching on, Misty asked, "What do you do for work, Wyatt?"

Wyatt gave Calla one last inscrutable look before turning his attention to Misty. "Firefighter," he said. "They recently changed the schedule, so I get every other week off. Before that, the most I'd get was three days, making it tough to do any serious peaks. With the new schedule, I couldn't pass up an opportunity to climb Torket. This mountain's legendary."

With Wyatt's attention focused on Misty, Brynn mouthed "firefighter" to the group, waggling her eyebrows suggestively. Looking at the two of them together, Tana supposed she saw the attraction. It was difficult to tell his age, based on all the facial hair, but she guessed late twenties, maybe early thirties, a good match for Brynn. They were both fit, both conventionally attractive, and both open-minded to the paranormal. Plus, if there was one thing pop culture had taught her, it was that every woman—besides herself—loved a firefighter. She wondered if she'd ever get to experience what was unfolding in front of her. That quick spark of attraction always seemed outlandishly fun, like a scene out of a movie. It was something she'd only ever dreamed about.

"Ever had to pull a kitten out of a tree?" Brynn asked. She leaned toward him, elbow resting on her knee, face cupped in her palm. This time, Tana had no doubts. Brynn was definitely flirting.

Laughing, Wyatt mimicked her gesture, leaning in close. "They don't really have us do that anymore, which is a damn shame. I've been told I have a knack with the kitties." He winked, eliciting a snort of laughter from Brynn and a gagging noise from Misty.

"Maybe it's time you hit the trail," Misty said. "The light's fading fast."

Wyatt stretched out his long limbs, leisurely folding his arms behind his head and surveying the women around him, a casually confident gesture that rang Tana's alarm bells. It was the pose of a man who knew he had nothing to fear.

"Actually," he said, "you've all convinced me to stick around. It was a stupid idea to try for the next camp at night. And when you meet someone who's worth sticking around for..." He smiled at Brynn, the corners of his eyes crinkling, and she blushed under his gaze. "I'll go set up my tent, and uh...I saw the two-mans you guys have. Mine's a little more spacious. Had to buy the big one because I'm six, three. You should come join me if you want a little more personal space." He winked at Brynn. "Or less, your call."

Calla stood, her feet spread and hands curled into fists, a perfect rendition of a power pose. "I think you need to leave," she growled. "We've been polite and put up with you, but nobody here is hooking up with anyone on this trip. I think it's best if you stick to your plan and keep moving."

Pushing himself to his feet, Wyatt narrowed his eyes at Calla, scrutinizing, scanning for chinks in her armor. "And if I don't?"

Brynn tugged Calla's arm, urging her back to her seat. "Calla, it's fine. Leave him alone," she pleaded.

"If you won't go peacefully, we'll make you," Calla replied.

Wyatt laughed, surveying the four women. "Fat chance."

"Try me." Her tone was so deadly serious that the laughter dripped right off his face. In its absence, anger found a new home.

Tana's stomach dropped at the sight of his features clouding over. She'd never been in so much as a fistfight and didn't know if she had the stomach for anything even remotely violent. If Calla really was capable of killing a person—an idea that seemed both completely fitting and horrifying—then this was a situation that was far beyond Tana's comfort level.

To her incredible relief, Wyatt made no move to challenge them. "Fine," he growled, his voice low and menacing. "Not a problem. I can tell when I'm not wanted. I'll be up and down this thing in two days, and when I get back to the ladder, I'll be taking mine with me." He paused, his blue eyes boring into Calla's. "It'd be a damn shame if you couldn't find yours."

A cold silence settled over camp, and Tana wondered if she'd heard him correctly. He couldn't possibly stoop that low, intentionally stranding them in the wilderness, right? In this frozen landscape, with minimal supplies and inclement weather, he may as well have been threatening to kill them on the spot.

Brynn's mouth dropped open. "Are you serious?" she asked quietly. Color rose in her cheeks, and Tana wondered if it was from anger or embarrassment at buying his nice guy routine.

He shrugged. "Just saying, you never know what those ghosts get up to."

In two long strides, Calla crossed the kitchen dugout, hands raised, and shoved him hard, sending him careening backward, arms pinwheeling. One heel caught against a rock, and he tumbled to the ground, a look of shock on his face.

"Get out," she said, her voice low and all the more dangerous for it. "And when you get to the crossing, take your ladder and nothing else. If you touch ours, I'll destroy your life, and that's a goddamn promise. Tana's a cop, and we have your plates."

Tana sat up a little straighter, trying to add some authority to the flimsy lie. She hoped she was projecting the haughty confidence she associated with police officers.

"You have a minute to pack your shit and get out of our sight," Calla said. She pulled the can of mace from her pocket. "Otherwise, we start with this, and things only get uglier from there."

"You're fucking crazy," he said, back-crawling away. "All of you, a bunch of fucking crazy bitches."

Calla's eyes blazed. "You have no idea."

Wyatt lifted himself to his feet and jogged back to his side of camp, his eyes continuously darting back to Calla and the mace in her hand. His bag lay open, a few items scattered about his campsite. He threw them inside his pack haphazardly, then cinched it shut, slipping the straps over his shoulders. He paused, his mouth open to say something, maybe plead his case, maybe ask for forgiveness, maybe call them a bunch of raging cunts. Instead, he shook his head and turned, disappearing into the dark gloom that led to Camp Three.

The silence stretched on for several minutes—the women alert for the sound of returning footsteps. Calla stood ready at the edge of the camp, her muscles tensed and an ear cocked against the growing wind. When it seemed like he was gone for good, she returned to their circle, stashing the mace back in her pocket. She glared at Brynn.

"Give him a chance, huh?"

"I'm really sorry," Brynn said and certainly looked it. With her skin flushed and eyes mournful, Tana had the fleeting impression of a puppy who knew they'd been caught tearing into an expensive shoe. "I should've listened."

"Do us all a favor and remember that next time."

Brynn stared at her feet, rebuked, and gave a tiny nod.

Misty placed a hand on her shoulder. "We've all had it happen, Brynn. The sweet, charming guy you want to show off to your parents turns out to be a dickwad. You had the rotten luck to find one in probably the worst possible place to piss someone off."

"What if he steals the ladder?" Brynn asked. "Should we go back?"

"Obviously," Misty said.

Calla shook her head. "I think we scared some sense into him. Me and Officer Tanaraq, two badass bitches out to fuck him up."

Tana smiled at the absurdity of her being a cop. She'd never be able to stand up to anyone, let alone a giant like Wyatt. Once again, she found herself grateful for Calla's presence. Without her, would Brynn be in his tent right now?

"Plus, we have the sat phone," Calla said. "A rescue would be expensive as hell, not to mention embarrassing. And with the weather kicking up, it might take a few days. But eventually, someone would come find us."

"Very reassuring," Misty grumbled. She pulled her backpack close and unearthed her medical kit from inside. Flipping through the baggies of pills, she whispered, seemingly to herself, "If I wanted this much stress, I would've stayed home with the kids."

Calla's gaze shifted to the trail that led to Camp Three, all traces of joviality melting from her face. Her head dipped a fraction of an inch as if confirming a decision with her own thoughts. She stood, the stress of the encounter showing in her tight features, and addressed the group, "Let's try to get some shut-eye. A little sleep'll do us all some good. And maybe tomorrow, if we're lucky, we can have a day where nothing spirals out of control."

While the other three headed for their tents, Calla took one last uneasy look around camp. The deepening shadows added to the sense of someone watching them, waiting for the perfect moment to pounce.

Chapter Ten

A howling wind tore across the mountainside, low and melancholy. Snow swirled on the currents, creating patterns that would be beautiful if they weren't blinding. A small girl, her face nearly as white as the snow, stumbled through the growing drifts. She pulled her hood lower on her forehead, trying to keep the flakes from stinging her face.

Her tiny feet ached with fatigue, and a cramp throbbed against her ribcage. She had no idea how long she'd been walking, but the rumble in her stomach suggested she'd missed lunch, possibly breakfast as well. Even scarier, she had no idea how much longer she'd be out here in the cold.

Despite the bright white light, her skin looked dingy, almost gray. She held her hand in front of her face, unable to shake the crazy thought that she'd been sucked into one of those old black-and-white TV shows. Her red boots were half buried in snow. She lifted a foot and shook off the powder, eyes widening to see that the boot seemed to have lost most of its color as well. The surrounding wilderness was snow-covered, a bleak and inhospitable landscape. What was she doing here?

She struggled to grasp any shred of memory, any clue as to where she was and, more importantly, where she was meant to be going. She spun on the spot, gray eyes sweeping over her surroundings. The outline of a huge peak stood stark against the white sky, jolting something loose in her mind.

The peak. She'd been standing on the peak. Two figures flashed into her head, their faces obscured, bodies fuzzy and undefined.

She remembered the summit, the loneliness that crashed over her when she woke up to realize that she was alone, abandoned. Her layers were soaked through with snow and water. She had no supplies, no backpack, only the damp clothes on her back. She'd cried out without knowing for whom.

Panic set in as she ran across the flat summit, peering down each side, checking for any sign of her family, yelling their names into the wind. No voices called back to her, and in the falling snow, any tracks they may have left behind were invisible. She had no idea which way led back home. Eventually, her throat hoarse from yelling, she chose a path at random and trekked down the side of the mountain, desperate to escape the frigid gusts. Despite her thick parka packed tight with down feathers, the chill seeped inside, sending shivers up her spine.

Tears fell freely down her cheeks, whisked away by strands of hair as they billowed around her head. Her dark hair, which had always shone with hints of red in the sunlight, was now a subdued, mousy brown.

Terrible thoughts swirled through her mind. What had happened to her family? Had they abandoned her? Didn't they like her enough to keep her? If she kept calling out, would they change their minds and come back?

The snowdrifts were growing larger with the gusts of wind, and she stepped into one, only to sink up to her waist. Snow poured into the tops of her boots and bunched under her parka, the icy cold nearly burning.

Finally, it was all too much. She screamed.

A wail of agony and terror, the verbal outpouring of fear that she was never going to see her family—or anyone—ever again. She scrambled out of the snow, clawing her way forward blind as tears blurred her vision.

It was then that she heard them. Voices flit through the sparse tree cover, rising and falling with the wind. Hurriedly wiping her eyes on her parka sleeve, she stumbled through the snow, racing toward the sound, praying they wouldn't leave before she reached them.

The man saw her first, tapping the woman's arm and pointing. Their faces were identical, all wide eyes and open mouths. She ran to them, not knowing or caring who they were, only wanting someone to rescue her from this frigid, lonely nightmare.

Tana bolted upright with a gasp. The dream, or as she liked to think of it, the memory, for this wasn't the first time she'd relived it, was still so fresh she could almost feel that bitter cold. Or maybe, she realized, it was actually that cold in the tent. Tears trickled down her cheeks, and she swiped them away, feeling foolish for getting this emotional, even in her dreams.

The likelihood of it being an accurate memory was slim to none. The central premise that someone had taken her to Torket's summit as a small child was preposterous. What parent would be so irresponsible?

And yet, the two figures in the dream were no doubt her adoptive parents. She'd dug up old photos from their time in Alaska, and their coats matched her dream. Her dad was wearing hunter green, and her mom navy blue. And they'd always talked about finding her as a child on Torket. If this part of her dream was a true memory, why not the rest of it?

Because it's impossible, that's why, she reminded herself. *People don't disappear into thin air.*

The dark mass on the other side of the tent rolled over. "Can't sleep?" Calla asked. "Feel like taking a shift for me? I've been awake, waiting for that asshole to come back."

"You haven't slept?" Tana asked, trying to shake the remnants of her dream and return to reality. "You're going to feel like shit tomorrow."

Calla shrugged, or what Tana assumed was a shrug inside her sleeping bag. "Did you honestly think I wasn't going to stand guard after what he said to us? If the options are feeling like shit or being beaten to death in your sleep, I know what I'd pick."

A wave of shame crashed over Tana. She'd assumed everything would be fine without taking any measures to actually keep her teammates safe. Once again, leaving Calla to pull their weight. "Why didn't you ask us to take turns keeping watch?"

Calla scoffed. "And make Misty even more paranoid? No thanks. I'd rather suck it up and pull the all-nighter."

I can't believe you were doing that for us." At Calla's bemused look, Tana laughed. "Ok, I guess I can. Still, it's really nice of you."

"Yeah, I'm a real softie," she said. "Don't tell the others. I prefer to rule through fear." She yawned. "What do you say? While you're fighting insomnia, feel like listening for Wyatt?"

"I can handle that."

"You're the best." She shot Tana an exhausted smile of thanks before rolling onto her side, pulling her beanie over her eyes to block the moonlight.

Within minutes, a low rumble of snores drifted from her side of the tent, and Tana realized with a pang of gratitude how drained Calla must have been. Pulling an all-nighter for their sake was so touching that Tana had to force herself not to roll over to hug her friend—a move that certainly would have earned either a snort of derisive laughter or an irritated sigh.

Now that she thought about it, the fact that Calla wasn't completely wrung out with nerves was astounding. With her take-charge personality, she was their de-facto leader, always had been, and had a habit of assuming far more than her share of responsibility. Since these reunion climbs had been her idea, the pressure of making sure each one went off without a hitch was undoubtedly weighing on her, especially now that it had already gone horribly wrong. The terror of nearly losing Brynn and Tana to falls on the same day, followed by their encounter with Wyatt, was enough to make anyone throw in the towel.

When you added unearthly specters to the mix, the only possible explanation for how they were still climbing was that Calla was superhuman.

Tana lay back, pulling the hood of her mummy bag up over her head. Giving in to creature comforts was bound to make her doze off, but the desire to be snuggled up, especially after being emotionally ravaged by her dream, was too strong to ignore. She wasn't as strong as Calla, and she could accept that.

Her bag, rated for minus twenty degrees, was like a warm, fluffy cloud. She wiggled her toes, relishing the layer of down encircling them. The wind whistled through their campsite and, coupled with Calla's snoring, acted as white noise, soothing away her anxieties. Her eyelids drifted shut, and she promised herself it was okay. She was only resting them.

The sound of footsteps jerked her awake. Shit. How could she have let herself fall asleep? Calla had been prepared to stay up all night to protect them, and she couldn't even manage fifteen minutes.

Struggling out of her sleeping bag, she paused, one ear raised. The wind was howling again. Could that be what she'd heard? Would Wyatt really come back to bother them at—she checked her watch—3:30 in the morning? A quick patter of steps made her head rise in alarm. She opened her mouth to wake Calla, then stopped at the thought of how quickly Calla had dropped into sleep. It seemed pointlessly cruel to wake her up for what was most likely a marmot or deer wandering through camp.

She unzipped her bag, one hand covering the zipper to muffle the sound, and slipped on her boots. A quick walkthrough of their camp would probably scare off whatever was out there. And if not, a good scream would bring everyone running. Yanking on her parka, she unzipped the tent and crawled into the open air, immediately regretting the move and wishing she could return to her warm sleeping bag.

Her headlamp was in her pocket. She grabbed it and flicked it on, surveying the site. Nothing seemed out of place. The stove and pot were still in their kitchen pit, undisturbed. The ice axes and crampons were all still arranged in a neat line. No shadowy figures lurked beyond the tents. She scanned the ground for footprints, searching for Wyatt's gigantic telltale boots, but except for his path leading away from camp, all the fresh prints were theirs.

The wind picked up again, the gusts causing the nylon tents to ripple, emitting a low, steady thrum.

And then, out of the darkness, a voice.

Tana spun around, headlamp raised. "Hello?" she asked, her voice thin with fear. "Wyatt?" She racked her brain for any threat that would stop him from inching closer. "Trust me, assaulting a cop is the last thing you want to do. They'll put you in a cell for the rest of your life, no questions asked."

Another voice chimed in, too high pitched to be Wyatt's, the words unintelligible. They danced around her, their meaning unclear but their tone urgent, wanting. She could almost feel the desperation in them. Was it the spirits? Did they need something from her? That's how it always seemed to work in the movies: a ghost who couldn't move on to the afterlife until a living person helped them find closure to some trauma in their past. But what help could she possibly offer these spirits, especially when she couldn't even understand the language?

A tent unzipped, and Brynn crawled out, Misty close behind. "Is he back?" Misty asked, flicking on her own light.

"Listen," Tana instructed, and they fell quiet.

The voices circled, drifting in and out of camp on the wind. Instinctively, the women huddled together, their backs inward, and the lights facing out.

One of the voices rose to a scream, a terrifying shriek that raised the hair on the back of Tana's neck. She pointed her headlamp in all directions, the light trembling as it combed over the surrounding rocks and ice.

"Leave us alone," Brynn screamed, her voice cracking, close to panic.

The voices grew louder in response, and Tana's knees nearly buckled at the return of footsteps, dozens of them moving closer, closer...

Calla burst from the tent, headlamp held in her left hand, a black handgun in her right. A snarl of rage was plastered across her face, her eyes bloodshot and shining. She charged toward her friends, gun held aloft, and fired a warning shot to the sky.

The blast echoed around camp, and Tana instinctively ducked, her eardrums ringing. Beside her, Misty and Brynn screamed. "You brought a gun?" Misty cried.

Calla wasn't listening, already stalking the perimeter of the camp, which had gone deathly quiet. Her steps were slow and calculating, the gun steady in her hand, and Tana found herself wondering if this wasn't the first time she'd needed a weapon on the trails. Calla's voice drifted over to them. "What the hell?"

Tana left Misty and Brynn, rushing over to Calla's side. "What is it?"

"I thought I saw—" Calla arced her light from side to side. "I swear I saw something."

Peering into the half-darkness, Tana scanned the same area, looking for anything out of the ordinary. She reminded herself it was possible Calla was hallucinating, given her lack of sleep. The thought, while concerning, was a mild comfort that she grasped onto, since the alternative was terrifying.

The landscape was a white expanse of snow and ice, broken up by the occasional boulder. Shining her light in a slow arc, she thought she could make out shadows moving between the rocks, but every time she stopped to focus on them, they disappeared. Turning her head slowly from side to side, she could make them reappear and disappear as her vision shifted. "I think I see them."

Goosebumps broke out over her entire body. The shadows were large, the size of grown men and women, and they shifted while she watched out of the corner of her eye. Something about their movements made her feel as though they were observing, returning her gaze.

Beside her, Calla was turning her head from side to side, mimicking her movements. "Holy shit," she whispered. "What the hell are they? I can't look directly at them. They disappear."

"Dunno," Tana whispered, mesmerized. The shadows were circling, their footsteps crunching along the camp's perimeter, though no tracks appeared in the snow. Panic leaked into her trembling voice. "Calla, what's happening?" She was close to tears now, knowing they were being surrounded. Though there had been no indication they meant any harm, Tana couldn't shake the uncomfortable feeling that she was being corralled in, that she and her team had slipped a notch down the food chain.

She turned her head, hoping for some glimpse of them, as if seeing the monsters would give her any sort of comfort. Yet the shadows had disappeared. In their place, the air and snow seemed to gather, lifting and taking shape into a pale, mottled figure. Her eyes bulged as the shape solidified, and she found herself staring at the sunken face of a fully grown man.

Her heart leaped to her throat, and the scream that threatened to erupt was choked back. All she could focus on were his eyes—

cold gray, surrounded by deathly pale skin. It was like staring into the eyes of a corpse. She backed away, her stomach turning to liquid, her face going numb.

Beside her, Calla fired.

Round after round, the explosions echoed across the mountain, Calla's screams of rage lost in the chorus. Both hands had a white-knuckled grip on the gun like she was afraid it would leap away from her. Tana involuntarily closed her eyes, horrified at finding herself caught between a ghoulish apparition and Calla's murderous response.

Blasts erupted around them, Calla pulling the trigger until all that was left was the dull click of an empty magazine.

Silence settled like a fog over the camp. Tana slowly opened her eyes, searching out the spot where the face had appeared, seeing nothing more than ice and rocks draped in shadows. She forced herself to remain still against every bodily instinct telling her to run hysterically back down the mountain.

"You saw it?" Tana asked, her voice no more than a wisp.

Calla nodded, struggling to catch her breath. Her skin was pale, and the gun trembled in her grip. She turned back to Brynn and Misty, both on the ground, half-ducked for cover behind a boulder.

"I really hate to say it, Brynn. But about that whole ghost thing, I think you might be right."

Chapter Eleven

Huddled around the camp stove, four bleary-eyed, puffy faces were evidence of a night without sleep—for anyone. Each woman nursed a cup of coffee, their bowls of oatmeal sitting untouched. Once again, Tana questioned the night's events when, in the daylight, they seemed far less terrifying. Was it really possible they'd seen a ghost? One of the mountain spirits Torket was named for?

She'd been raised without religion and, as an adult, found the whole idea of hidden deities and satanic demons to be ridiculous. Religion was nothing more than a means to control the uneducated masses, or so her parents had taught her. They'd always claimed to be spiritual instead, choosing bits and pieces of different religions and philosophies to illustrate points, always omitting anything that touched on fire and brimstone. Their views on the afterlife were skeptical at best, leading Tana to wonder if there even was a life after death. If so, had she and her friends been given a glimpse into it? The idea seemed absurd, and yet, considering the lack of alternatives, strangely compelling.

A nagging thought had plagued her all night. If they were, in fact, glimpsing some type of afterlife, would these spirits have some knowledge of her family's whereabouts, whether hellbound or heavenward? Or—Tana sucked in a deep breath—were her parents somewhere inside that swarm of spirits, long dead, desperate to reach out and make contact with their daughter? It was a theory that she kept pushing away lest it take root and inevitably lead to crushing disappointment.

Calla was uncharacteristically quiet. She stared into her mug of coffee with the haunted gaze of a soldier returning from war. Tana could only imagine the swirl of conflicting thoughts, her need to rationalize what she'd seen butting against the glaring fact that there was no rational explanation.

Misty broke the silence. "If you saw what you think you saw—a spirit—then why would it be scared off by a gun? That makes no sense."

"None of this makes any sense," Calla grunted.

"It was definitely a man?" Brynn asked. Of the four of them, she was the only one who didn't seem disturbed by the night's events. Confirmation that she'd been right all along had only bolstered her enthusiasm.

Tana nodded. "Definitely a guy. Older than us, super pale. Big, scary eyes." She shuddered. "Like a zombie."

"Interesting." Brynn jotted down another note in her journal. She already had several pages of their accounts, all written in painstaking detail.

"I'm glad at least someone thinks so," Misty said, rubbing her temple. "Man, the lack of sleep is killing me. I think I'm getting a migraine."

Tana was thankful that, for the time being, Misty hadn't resumed her call for them to turn back. Maybe she was tired of being outnumbered. Maybe she assumed that Calla had finally seen the light and would pull the plug on this whole affair. Whatever the reason, she held her tongue, which Tana regarded as a small blessing. Between their injuries, their anxiety about Wyatt, and the sighting of this new creature, the last thing they needed was another fight amongst themselves.

"I wonder what sort of spirits they are," Brynn said, staring dreamily into space. "Long-lost Native ancestors? It's possible they used to bury the dead up here. Or something more nature-focused? Like forest sprites or wood gnomes. You did say it seemed like it was made of the snow, right? Or something darker? Like a demon. Have you guys seen *Paranormal Activity*?" When no one answered, she shrugged and scribbled a few more lines in her notebook.

"Can we hit the trail?" Calla asked. "This whole thing is messing with my head in a big way. Sometimes, getting the blood flowing helps sort things out."

Misty's head dropped in exasperation. "I'm sick of saying this," she started.

Calla groaned. "Then don't."

"No, we're not going back," Brynn said. "And I can't believe you'd ask. Again. This is an incredible story and might be the big break I need to finally get my name out there. Mist, this could be my novel." Her eyes shone so brightly, and her smile was so hopeful that Misty could only sit in silence, unwilling to wipe away her sister's enthusiasm. Either that, or she'd finally lost the will to fight.

"How about a rest day?" Tana asked, hoping to find some sort of compromise. "Nobody slept last night, we're all exhausted, and that's probably not helping anyone's mood. Let's take a breather, let our bodies heal up, and head to Camp Three tomorrow instead."

Calla swiped her phone open, frowning at the glowing screen. "Weather's crappy whether we leave today or tomorrow. It's not bad enough to abandon the summit, but it won't be pleasant."

"You guys seriously want to stay here another night? After what you two saw?" Misty stared at them, unbelieving. "We're too far into this thing to say it's all a figment of our imaginations. Something's really out there."

"And you think we can outwalk it?" Brynn asked. "Moving—whether to Camp Three or back to the truck—does nothing for us. This thing lives on the mountain. If it wants to attack, it will."

Misty's tone turned sour. "There's nothing I could say to change your mind, is there? No logic or common sense. Hell, even me getting down on my knees and begging would be pointless, wouldn't it? You're going to keep going." At all three of their solemn nods, Misty threw up her hands. "Fuck it, do whatever you want then. Set up a permanent camp and live here for all I care. I'm going back to bed. It feels like I haven't slept in days."

With an irritated flick of the wrist, she tossed the remainder of her coffee into the snow, then rose and headed for her tent.

"Maybe it's all those pills you've been taking," Brynn mumbled under her breath.

Misty froze in the open tent flap. "What did you say?" she asked. She turned back, her gaze boring into her younger sister.

Brynn shifted uncomfortably, leaving Tana to wonder if she'd actually meant for Misty to hear. "I..." Brynn struggled to find the right words. "I knew you were taking sleeping pills, but I didn't think it was every night. That stuff can really mess you up. And it's addicting."

Misty rose to her feet, her cheeks flaming. "I'm taking them every night here because we're in a new environment. I'm exhausted, and with everything that's happened, I'm stressed to the limit. I'm fine, and you can do me a favor and keep your nose out of my business."

"I'm your sister, Misty. It's my job to be up in your business. You've been talking in your sleep the last three nights. Sometimes, you thrash around like a crazy person. You kicked me super hard last night—want to see the bruise?"

Misty stood and stalked toward Brynn, towering over her in a power move she'd no doubt learned from parenting. "You don't get to judge me, all right?" Her eyes moved to Tana, then Calla. "None of you do. When you've gotten married, popped out a couple of kids, and suddenly, you're expected to drop everything and make this perfect life for everyone else, then—and only then—you can lecture me."

Brynn opened her mouth to respond, but Misty cut across her.

"Don't start, Brynn. Every single day, I deal with dishes, laundry, lunches, play-dates, trying to find preschools that don't have some insane leftist agenda, dinner, all the Todd BS, and then do it all over again the next day. Now I'm finally getting a break from that routine, and instead of getting a second to relax, I've wound up in a goddamn ghost story. And you have the gall to lecture me on the one thing that takes the edge off at night?"

She scoffed at the notebook in Brynn's hands. "Everything's always been so easy for you, not a care in the world, floating around with your head in the clouds. No one ever expected anything of you."

At this, Brynn flinched, a burst of color appearing in her cheeks.

"You go focus on your dreams." Misty spat the word like it was dirty. "And I'll worry about the grown-up problems." She turned on her heel and marched back to the tent, crawling inside.

Brynn sat for a moment, collecting herself. She let out a deep sigh before turning to the others, her gaze accusatory. "Why didn't you guys back me up?" she whispered angrily. "You know those things are bad for her. And it's not only the sleeping pills. She takes some other stuff during the day. Anti-depression, anti-anxiety, plus some little white ones that make her perky. Could be crack for all I know."

Calla shook her head, dropping her voice to match Brynn's volume. "As long as she's still able to climb, I'm not getting involved. Maybe back on solid ground, we can have an intervention if—and that's a big if—she actually needs one. Until then, let's keep the fighting to a minimum, huh? She's barely hanging in as is."

"Fine. When she ends up in rehab for an Ambien and coke addiction, I want you to remember this moment." With that, Brynn scooped up her notebook and stomped to the edge of camp, plopping down on a rock to consult her notes.

Calla turned back to Tana, a cloud of weariness surrounding her like fog. In the morning light, purplish circles were visible beneath her eyes. Despite the stress of leading such a turbulent team, she managed a small smile. "Not a terrible idea," she said, nodding at the tent where Misty, presumably, was trying to get a little shut-eye. "I could use a nap too. Tana, you want to?" She jerked her head toward their tent.

"What do you need me for?"

"I just like having you around."

With the admiration she felt for Calla, any compliment directed her way felt like sunshine, warming her from the inside out. The thought of someone so wickedly capable and independent wanting to be in her company pulled her lips into a bashful grin. "Yeah?"

"Yeah," Calla said. "You're a great roommate. You give off a ton of body heat."

The smile melted right off Tana's face.

With sunlight streaming through the thin nylon, the tent was cooked to a balmy forty-five degrees, a luxurious temperature at their current altitude of over fourteen thousand feet. The wind continued to blow outside, but snuggled into her sleeping bag, Tana felt safe and cozy. Compounding the comfort, Calla was pressed against her back, no doubt savoring the extra heat that Tana apparently emitted. And while Tana wasn't exactly fond of being used as a personal heater, she certainly enjoyed the human contact.

She checked her watch: one thirty, meaning they'd managed a solid five hours of uninterrupted rest.

In her sleep, Calla pressed tighter against her, the two women now practically spooning. In warmer conditions, Tana might have shoved her back to her own side of the tent, maintaining her small slice of personal space. But with the chilly air nipping her face, she gratefully nestled into the curve of Calla's body.

A sudden flash of heat scorched through her belly, making Tana double over, her hands instinctively grabbing her stomach. The burst of fire burned lower, smoldering between her thighs, and then, within seconds, it disappeared. Snuffed out by forces as mysterious as those that had started it. Tana lay still, her mouth agape, desperately trying to understand what had just happened to her.

Her first thought was food poisoning or a touch of altitude sickness, both of which could cause stomach distress. And yet, there had been more than simply a physical burning. She tried to put her finger on the foreign sensation. It was a sense of longing, a desire to somehow be even closer to Calla than she already was. She froze, remembering her few friends back in high school recounting tales of their first exploratory dates. What they'd felt as they'd leaned in for their first kiss or as a boy hastily fumbled with unhooking their bra.

Was this lust?

The idea that this could be happening now, in her late twenties, was preposterous. She'd been in this exact situation before—cramped in a tent beside Calla and Misty—and had never experienced anything beyond physical comfort from their body heat. A pang of lust, or even more ridiculous, love, was too outlandish to take seriously.

The more she turned it over in her mind, the more convinced she became that it had been a stomach cramp, nothing more. A sudden crush was out of the question. As a teenager, she'd assumed she was gay, unable to feel anything close to love or lust for the boys in her school. The lack of attraction had been reciprocated, so that was fine with her.

Once she reached college and allowed herself to chase whomever she liked—male, female, or fluid—she'd been shocked to learn that she didn't have those feelings for anybody. She remembered watching Misty and Calla from her bunk, their toned bodies sweat-slicked from a workout, trying to force herself to find them attractive and coming up empty. In the years since, she'd chalked romantic feelings up to one more normal experience she simply wasn't capable of.

Calla, on the other hand, was a complete mystery. With no lack of attention aimed her way, she was constantly fending off suitors in college, a fact that, although Misty tried to hide it, obviously made her jealous. Tana had no recollection of seeing her actually go on a date with someone, much less spend the night at their place. Their group emails back and forth always included updates on Misty's love life, even the gloomy snippets after marrying Todd, but Calla was conspicuously silent on details. Tana wondered if Calla was secretly like her. Not in looks or strength or anything like that. But maybe in this one small area.

Now was as good a time as ever to find out. "You awake?" Tana asked.

"Mmm," came the reply from deep inside Calla's sleeping bag. "Am now."

"Sorry. I wanted to ask you something."

"Yeah?"

"Are...are you asexual?"

Calla popped her head out of her bag, her eyes bleary and one eyebrow raised in question. "What? No."

"Are you gay?"

At this, Calla laughed. "Are you? Is this your way of propositioning me? I thought you'd be a little smoother. Actually..." She considered for a moment. "No, this is about how I figured it'd go."

"Be serious, Cal."

Calla wiped the smirk off her face. "Christ, it's too early for this."

"It's almost two in the afternoon."

Calla shot her a look, then dropped her gaze to the tent floor. "I, uh...fuck. Give me a sec, I wasn't prepared for this." She shifted in her sleeping bag, propping herself up on an elbow. "I'm not asexual. Beyond that, I'm not really comfortable putting a label on anything, okay? The town I grew up in, you didn't talk about that sort of thing unless you wanted to be called a queer every time you stepped foot in the grocery store. Or worse." She paused, her eyes glazing over. "A lot worse, actually. And I certainly wasn't going to bug my dad with it. He loves me, but...you know. I didn't want to put it to the test."

She frowned, absentmindedly tracing the seam of the tent with her finger. "Old habits die hard, I guess. Even now, I hate talking about it. Not that there's much to tell. Every now and then, I'll take someone home. It's rare, and I keep it short. I don't want any attachments. Not now, anyway."

"Why, though? That's what I don't understand. You could have anyone you wanted."

"Where's all this coming from?" Calla struggled out of her snug mummy bag, rubbing her bleary eyes. "And why couldn't it wait 'til later?"

Tana shrugged, not wanting to push the issue, yet now that it was out in the open, unable to let it go. "It doesn't make any sense. You have people throwing themselves at you, but you want nothing to do with them."

At this, Calla's gaze dropped to the tent floor. "God, this is going to sound stupid," she said, her tone sour. "Woe is me, I'm so goddamn pretty." She scowled, all traces of her former joviality gone. "I got a lot of attention from my dad's friends growing up. He was blue-collar, uneducated, a man's man—you know the type. And he had some real shitheels for friends. They'd make comments, pinch me when I walked by, that sort of thing. Then, when I was fourteen, one of them took it way too far. I'll spare you the details—I don't like talking about it. I told my dad, and I honestly thought he was going to murder him. The next day, he had me enrolled in the local Tae Kwan Do classes."

She smiled, but the joy didn't reach her eyes. "Best thing he ever did for me. I learned how to take care of myself and how to be self-reliant. The mountains were the next step, a way to learn how to deal with danger and come out on top. Then, moving up here and living off the land. It became an addiction, honestly. Proving to myself that I didn't need anyone, that I was tough.

More than that. Invincible. Emotions, partners, spouses—that all feels like a step in the wrong direction. Like it would make me softer."

She paused, biting the inside of her cheek. "I thought if I made myself tough enough, nobody'd ever be able to hurt me. But what happened all those years ago with my dad's friend, it happened here too." Her dark eyes bored into Tana's, anger etched into the fine lines around them. "Some guy at the local dive didn't take a rejection well, and he followed me out to my truck. It was a crappy night, and I thought maybe he was running to his car to get out of the storm. He grabbed me, pinned me against the seat, started undoing my belt. I was screaming like crazy, and nobody heard me from inside." Her expression darkened. "Or nobody cared. No matter how strong you are, there's always some guy ready to put you in your place."

A slightly deranged grin spread across her face. "And that's why God invented the Glock. So we can put them right back in theirs."

"You didn't."

Calla nodded. "I keep it in the glovebox. Never leave home without it now. Before he even knew what was happening, he had a bullet through his chest." She paused. "About a week later, I planted the new apple trees—the ones along the front walk. They're growing like weeds. Must be that new fertilizer I dragged home."

Tana was at a loss for words. She wanted to comfort her, to offer some kind of support—to ask why the hell she'd served them homemade applesauce at the cabin—but had no clue how to respond.

As the silence stretched on, Calla laughed nervously. "Well, shit Tana. Say something. I just told you my deep, dark secrets."

"That's uh...you're...you're really fucking scary."

Calla nodded. "Alas, another roadblock to marital bliss." She frowned at Tana. "We cool though? You're not going to run away and report me to the police or anything, right?"

"God, no. Of course not. I feel awful that you had to go through all that." She hesitated for a second, then pulled Calla into a tight hug. Beneath Calla's thick layers, Tana heard her heart pounding against her ribs. "Thanks for telling me," she said, her voice muffled by Calla's shoulder. Though she may have been incapable of romantic feelings, there was no doubt in her mind as to how much she loved Calla. Her heart ached to think of Calla's stony, sarcastic shell, a buffer from the cruelty of the outside world and a vault to bury her skeletons inside. More than anything, Tana wanted to relieve her of that heavy burden.

To her surprise, she felt Calla's arms wrap around her back, drawing them even closer. One hand gripped Tana's waist, fingers tracing the sliver of exposed skin at her midriff. Her other hand snaked up Tana's back, nails lightly grazing her neck. A shiver ran down the length of Tana's body, and she found herself suddenly wishing their legs weren't wrapped in separate sleeping bags.

Calla's voice was low in her ear. "It's not true, you know. That I could have anyone I wanted. I—"

"Guys! Guys, you awake?" Brynn's voice cut through the tent, yanking Tana and Calla from their embrace.

"What's going on?" Calla asked, pushing herself upright. "Is someone out there?"

Tana reeled at the return of her sharp, no-nonsense tone. Had she imagined the tenderness in Calla's touch? Was it simply a hug of gratitude for empathizing with such a terrible secret? What was the alternative? That Calla was making a move on her?

The zipper of their tent pulled apart, and Brynn's deliriously happy face poked inside. "What? No, nothing like that. While you were sleeping, I used the sat phone to get online and do some googling. I think I know what's chasing us."

"You what?" Calla was fully awake now, her eyes wide. "That's for emergencies! Which, if you haven't noticed, this trip is prone to."

The smile dropped off Brynn's face. "I thought you had a solar charger for it."

"Does it look sunny to you?"

Chancing a peek over her shoulder at the gray sky, Brynn admitted, "Fair point." She turned back to Calla with a sheepish grin. "I made lunch, some spaghetti and meatballs. Truce? Come eat, and I'll tell you what I found."

"That does sound good," Tana said, hating the strangely high pitch in her voice. Christ, was she still blushing?

Clearly outnumbered, the will to fight drained out of Calla. Tana saw her posture, all hard ridges and angles, softening. "Fine," she said. "But don't ever let me catch you using up the batteries for something this dumb again."

"Aye, aye, cap'n," Brynn smirked at Tana, including her in the joke. "Now, c'mon, before it gets cold."

As Brynn retreated from the tent, Tana tried to make eye contact with Calla, if only to confirm the moment they'd shared was indeed something special, not a figment of her imagination. Rather than return her gaze, Calla kept her head ducked as she pulled on her boots, a red flush on her cheeks. Seconds later, she crawled out the tent door.

Face burning at her obvious misread of the situation, Tana ducked out of the tent, pulling on her extra layers against the sting of the wind. Misty was already sitting beside the stove, spooning herself a bowl of pasta. "Afternoon, sleepyheads," she said. Tana was relieved to hear that most of the anger had vacated her tone.

Tana and Calla pulled their bowls from the snow and held them out for a serving, and Brynn scooped a hearty helping into each. "Did you get any sleep?" Tana asked, digging into a meatball. The heat of it warmed her belly, radiating outward through her body. After a few days out in the cold, it was amazing how something as ordinary as a hot bite of food felt so luxurious.

"A couple hours," Misty answered. "That's when this one"—she jerked her head at Brynn—"decided she had to tell me about what she found online. It couldn't wait until I'd caught up on sleep." She shook her head in that disappointed way that only mothers seemed to excel at. "Now you've got your audience. Spill the beans."

Brynn stood, notebook in hand, an excited smile plastered on her face, clearly relishing all eyes on her. "You will not believe what I found," she began.

Tana had to bite back a laugh, picturing the children at school who loved being the center of attention—their class presentations were always theatrical. No wonder she wanted to be a writer. Brynn had a flair for the dramatic.

"There are a ridiculous amount of creatures in Alaskan and Inuit myths. The Sasquatch, of course. Witches and demons and spirits too, some good, some evil. It's a mixed bag. Nothing really matched what we were looking for until I came across the Tak—" She consulted her notes again. "Taqriaqsuit," she said, carefully sounding out each syllable. "They're Alaska's version of shadow people, and early versions of the mythology have been traced to this exact area: Torket and Denali. Plus, shadow people actually have some validity as a myth. They show up across cultures all around the globe. Sort of like the Noah story."

"Noah? Like, from the Bible?" Misty asked.

"Yeah, Noah and the ark. You know there are a zillion versions of that story, right?" Brynn asked. The only response was her teammates' blank stares. "Don't any of you read? Stories of great floods are staples in mythologies around the world. There's a version of Noah in Native American stories, Asian, South American, you name it. This means that at some point in history, there probably was a giant flood. It's not just some stupid Bible lesson. Same goes for these shadow people. If every culture has a version of them, they're probably real."

"What are they though?" Tana asked. "Are they ghosts? Are they good guys or bad guys?"

Misty laughed. "What are you, five?"

"I'm sleep-deprived, leave me alone."

"Well, that's where it gets interesting," Brynn said, "or rather, very uninteresting. They're not good or bad. They're people, like us, living their lives. And occasionally, you can catch glimpses of them in shadow form, but not if you stare directly at them. If you do that, they disappear."

Tana caught Calla's eye, remembering how the shadowy silhouettes had only appeared for a second and only when they turned their heads back and forth. "Sounds about right," she said. Calla nodded in agreement.

Brynn looked down at her notes. "There are a bunch of details that seem like they were tacked on over the years, and they change depending on who's telling the story. Some people think they only become visible if you kill them and that they take on a half-man, half-caribou form."

"Doesn't quite match up," Tana said. "We only saw his face, but he looked like a zombie, definitely not a caribou. Plus, he was still alive."

"Another detail I found was that they can only eat food they caught themselves."

Calla nodded in approval. "My kind of people."

"So they're not trying to hurt us?" Misty asked.

Brynn shook her head. "Nope. And actually, they couldn't even if they tried. They're stuck over there, and we're stuck here. The most they can do is spook us in places where the barrier is thin, which I'm guessing is here because of the name Torket. For all we know, we're scaring the bejeezus out of them too."

Calla piped up. "What about the one who popped through? We didn't see his shadow. We saw him. Seems like he made it through the barrier, no problem."

Brynn consulted her notes thoughtfully. "Maybe he was really close to the barrier, like when you press up against a window," she said. "I don't think they're supposed to be able to cross over. There were a couple firsthand accounts of people saying they've made contact, although they sounded a bit kooky. Like those weirdos who claim aliens abducted them. One lady said she was attacked up in northwest Alaska, but nobody could back up her story."

"Why are there so many of them?" Misty asked. "We're on a mountain, and presumably, they are too. Why's it so damn loud on their side?"

At this, Brynn shrugged. "No idea. My guess is the worlds aren't exactly identical. For all we know, our mountain is their shopping center or an amusement park. That'd explain all the yelling."

They fell into silence, each woman lost in her own thoughts. To Tana, the idea of another world, a parallel universe, filled her with a childlike wonder. Even if it was as painfully dreary as this one, it gave her hope that there was more to explore. Eventually, one of those worlds had to be something worth seeing. A split-second fantasy danced through her mind—Tanaraq: Multiverse Explorer. Jumping through universes, always ready for a new adventure.

The dream was squashed as quickly as it arose. Surely, such a life should be reserved for someone brave like Calla, curious like Brynn, or competent like Misty.

"This is going to be such a good book," Brynn said, her eyes unfocused as the possibilities of fame and fortune wafted through her head. "Bill Bryson never had anything as good as shadow people."

"People will think you're insane," Misty said.

"Let them. All they need to do is look up Torket, see how many people have vanished here, and the story puts itself together." A hopeful smile danced across her lips. "Dad's going to love this. He's always had a soft spot for horror. And it's the perfect amount of scary. Deadly shadow people luring climbers to their deaths."

Calla's head shot up. "Wait a sec. I thought they couldn't interfere on our side."

"Oh, right." Brynn's enthusiasm dimmed. "I might need to fudge some details to make the story more exciting."

"Hold up. We only know a few things for certain," Misty said. "Torket has a ridiculously high disappearance rate, even considering how technical it is. And we're being followed by some weird voices. Beyond that, we don't understand the rules, and it would be stupid to assume them. For all we know, these things are crossing over and throwing people off the cliffs or hell, eating them. I don't know. And even if they are these Taki-whatsis—"

"Taqriaqsuit," Brynn corrected.

"Whatever. Even if they are what you say, we shouldn't assume they're harmless. Did you forget what happened to Tana? Somehow, these...things managed to possess her, and she almost died because of it. I'd rather assume they're trying to kill us and be pleasantly surprised if they don't."

Brynn crossed her arms. A smirk flitted across her face. "So now you believe she was possessed? Glad to see you're finally onboard."

Misty huffed. "I don't know what I believe anymore. This whole thing is insane."

"Calla believes," Brynn said. She looked to Calla for support. "She saw it with her own eyes, and she's the last person who'd make something like that up."

Calla's tone was thoughtful. "It's possible we were hallucinating—"

"Oh, come on!" Brynn interrupted. "You can't seriously believe that. Tana saw it too."

"I'm trying to consider every possible angle."

Brynn's tone was sour. "You know, at a certain point, playing the devil's advocate just makes you ignorant."

Calla's eyes flashed, locking onto Brynn. "Excuse me?"

Sensing another eruption, Misty intervened. "Let's drop the supernatural element for a second, okay?" Her gaze darted between Calla and Brynn, making sure that another argument wasn't about to break out. Satisfied, she asked, "Have you all forgotten that there's a very real threat on the mountain? And that he seemed more than willing to strand us out here? This ghost stuff is all fun and exciting, but we have bigger issues to worry about."

Tana nodded, more out of habit than agreement. The last thing she wanted to exercise right now was caution. She yearned to push against the barrier between worlds, to see what lay beyond. Her childhood fantasies of magical lands butted against her parents' practical, atheistic teachings. This was her one chance to see the truth for herself. More than anything, she wanted to abandon any sense of prudence and catch a glimpse of the other side, regardless of what obstacle, real or imagined, stood in their way.

As an antidote to Misty's worries, she tried to inject her voice with a casual nonchalance, as though they faced such dangers regularly. "Then it's a good thing we have someone who knows how to protect themselves." She glanced at Calla. "And someone who can patch us up." She turned to Misty. "And someone to document the whole thing." She nodded at Brynn. "If there was ever a team that's well equipped for this mission, it's us." She sloshed some snow into her empty dish to clean it out and then stood. "Let's get a good night's sleep so we're ready for whatever tomorrow holds."

Misty opened her mouth to protest, clearly unhappy with how the conversation had suddenly flipped against her interests. Her objections caught in her throat as Calla and Brynn rose, following Tana's lead to the tents.

"Goodnight, Misty," Calla called, a grin threatening to surface on her lips.

The three women hustled into their tents before Misty could say another word, Calla clapping Tana on the back as they crawled inside. As Tana pawed through her toiletry kit for her toothbrush, her sense of victory was cut short by the muffled sounds from beyond the tent walls. She tried to tell herself that she was imagining it or that perhaps it was only the wind. But deep down, she knew that outside, alone in the kitchen dugout, Misty was crying.

Chapter Twelve

2013

White, all around her. White ceiling, white floor, white walls. The table her examination rested upon was white. The pages were so starkly white they were nearly blinding.

A dizziness settled over her, a sudden urge to either run screaming from the room or lean over and vomit onto the pristine floor.

"Ladies and gentlemen, this concludes your exam time. Please bring your booklet to the front of the room."

Misty stood on trembling legs, clutching her exam booklet in clammy fingers, with no doubt in her mind that she'd failed. College, her career, her dreams: all gone. Any future prospects in the medical field were laughable. If she was lucky, she'd be able to manage a hostess job at the local watering hole.

She dropped off the booklet, her stomach flip-flopping as it left her hands. What would her parents say? All those perfect grades dissolved in one failed exam. How could she have been so stupid? Taking a pill to try and cheat her way to a perfect score, and from Jamie Tower, no less. Everyone knew he was a liar. For all she knew, he'd given her a baggie of crack instead of Adderall. And then she'd topped it off with an espresso for good measure.

She rubbed her eyes with the heels of her hands, wishing she could jam them into her brain and sort out the swirling chaos in its depths. Answers had come and gone with lightning speed before she had a chance to record them on the page. All those tutoring sessions her parents had paid for were wasted in the span of a day.

Her parents.

The thought of their disappointed faces made the walls spin, and she braced herself against the door frame, closing her eyes against the tilt of the room.

"Hey, Mist, how'd you do?"

Her eyes cracked open, taking in the sight of her boyfriend, an affable grin beneath his spiky, tousled locks.

"I need to get out of here, Ryan," she said. "I think I'm gonna be sick."

"I've got you." He wrapped an arm around her waist, the smile melting from his face. "Let's get some air."

She allowed herself to be led out of the building into the blissfully un-white surroundings. Ryan's car, a 1984 Chevy, sat in front of the building, its cherry red paint peeling off in sheets. He opened the passenger side door, and Misty dropped into the seat like a stone.

He ran around the car and entered the driver's side. "That bad, huh?" he asked.

"Worse," she groaned.

"You always say that. Right before you get a perfect score."

Misty shook her head, burying her face in her palms. "For real this time." She paused, her nails digging into her skin, the sharp pain a salve for the oncoming wave of despair. Why hadn't she stuck with the caffeine pills—the ones her dad kept tucked into his desk drawer for late nights? His little helpers, he called them, before popping one into his mouth and giving Misty a wink. The ones she'd been sneaking for years whenever she needed a little helper herself. A quick jolt before a math test or a late-night buzz the evening before a report was due. A precise dosage she'd calculated for maximum focus without the jitters. After all, drugs were only safe as long as you maintained control.

But this morning, in a moment of desperation, she'd thrown caution to the wind. No experimentation, no rigorous testing for side effects in the safety of her bedroom. Just opened her mouth and popped them down the hatch, like a junkie. She shuddered.

"I, uh, I took some pills before the test."

"You what?"

"I needed the boost! If I get anything below 2200, hell, probably 2300, you know I'd never hear the end of it. But it messed with my head. I guessed on almost everything." A tear leaked from her eye, wetting her fingers. "I'm never getting into college. I'm never getting out of this shithole town!"

Ryan stared at her, his blue eyes calculating. Finally, he placed the key in the ignition and revved the engine. "I know exactly what you need."

A half-hour later, they pulled up at the base of Blue Mountain, a popular make-out spot thanks to its seclusion, while still an easy drive from town.

Misty rolled her head to glare at Ryan. "My life is basically over, and you think I'm in the mood for this?"

His triumphant grin disappeared. "Oh. No, I thought…"

"That I'm depressed enough to go all the way with you?" She let out a huff, glowering at the surrounding woods. "Guys are disgusting."

"Wait, what?" The confusion in his voice made her turn. "I wasn't expecting anything like that. I just wanted to go to the top. Since you like hiking, I thought it might be fun. You know, something to take your mind off things."

"Oh." Misty's cheeks flamed, matching her hair. "I guess that's fine then." She thought of her parents waiting for her at home, no doubt wanting to hear how wonderfully she'd done. "That sounds great, actually."

"Lucky for me, I had gym yesterday and forgot to take my clothes inside. I'm sure you could tell by the smell." When Misty didn't react, he reached behind the seat to retrieve a crumpled pair of sweatpants. "Gimme a sec."

He exited the car, letting his Abercrombie jeans—the ones he'd spent months saving for—drop around his ankles. Even the sight of his pale, skinny legs protruding from checkered boxer shorts couldn't coax a smile onto Misty's face.

She pulled a water bottle from her backpack and left the car, letting the springtime breeze kiss her face. Her thoughts were still racing a mile a minute, but at least here, secluded from civilization, no one was around to witness her inevitable breakdown.

Ryan sidled up to her, pulling a baggie from his pocket. "Gym clothes weren't the only smelly thing in my car," he admitted, shaking the leafy contents. "I know you don't smoke, but I think this might make you feel better. Once we get to the top, I'll set it up for you."

"Can we do it now?" Misty begged. She'd never even touched a cigarette, let alone marijuana. With no obvious benefit to her grades, the appeal eluded her. But she was desperate for relief from her thoughts, the crushing weight of her impending failure.

Ryan laughed. "If you smoke it now, you'll never make it up there. C'mon, walk, you'll feel better." He grasped her hand and pulled her toward the trailhead, her steps sluggish and heavy.

The trail unfolded before them, a route they both knew by heart after a lifetime of hiking in Pennsylvania's Appalachian hills. Misty's heart hammered against her ribs, far too violent a pounding for their casual pace. "I need you to listen to me," she said, her voice shaky. "Don't interrupt, don't offer advice. I need to let this all out, or I feel like I'm going to explode."

At his nod, she took a deep breath and began, "I have no idea what I'm going to do now. I—"

As Ryan opened his mouth, she slapped him on the arm. "No! You promised!"

He shut his mouth, turning to the trail ahead.

"It feels like I've been training my whole life for the Olympics, and I finally made it, only to trip over my own feet in the first race. Everything I've ever worked for is gone. And there's no excuse." Her voice wavered. "My GPA is perfect. I joined all the right clubs—stuff I couldn't care less about, just to show how cultured and well-rounded I am." She kicked a spray of rocks into the brush. "I hate Model UN," she cried. "I hate it!"

Her voice broke, and she bit the inside of her cheek to try and stifle the tears welling up in her eyes. "You know what my parents tell everyone? That I'm their little go-getter. They never need to worry about me because I'll always make the right decision." Her lip quivered. "Maybe they should've spent a little more time worrying."

Her stomach rolled, the experimental poisons of the morning demanding to be released. Misty dropped to her knees, clutching a moss-covered rock for support, and vomited into the leaves. Her stomach heaved again and again until she was retching up nothing but air.

She turned, wiping the mess from her lips, her bloodshot gaze finding Ryan. "You didn't hold my hair."

He laughed. "I thought I was supposed to let this run its course without interfering. C'mere." He extended a hand, pulling her to her feet. "You want to go back?"

Misty shook her head, stubbornly continuing up the trail, Ryan following suit. They walked in silence, the late afternoon sun filtering through the leaves, dappling their bodies with light.

Misty took a swig of water, swished it around her mouth and spit. The scents of the forest—her childhood—filled her lungs. She had to admit, she actually felt better. As though eliminating the drugs from her body had purged some of their consequences. With her rigorous tutoring schedule, she'd spent most of the past few months cooped up inside with her textbooks. The fresh air clarified her thoughts, helping to sort through the jumble. She let her fingers trail over the rocks and tree trunks, so rough and untamed, unlike the sterile world of academia. God, how she'd missed this.

"Am I allowed to talk now?" Ryan asked.

"Yeah, sorry."

He waved off her apology. "Ok, let's assume it's as bad as you think. A total catastrophe. Can't you retake it?"

"Not if I want to do early applications."

"Ok, you miss the early deadline. So what? Apply like the rest of us mere mortals. And if they're already full? Fuck 'em. You don't need Harvard or Yale or any of that upper-crust bullshit to be special, Misty."

"I do if I want to be at the top of my field."

He cocked an eyebrow at her. "Mist, you haven't even decided what you want to be yet. All you know is it's something vaguely medical. Even if you failed horrendously enough that every college in the country blacklisted you, guess what? You can still go to nursing school. And you'd be amazing at it."

"I can't be a nurse," she muttered.

"Why not?"

"It's not...you know."

"Prestigious?" At her reddening cheeks, he threw up his hands. "Seriously? Is this your parents talking, or you? Because the Misty I know wouldn't give a damn. The Misty I know wants to make a difference in this world and cares more about everyone else than herself. She's smart and protective and would make one hell of a nurse. If that's her worst-case scenario, I think she's doing A-OK."

She considered his words, trying to picture herself as a nurse and not feel the crushing weight of shame at the sight of herself in white sneakers and colorful scrubs. It wasn't so bad, right?

Within seconds, the onslaught of humiliation was painful enough to draw a wince. What would people say behind her back? What would her parents think? All that talent, all those long nights studying, wasted. She was meant for greater things, for curing cancer or unraveling the mysteries of the human brain. Not for poking people with needles or checking to see if a patient had finally filled their bedpan.

The leftover Adderall in her pocket seemed to burn into her skin, a reminder that there was still a way out of this mortifying future. If she put the proper time and research into the correct dosage, maybe she could retake the test and still come out on top. She needed a few weeks—and some more cash to pay off Jamie Tower—and she'd be ready to try again.

The trees opened up, giving way to the view below. Miles upon miles of Pennsylvania forest, dotted with a smattering of farms, stretched in every direction. The vivid, electric green of springtime leaves cut through the dark emerald of the evergreens.

The sight was cathartic after months of going to sleep at night, only to still see trigonometry equations scribbled across her eyelids. "God, it's been too long," she breathed.

Ryan pulled her close, kissing her on the cheek. "You're a backcountry girl, Mist. Like it or not, you need this like a plant needs the sun."

She leaned her head against his shoulder, wishing she could hold onto this moment forever. No pressure, no expectations. Just the woods and someone who completely, thoroughly understood her down to her core. She turned her head, giving him a small peck on the lips.

"Mmm, puke flavored, my favorite."

She pulled away, one hand covering her mouth. "I'm sorry! I forgot! Oh my God, that's so gross."

"Relax, I'm kidding." He took her hand, gesturing to the bald hilltop above them. "Shall we? We're almost there. May as well get the best view in the house."

They climbed up the grassy knoll, clutching at the overgrown grasses to haul themselves up the steep face. Insects scattered to the winds as their perches swayed, a confetti of iridescent jewel tones. Finally, they collapsed in a heap atop the highest point, marked only by a tiny, half-toppled cairn.

"Watch out for condoms," Ryan said, peering into the grass. "Can't be too careful up here."

Misty chuckled. "Do you always have to ruin the moment?"

Ryan grabbed her around the waist and pulled her onto his chest, her head coming to rest right below his chin. "Just trying to make you laugh. That's all I have to offer since, you know, you're smarter, hotter, stronger..."

Misty smacked his arm. "Oh, stop it." She snuggled into his embrace, enjoying the feel of his arms wrapped protectively around her. "I'm really glad you brought me here. I needed this."

"I know."

A cluster of birds soared overhead, dipping and twirling in the wind, not a care in the world besides how many bugs they could fit in their bellies. No SATs, no college prep, no adoring parents to please. Pure freedom.

Ryan reached into his pants pocket and pulled out the baggie of marijuana, giving it a little shake. "What do you think? Still need something to take the edge off?"

Misty shook her head, breathing in the scent of pine and damp earth. Her fingers traced the slight bulge in her jeans pocket, the baggie of leftover pills a warm comfort. Tonight, she'd face her parent's well-deserved wrath. Tomorrow, the experimentation—her road to redemption—would begin.

"This is all I need."

Chapter Thirteen

An ocean of clouds blocked out the stars. The moon was dampened to a wisp of gray light, leaving Torket swathed in a pitch-black cloak. The only visible signs of life for miles in all directions were four identical pinpricks of light inching their way up the mountainside.

Clambering up the ice and snow, the four women surveyed the trail ahead, their headlamps illuminating the inhospitable terrain before petering out into predawn darkness. Before them lay a painfully steep ascent up the glacier. Veering too far to the right led to a patchwork of crevasses, where, presumably, several frozen climbers had experienced their last, painful moments. Too far to the left put them in the path of avalanches. A perfect forty-degree angle slope, packed high with the recent storms' worth of snow, made it a disaster waiting to happen. The slightest provocation could cause a collapse. Starting before sunrise was the safest option, even if it meant limited visibility, as the warmth of daylight could cause the snow to melt and shift position.

With no sunlight to brighten their route for at least another hour, it was too dangerous to veer to either side lest they find themselves in inhospitable territory. A straight shot up the middle was their only reasonable path, meaning a long, arduous slog with minimal zigzagging switchbacks to ease the incline.

Their final camp waited above, meaning this would be their last haul with their fully loaded packs. One ultimate strain on their aching muscles before they could switch to their lightweight summit backpacks. Even with their rest day, Misty still showed signs of fatigue, gratefully taking Calla up on her offer to carry some of her weight. Not to be outdone, Brynn also took Misty's share of the food and placed it in her own bag.

"Thanks, and sorry," Misty said. "It's the kids, I swear they suck the life out of your body. They're little vampires. Since having them, I don't handle altitude as well as I used to. I've been popping Diamox like candy this whole time."

"Keep breathing, and don't be afraid to ask for a break," Calla encouraged. "We're all making it up there. As a team." She started along the trail, then stopped, turning back to address the group. "Actually, Tana, get your ass up here." She stepped to the side of the trail, gesturing at the vacated space. "Brynn, hold up, we're taking the lead here."

With a huff, Brynn stopped in her tracks. Several paces ahead, she'd been quietly urging her small team of herself and Misty into the front position.

"You sure?" Tana asked. "I never lead."

"Exactly, it's about damn time. You've been doing this as long as I have. Besides, we're in topsy-turvy land now. Shadow people and whatnot. If there was ever a time to go hog wild, this is it." When Tana continued to hesitate, Calla said, "I'll have the GPS out. I promise to yell at you if you veer off trail. C'mon, give it a shot."

Tana walked up the trail, feeling the burden of responsibility as she passed Calla, moving into the lead position. To have Calla, and by extension, Misty and Brynn, put faith in her, especially on this portion of the trail, made her chest swell with pride, though the thought of leading them into serious peril was a crushing weight on her shoulders.

"Lead the way," Calla said, clapping her on the back.

"Not too fast," Misty called up the line.

She needn't have bothered with the warning as the trail lifted sharply within minutes. Tana couldn't have maintained a quick pace even if she wanted to. The snow was slicked over with an icy crust, and each step required Tana to kick into the ice, sometimes multiple times, until there was a solid shelf for her crampons to grip. The process was draining and forced her to stay mentally alert, searching for dips and grooves that would serve as promising footholds. Occasionally, she'd come across a footprint that hadn't been completely smoothed over by the weather, and she assumed it must belong to Wyatt. Whenever possible, she'd use his wide, flat prints as her own, taking advantage of how he'd pressed the snow into perfect steps.

Calla, too, took notice. "That bastard's up here somewhere," she panted. "I was probably a little harsh on him, but he really showed his true colors with the whole ladder thing. I wouldn't mind if he was one of the climbers who disappears."

"Calla," Misty's shocked voice rang out. "Don't say things like that."

Glancing over her shoulder, a grin spreading above her neck buff, Calla's tone was syrupy sweet. "What? I didn't say I wanted him dead. Just to go missing. Maybe cross over to our shadow pals and let them deal with him." She checked her GPS. "Too far right, Tana. Rein it in a little. I'd hate for Brynn to end up in a second crevasse this trip."

"You're hilarious," Brynn grumbled.

Tana steered them slightly to the left, noticing that Wyatt's footsteps continued to the right. Was he trapped in a crevasse at that very moment? Arms broken, legs twisted? Hypothermic, with maybe a few precious minutes left to live? She pushed the thought from her mind. He knew the risks—they all did. The mountains were unforgiving, a vast playground dominated by those with a love for life who chose to embrace the thrill or those with nothing to live for who chose to risk it all. Tana often wondered which group she and her friends fell into.

Whatever someone's reasons for climbing, the mountains chewed them up the same. Wyatt chose to come alone, so his fate was in his own hands. If he was trapped in a crevasse, it was a prison of his own making. Most climbers would do nearly anything to rescue one of their own, but not if it meant putting their team in jeopardy.

The sun was beginning to peek over the horizon, casting a pink flush over the snow. This was Tana's favorite time of day in the mountains, when the darkness was cast aside and the trails that had seemed terrifying and mysterious hours ago were now a thing of beauty. Bright purples and reds dashed across the clouds, reflecting their brilliance in the snow. Tana switched off her headlamp to fully appreciate the kaleidoscope around her. They were now above the sea of clouds, a cotton-candy rainbow stretching in all directions, broken up by the hulking mass of Denali, which sliced through them like a knife. Sights like these could make anyone believe in worlds beyond the ordinary.

"Turn around," Misty called up to them.

They spun on the spot, faces brightening in unison. Behind them, a perfect triangle lay across the clouds, its deep violet a stark contrast to the pinks and oranges surrounding it.

"Torket's shadow," Brynn said. "It's beautiful." She pulled out her cell phone to snap a photo, then looked at the screen in disgust. "Photos never do it justice."

"Maybe that's for the best," Calla said. "Something like this should be reserved for the people who've earned it."

It was typical Calla snobbery, though Tana couldn't help but agree with her. They'd fought tooth and nail for this sunrise, and she wanted it to remain theirs, not an Instagram post with a cutesy caption for the masses. Keeping it between the four of them meant more to her than all the validation the internet could provide.

The sound of trickling water pulled Tana's attention to the end of the line, where Misty was squatting in the snow, her bare ass on display.

"Sorry," she called out. "That friggin' Diamox makes me pee like crazy."

Once Misty had cleaned up and readjusted her harness, Tana turned back to the trail. While cloaked in darkness, she'd been able to pretend that they were nearing camp, even though she knew it was still hours away. It was a tactic that made the hours drag considerably less. But in full sunlight, there was no deceiving themselves. The glacier stretched on for what seemed like an infinity, a solid mass piercing the sky.

With a deep breath to regain focus, Tana kicked into the ice and continued up the trail. The higher they climbed, the more nervously she gripped her ice ax, her one defense against a fatal fall. If either Calla or herself were to slip, it would send them careening down the slope. Between their slippery snow pants and the slick, icy ground, they'd only have a fraction of a second to self-arrest before they'd be moving too quickly to recover. She glanced over her shoulder, evaluating how far they'd drop if that terrible scenario came to pass.

The ground disappeared into the clouds, leaving the exact distance—and the final crash landing point—to the imagination. Tana ballparked it at several hundred feet. The thought of falling for so many endless seconds, knowing you were powerless against the pull of gravity...a shudder ran up her spine. It was too awful to imagine.

The Innuksuk Rocks lay ahead, named for the first known summiter, Oudlanak Innuksuk, a 19th-century trapper with a zest for the untamed wilderness. An enthusiasm that, sadly, wasn't shared by his young wife. Oudlanak returned from his successful Torket expedition to find their home abandoned, his wife having run off with his cousin, a steady, reliable fisherman with no trace of that troublesome wanderlust. The namesake rocks were an appreciated consolation prize, though even this achievement was debated by locals, who claimed Torket had been scaled thousands of times by previous generations.

Despite their disputed history, the rocks were a welcome sign, signaling that their steep ascent was finally coming to a close. They'd been climbing for hours, and the rising sun was beginning to make Tana's thick layers feel uncomfortably heavy. Drips of sweat rolled down her chest.

She knew she ought to stop the team rather than let her layers get damp, as they'd inevitably freeze once they stopped moving. But her reign as team leader had gone surprisingly well, even better than Brynn and Calla's, and she wanted to keep up the momentum, pushing them up to camp with minimal interruptions.

"Just a little farther," she called down the line.

"That's what you said half an hour ago," Misty muttered.

Brynn pointed up to the rocks. "She's right, Mist. Hold it together. We'll be up there in, like, twenty minutes. Ten if you stop holding us back."

Misty's reply was a snowball to the back of Brynn's head.

"Hey!" Laughing, Brynn spun, kicking a cloud of ice shards toward her sister.

Calla glared down at the two of them. "Knock it off, guys," she said, her voice low and serious. "This definitely isn't a place we want to be screwing around."

Tana stopped, a blur of movement catching her eye from above. "Is that..." she asked, squinting at a figure dashing through the Innuksuk Rocks. As his bright yellow coat swam into view, she finished, "Wyatt?"

He careened toward them, his pack bouncing against his back as he raced through the boulder-strewn terrain. His ax scraped against the rocks as he flew down, raising sparks that nipped at his heels. Every ten steps or so, he looked back over his shoulder, nearly tripping himself in the process. His voice echoed across the mountain, though it was difficult to make out the words. From what the wind carried down to them, Tana guessed it was "Shit, shit, shit, shit!"

At the edge of the rocks, his stride lengthened, perhaps taking advantage of the smoother terrain. But in his haste to flee whatever unseen foe was bearing down on him, his crampon caught the laces of his opposite boot, sending him sprawling headfirst into the snow.

"SHIT." His scream rang clearly down to them as he slid down the icy face.

Brynn gasped, her hands instinctively gripping her ax as though she could somehow help control his slide. "Dig your ax in," she screamed up at him.

Wyatt grabbed his ax with both hands, rolling the pick into the snow, but he'd already picked up too much speed. Instead of stopping him, the pick tore easily through the top crust of ice, gravity now dragging him down the slope.

"Now your crampons," Brynn yelled. If Wyatt heard her, he gave no indication. He continued to slide in their direction.

"He's moving too fast," Tana said. "He'd probably snap an ankle if he tried dropping his feet right now."

"Better a broken ankle than dead!"

Misty shook her head. "If he drops his feet and starts cartwheeling down, he's as good as dead."

Calla hurried to the side of his trajectory, her eyes never leaving his yellow parka. "He's going to pass right by us," she said. She dug her crampons into the snow, bracing herself against the slope of the mountain. "Tana," she barked. "Get ready. We're going to grab him."

"Are you crazy?" Misty yelled. "He's going to drag us all down with him."

"If you don't want to help, then back up," Calla replied. "Otherwise, get ready for a rough impact."

Wyatt's screams preceded him down the slope, a mix of gibberish and obscenities. The rough grind of his ax tearing through the ice grew louder, his body twenty feet away, then ten, then five.

"Now," Calla screamed, lurching forward and grasping the straps of his backpack. Tana did the same on his other side, his bulk nearly yanking her right off her feet. She dropped to her stomach, pushing her weight onto her own ax, praying it was enough friction to slow his momentum, and horrified to see that he was dragging both her and Calla down with him.

Then Misty's bulk was beside her in the snow, grasping at Wyatt and thrusting her own ax into the ice as he pulled them into a V-shaped formation, his body at the lowest point. There was one last tug, and then the shriek of their axes against ice quieted. At last, their bodies stilled.

Tana lifted her head to see that Brynn had added her weight to Calla's side, the two women bunched together, each with one hand on their axes, the other firmly gripping Wyatt's pack. A look of ecstatic relief swept over Brynn's features. Her joy was contagious, spreading across the women like wildfire. Calla laughed, the sound rippling across her teammates before morphing into a chorus of victorious war whoops, their cries echoing off the rocks above.

"And my dad thought I'd never catch myself a man." She cackled, grinning down at Wyatt. "You're one lucky SOB. What if we hadn't been here?"

Wyatt wasn't listening. Crouched on his knees, he stared up at the rocks he'd fallen from, skin pale and pupils dilated with terror. "Run," he said, his voice no more than a hoarse whisper.

"Everybody, run!"

Chapter Fourteen

Wyatt attempted to lift himself from the ground, but the climbing rope had snaked its way around his body. Struggling to untangle himself, he moved with a panicked jerkiness, his gloved hands fumbling over the rope's twists. With an irritated huff, he pulled off the gloves and threw them to the ground.

Brynn put a comforting hand on his shoulder. "It's okay, we saw them too. They're scary, but they're not evil. Not even spirits, we think. More like a parallel dimension."

"What the hell are you talking about?" he asked, finally freeing himself and tossing the rope to the side. "We need to get out of here, now."

"No, you don't understand," Brynn explained. "We think we've narrowed it down to Taqriaqsuit, in layman's terms: shadow people. They don't mean us any harm—"

A bellowing roar cut across their chatter, their heads turning simultaneously to the rocks above. Blending seamlessly into the brown, crumbly stone, a hulking mass lumbered toward the edge of the Innuksuk Rocks.

Tana's stomach dropped at the sight. Was it the shadow people? Could they do more than peek across the barrier? Were they moving rocks right before her eyes?

But as it moved beyond the boundary of the rocks, she realized this had nothing to do with the paranormal. She was staring straight into the face of an enormous grizzly.

"Oh shit," Brynn said, echoing Wyatt. "Why's it up this high?"

"She has a cub," Wyatt said. "I didn't know. I only saw the mother at first. She was down lower on the trail. I had a leftover hotdog, so I threw it to her. You don't have to tell me. I know it was stupid—even without the cub. She's been chasing me since camp, and I don't think she's going to give up."

"Everyone on your feet," Calla said. "Don't make any sudden movements. Tana, you're going to lead us out of here, okay? Brynn, reach into my top pocket—nice and slow—and pull out the gun." She angled her back to Brynn, never taking her eyes off the grizzly.

"Please don't try to shoot it," Brynn pleaded. "It's too far away, and if you miss, you'll just piss it off."

"Trust me, I won't miss."

Misty's words dripped with sarcasm. "Did you forget we're in an avalanche zone? You think maybe a gunshot isn't the greatest idea?"

Tana's brain, overloaded with adrenaline, struggled to remember what to do when faced with a grizzly. Stand tall, make a lot of noise, and hold their ground? No, that was for black bears. "I think we're supposed to play dead," she said.

The bear sniffed the air, then let out another terrible roar, its lips pulled back to reveal a row of massive teeth.

Then it charged.

"Good luck with that," Wyatt said, then took off running.

"Tana, go," Misty screamed, giving her a rough shove after Wyatt.

Tana stumbled to her feet, the overloaded pack making her footing unstable. The slope was so steep that Wyatt was cutting a diagonal across the trail rather than charging straight down. Figuring there was strength in numbers, or at least a smaller chance of being the one who got mauled, Tana ran after him, slamming her heels into the ice to try and maintain some type of footing. Though Wyatt had a head start and the benefit of longer legs, the fear of another fall seemed to have scared him from moving too quickly, and Tana was easily closing the gap between them.

The grizzly was taking no chances either. Instead of dropping onto the steep trail and chasing the tail end of their line, it raced laterally, twenty feet above the rope team. Within ten seconds, it had passed Misty, then Brynn and Calla, until it loomed directly above Tana. Terrified to turn her head and yet somehow unable to resist, Tana found herself gazing directly at the beast, all muscles and fur and slobbering breaths. The bear's head alone was larger than her torso, its paws wide as tree trunks as they pounded against the earth. She forced her legs to keep pumping, though she could no longer think of a good reason why. The bear had outrun them. If it wanted to start picking them off, there was nothing left to stop it.

Why didn't we play dead?

And yet, it seemed the grizzly only had eyes for Wyatt, drawn to his bright parka like a beacon. It let out another ear-shattering roar, charging past Tana until it was directly above his head. Tana's legs went weak with relief. She wasn't proud to admit it, but if it was going to tear anyone to shreds, she'd prefer it not be her.

Slowing her pace, she let the bear and Wyatt continue ahead. She no longer trusted her wobbly legs to hold her upright. She must have been even more terrified than she imagined because her knees were buckling, barely keeping her from sinking to the ground.

"Oh fuck," came a voice from behind, and the sudden realization drained the blood from Tana's face. The problem wasn't her legs. It was the ground beneath them. The snow and ice were giving way, dissolving down the steep slope.

The world dropped into slow motion. She heard screams behind her and felt the rope tugging her waist. Wyatt dropped to the ground, his feet pulled out from under him by the shifting snow. The grizzly struggled to maintain its footing, but as the crust of ice beneath it gave way, it slid down the slope, bellowing as it tumbled after Wyatt. Tana spun back the way she'd come, now realizing that in their panic, they had crossed to the left side of the trail, that perfectly angled slope that was waiting for any excuse to release an avalanche.

And a massive, lumbering bear was as good a catalyst as any.

Misty streaked across the trail, probably the fastest Tana had ever seen her move, Brynn close behind, the rope bunching at their feet as they fought to escape the collapsing snow. Calla raced after them, but the rope between her and Tana was pulled taut, Tana struggling to gain footing as the ground beneath her gave way. Her stomach sank at the realization that she wasn't going to make it.

Time slowed to a crawl as she stared at her friends' retreating backs. They still had a chance. How could she possibly take that away from them out of a pathetic, desperate grasp at survival? They had families, dreams, and ambitions. What did Tana have to live for?

A wave of hopeless defeat crashed over her as she realized there was no real choice to be made. Her hand—which no longer even felt like part of her body—reached for the carabiner at her waist. With her other, she pulled on the rope to give herself some slack. Her fingers fumbled over the locking mechanism, struggling to twist it open as it vibrated with each pounding footstep. Finally, just as she was about to give it up as hopeless, the lock spun free. With a quick flick of her thumb, she unclipped the carabiner, releasing herself from the safety line. Her last view was of Calla, still running for her life, not yet aware of the change in pressure on the rope. She prayed they'd make it, that this one last gesture wasn't all for nothing.

Then, the world went white.

Her feet were pulled out from under her, and she was knocked onto her back, but only for a second, as the churning snow quickly pitched her forward. Her face slammed into the mess of powder and ice. The sharp crystals pushed into her open mouth and nostrils, grinding against her eyelids. She instinctively fought to inhale, sucking in more snow. Her pack snagged a rock hidden beneath the snow and yanked her upright, her head popping above the surface. She spat out the snow and sucked in a lungful of air, scraping the icy crust from her eyes. Below her, she saw the bright yellow of Wyatt's jacket and the dark brown of the grizzly's fur as they were tossed just as mercilessly.

She rolled forward again, a wave of powder engulfing her from behind. Tana struggled to remember her avalanche training, searching her panic-soaked brain for any shred of useful information. She needed to keep her head above the snow, a seemingly impossible task as the force of the avalanche dragged her under like a breaking wave tumbling a swimmer against the sea floor. Swimming. That's what her instructor had drilled into them. Pretend as though you're swimming to stay above the surface. Make sure your face has an air pocket.

Shooting out her arms and legs, she began to paddle, her limbs pawing ineffectually against the turbulence. A chunk of ice sliced the side of her face, making her gasp in pain and suck in another mouthful of snow. She coughed, only managing to plug up her nostrils even further. *So this is what it's like to die*, she thought. Her ordinary, meaningless existence, wiped out because some idiot gave a hotdog to a bear. It seemed fitting.

A numbness spread up her limbs, even as they continued to paddle frantically. She wondered if her body knew the end was near and was pulling all remaining life to her core in a last ditch effort at survival. Even her face was frozen, though it was possibly a side effect from the snow packed against it.

Finally, she surfaced, her upper body breaking into open air. She clawed the snow from her face, coughing out chips of ice. Her burning lungs dragged in mouthfuls of air, each breath more precious than the last as the end of this horrific ride drew closer.

She was below the clouds now, the ground rockier. Tana bounced over the fist-sized stones, her legs slamming against their sharp edges. The pain barely registered as she focused on her final destination, a pile of boulders nearly a hundred feet below. They'd caught glimpses of it from camp yesterday, its jagged edges poking through the snow cover.

Tana was helpless to do anything besides watch as she was swept toward it, her hands still paddling through the snow of their own accord. This was it, then. She was going to die on the same mountain as her parents, no closer to knowing how they had disappeared. Would anyone find her body, or would she become yet another mysterious disappearance on Torket? She hated the thought of her adoptive parents enduring the same lack of closure she had. If the others survived this nightmare, they could at least tell them what had happened. She closed her eyes, desperate for a hint of solace but finding only the empty buzz of panic.

Her eyes snapped open at the sound of a lone voice. She whipped her head around to see who was beside her, but she saw nothing save the rushing snow. Again, the voice cried out, the words foreign to her ears.

"Where are you?" she shouted. "Help me!"

Adja bukira. The phrase repeated on a loop, the tone urgent, sounding as panicked as Tana felt.

"I don't know what you're saying," she shouted with frustration. Tears leaked from her eyes, melding with the blood and snow already dripping down her face.

Adja bukira. Adja bukira. Adja bukira.

The words began to take shape, not in a direct translation, but Tana swore she felt the emotion behind them, an urgency, a fear. And a desire to help. An image flickered through her mind, a foreign intrusion on her despair. Something dark and gray...a stone?

Adja bukira.

"A stone?" Something clicked into place. "The rocks! Grab the rocks!"

The boulders were less than fifty feet away. Tana sucked in a lungful of air, shut her eyes, then rolled onto her stomach. The snow immediately closed over her, clogging her nose and ears as it shrouded her in darkness. She grappled for the ground, her gloved hands searching for any kind of hold. The moving snow threatened to roll her sideways, but she dug her fingers into the earth, clawing at the loose rocks. One fist-sized stone jolted her finger, snapping the nail and sending a shockwave of pain up her hand.

Precious seconds ticked away, and each stone that she rolled over only served as a reminder that she was running out of runway. With a primal scream that filled her mouth with snow, Tana lifted both hands and slammed them into the ground, her fingers curved like talons. The rocks were larger now, and each one that bashed against her legs became an anchor point, something for her hands to latch on to. She grasped, missing the first but holding on to the second for a heartbeat before being tugged away. Finally, on the third, she managed to wrap her fingers around the head-sized stone and hang on for dear life.

The snow moved around her, but slower now. She felt the ice sliding past her body like a crowd of New Yorkers in a busy crosswalk—obtrusive but unharmful. Lungs burning, she released the rock and pushed herself from the ground, her head popping into sweet, life-giving air. She took a gasping breath as the snow gave her one final push—the raging menace now tamed to a lover's embrace—propping her gently against the boulders she'd assumed would be her gravestones.

She leaned her head back against the rock, her body still submerged in snow, and stared up at the sky in wonder.

She was alive.

The realization was so overwhelming, so surreal, she couldn't tell if she wanted to laugh or cry. Adrenaline still coursed through her bloodstream, muting any sense of pain, though she knew the effect would be short-lived. Dull throbs where the rocks and ice had made an impact were popping up all over her arms and legs, warnings of the oncoming agony.

Over the years, she'd had plenty of close calls while climbing, but the sheer amount of catastrophe on this trip no longer felt like a coincidence. Torket seemed determined to stop her from reaching its summit, even if it meant killing her in the process. While she'd won this battle, it was much too close for comfort. She was only alive because of the invisible voice that had followed her down the hill. Otherwise, she'd surely be dead due to her own panic.

At the sound of a low, gurgling groan, Tana twisted her neck to catch sight of the source. It was a man's voice, surely Wyatt. And by the sound of it, he hadn't been quite as lucky.

Chapter Fifteen

Stuck under nearly three feet of snow, Tana wriggled her body, wrenching each limb free from the oppressive weight. She berated herself for not shaking loose as soon as she'd stopped moving. Her avalanche instructor had droned on and on about how the friction of an avalanche created heat, partially melting the snow. When it finally stopped moving, it would freeze back together, sealing bodies inside as though they were trapped in cement. Timing was the most important factor for survival.

Grunting with the effort, she yanked her feet free and rushed toward the sound of Wyatt's voice. Snow was packed inside every inch of her clothes and boots, which she needed to remove before it melted and soaked to the skin. But finding Wyatt was now her top priority. His moans, weak and gurgly, were alarming.

"Wyatt?" she tried to yell, her voice cracking. "Where are you?"

Again came the moan, this time on her left. She crawled over the snow on her hands and knees, not wanting to pierce him with her crampons if he lay right below the surface. "Keep making noise," she urged, listening for another groan.

A flash of yellow a few feet beyond the next clump of rocks caught her eye. She jumped to her feet and ran through the pileup of debris, stumbling to where Wyatt's head and shoulders rose above the snow. His hat had fallen off, exposing a gash where his skull had impacted the rock beside him. Bits of hair and blood were plastered to the rock. A trickle of blood spilled down his cheek, but at a quick glance, the wound didn't look exceptionally deep.

Still wearing her backpack, Tana unclipped it and dropped it to the ground, pawing through one of the pockets until she found a bandana. "Hold still," she instructed, though there was no need. Wyatt was in a daze, his eyes unfocused. She doubted he could even hear her. Folding the bandana into a long strip, she wrapped it over the wound and tied it off tightly. Not perfect, and Misty would surely give her grief for not sanitizing the wound first, but it would at least slow the bleeding.

"I'm going to dig you out now," she said. "Does anything hurt? Can you move your arms and legs?"

No answer. Only the wet, labored breathing.

Tana lifted her foot and slammed it into the snow, using her steel crampons to break up the ice sheets holding him down. What had been a wave of slush and powder moments ago was now solidifying like a wall of concrete, a frozen tomb. "You're gonna be fine," she panted, lifting a large chunk of ice off his forearm. "We'll call for help and get a helicopter to take you down. As soon as I get you out of here, you can have my coat too." She laughed, trying to snap him out of his funk with her faux-cheery mood. "It's full of snow, so it's not helping me much anyway."

She scraped the snow away from his chest, her hands smacking something hard and metallic.

"What the..."

The snow here was bright red, little rivulets of color seeping into the surrounding ice. She quickened her pace, not wanting to see the extent of the damage but knowing that with this much blood loss, every second mattered.

"Oh, fuck," was all she could manage to say. Embedded halfway up the shaft, Wyatt's ice ax protruded from right below his ribcage. At some point during the avalanche, he must've fallen on it, impaling himself. Blood gushed from the wound, coating his yellow jacket in a crimson slick. The sight of it made her dizzy.

She looked up the slope they'd climbed that morning, where she prayed the rest of her team had found safety. The clouds obscured the upper reaches of the trail, but since her teammates didn't appear to be in the pileup of debris alongside her, she remained cautiously optimistic. Once they were sure the avalanche had stopped, she knew they'd come looking for her. Hell, Calla was probably already on her way. Until then, Wyatt was her responsibility.

Her hands fluttered nervously, unsure of whether or not she should remove the ax in case it was pressing up against an artery, holding blood inside his body. The last thing she wanted was to allow any more of it to escape. Not that it mattered. The growing pool of blood in his lap made the decision for her. How could things possibly get any worse?

"I'm sorry," she whispered, her fingers wrapping around the head of the ax. She squinted her eyes against the gore, took a deep breath, and then slid the metal shaft from his gut. Wyatt let out a gasp, his wide eyes finding hers as the pain seemed to pull him from his shock.

"Wh-wh-where's th-the b-b-bear?" he stuttered.

"It's gone," Tana said, slipping off her snow-crusted coat and pressing it against the wound. It was a lie, she knew. She could hear heavy rustling from the other side of the rocks. The bear must have been thrown over them or managed to crawl there after the crash landing. Either way, it was unlikely to attack after such a rough, painful fall, or so she hoped.

Slipping her hands beneath his armpits, she pulled Wyatt forward, knotting the coat around his back to keep pressure on the wound. She pulled out her cell phone and checked the signal—nothing. Without the satellite phone, all she could do was wait for help to arrive. She supposed she could start back up the hill, hoping to catch them as they ran down, but leaving Wyatt seemed as callous as it was pointless. Surely, they had called for rescue the moment she was swept out of sight.

Unless they, too, had been swept away, their final resting place a different cluster of rocks. Tana forced the thought from her mind. They were all well-trained and would probably do a better job of keeping their wits about them than she had. She had to believe they were fine if only to help soothe her raw nerves. Right now, all she needed to focus on was Wyatt.

"Can you tell me your name?" she asked, running through her first aid checklist of how to diagnose brain damage after a fall. Though, God forbid, he actually have a concussion—or worse. Tana was completely unequipped to actually treat the victim.

"Wyatt Ha-Halifax," he stuttered.

"Do you know where you are?"

He nodded. "Torket. One avalanche lower than the Innuksuk Rocks. That's the technical measurement." He tried to laugh, but the sound lodged in his throat, a liquid rasp.

Tana decided that was a good enough answer to rule out a concussion. She dug out his legs, careful not to move him and jostle his injury any more than she already had, pushing the snow into a low wall to block the wind. Then she settled into the nook beside him, hoping they'd keep each other warm while they waited. In an effort to take his mind off his current predicament, she said, "Tell me about your family. I know you can't be married, not with how you were hitting on Brynn." She smirked to show she was joking, a gesture he tried to replicate, only to wind up grimacing.

"That was stupid," he croaked. "I'm really sorry, I...I don't know what the hell I was thinking. I'm sorry."

Tana kicked herself for bringing up a sore subject. "I was kidding, don't worry about it. So, um, how'd you get into climbing? Your parents?"

Wyatt nodded, and Tana was horrified to see that his eyelids were drooping. Where the hell were the others?

"They used to take us out every weekend," he said. "Me and my brothers. They kind of grew out of it, but I got hooked. I love it out here." He let out a weary sigh. "Sorry, it...it's getting kind of hard to talk."

Tana gripped his hand, threading her fingers between his. Despite the gravity of the situation, she almost laughed. It was the first time she'd ever held hands with a man—of course it would be something horribly unromantic. "Relax," she said. "Try to focus on my voice and stay awake. The helicopter will be here soon."

She racked her brain for a better conversation topic. Her job? Boring. Her love life? Non-existent. Bucket list? Didn't have one. She settled on their surroundings. "My first mountain was actually this one," she said. "Though I'm not sure if I was ever on the summit. I was too little to really remember. After that, we moved to Seattle, and of course, I bounced around up there: Rainier, Hood, Baker, St. Helens, all the big ones. My parents didn't push it or anything. I think they were kind of over it, to be honest. They'd been climbing since they were teenagers. It's actually how they met.

"Anytime I saw a new mountain, I needed to be on top. It was like a compulsion. It's hard to explain, but as a kid, I thought there was something magical about the summits, like I'd reach the peak and suddenly, doors would open up. Like the wardrobe to Narnia or the tornado to Oz. My parents always said my imagination was out of control."

The light in her eyes dimmed. When had she lost that spark? The hope of escaping to a hidden magical world where she wouldn't have to be, well, herself. She supposed that, like most adults, the monotony of life had beaten it out of her. Bit by bit until, one day, you looked up from your quarterly spreadsheets to realize it was all gone.

A small chuckle bubbled out of Wyatt's throat. "I used to think that stuff too. Two peas in a pod, eh?" He coughed, and a small spatter of blood appeared on the corner of his lip. "I'm really glad it's you here and not the mean one," he whispered, giving her hand a squeeze. Then his eyes rolled up in his head, and he slumped forward.

"Shit." Tana grabbed his torso and lifted him upright. She'd been babbling away like an idiot while he was drifting into unconsciousness. How thoughtless could she be?

"Tana!"

"Tana, where are you?"

She turned toward the voices, popping her head over her makeshift wall. Calla and Brynn were running down the slope.

Brynn's pack had been left behind, no doubt so she could sprint, while Calla carried her entire bag, ready for whatever aftermath awaited them.

"Here," she shouted, waving her arms above the snow line, her bright red shirt like a flare against the landscape. "We're over here."

Brynn spotted her, pointing her out to Calla, and together, they raced the last hundred yards, kicking up shards of ice in their wake.

"Oh, thank God, you're alive! Are you okay?" Calla asked as soon as she was within yelling distance. "Why did you unhook? How goddamn stupid do you have to be to unhook? That's what the rope is for."

She slid into Tana's nook, barely sparing a glance at Wyatt. Her hands grasped Tana's shoulders. "I can't believe you're alive! You're okay?" At Tana's nod of assent, Calla pulled her into a shaky hug. "Don't you ever fucking do that again," she warned. "We don't need you to be a hero."

Brynn squatted down in front of Wyatt. She took one look at his pale face and tore off her gloves, lifting his chin to search for a pulse. "Oh no," she breathed. "I think he's dead."

"Are you serious?" Calla slipped a hand inside his shirt, feeling for a heartbeat. "Holy shit, I think you're right."

"Did someone call for help?" Tana demanded. "He landed on his ax when he fell. He's lost a ton of blood. If he doesn't get to a hospital soon…" Her last few moments with Wyatt had endeared him to her. The last thing she wanted was for him to die on her watch.

Brynn nodded. "Misty called as soon as she knew we definitely weren't going to slide. She was losing her mind, crying on the phone and everything. The helicopter should be here soon. I'm surprised it hasn't landed yet." She looked at Wyatt, her brows creasing with worry. "I think it's already too late."

They knelt around him, their eyes solemn with the knowledge there was nothing they could do. Even Calla, who wished only misfortune upon him, bowed her head. Like him or not, he was one of their own, a climber. His death was a loss to their community. Another number sacrificed to the mountains. It was an outcome that awaited all of them if they made even the slightest mistake on the quest for a peak. Tana knew how close she'd come to such a fate today.

They sat, heads bowed, silent and mournful, waiting for help to arrive.

Chapter Sixteen

Walking the expansive grounds of the Pacific Glass Gardens, Tana was engulfed in a kaleidoscope of color and shape. Glass swirls emerged from gardens of brilliant tropical flowers, including ruby-red ginger blossoms and exotic bird of paradise blooms. Up above, a dazzling display of handcrafted glass flowers hung above her like technicolor clouds.

A group of her classmates sprinted past, the ecstasy of a weekday field trip emblazoned on their faces.

"No running," their teacher, Mrs. Kim, hollered after them, seemingly only now realizing that bringing a class of middle school children to a museum of fragile glassware may have been an error in judgment.

She took chase, accidentally knocking Tana's shoulder. "Oops, sorry, sweetheart. Didn't see you there."

Tana shrugged, used to such offenses by now. She wandered down the hallway, where the tile floor gave way to rough stone, expanding into a full cavern of craggy rock. Woven through the cracks in the stone and arching across the ceiling were thin, ribbonlike swirls of glass. Her fingers trailed over the colorful pieces. They reminded her of photos she'd seen of her adoptive parents back in their rock climbing days, contorted into unnatural positions, stretching and straining to inch their way up the rock face.

A young couple entered the cavern, their voices echoing around the stone chamber, all delighted oohs and aahs. The man pointed to an intricately twisted piece, his hands gesticulating as he explained the process behind creating such a work of art.

Tana turned her attention to the glass, scrutinizing the dips and swells the artist had surely labored over. Vivid red gave way to violet and then a brilliant sapphire blue. It was objectively pleasing to the eye, a fact she couldn't dispute. And yet, she found herself unable to produce any appreciative reaction even close to what the couple displayed.

As she listened to the man ecstatically exclaim how each piece was more masterful than the last, she walked the length of the cavern, stopping at the very back. Here, instead of colorful glass ribbons, swoops of mirror-like reflective glass clung to the walls. Her own face reflected back to her, twisted and contorted, turning her ghostly pale features into something monstrous. She pulled back until her reflection disappeared from the glass depths.

"Tan-a-raq has no rack," a singsong voice cut across the man's gushing admiration.

Tana turned to see Bill Conley swaggering toward her. Though he was hardly popular, thanks to his threadbare hand-me-down clothes and dismal hygiene, he still ranked one rung higher than Tana on the social ladder. Since punching upward often landed him in detention, he tended to prey upon those on the lower levels of the middle school hierarchy.

Tana shrugged, barely acknowledging the weak insult. Half her class was still flat-chested. Frankly, it was a relief to be made fun of for something common, as opposed to, say, her grayish-brown hair color or nearly colorless eyes. She'd lost track of the number of insults targeting her unpigmented skin. Or even her adoption, as if losing her parents was shameful rather than tragic.

Not used to being ignored, Bill pressed on. "Tan-a-raq has no—"

"I heard you," Tana said quietly.

When she refused to react further, Bill spat out, "You're weird-looking, and nobody likes you." He turned and ran out of the cavern.

Tana felt the couple's eyes on her back. She turned to meet their gaze, and they pivoted away, pretending to be lost in the beauty of the art.

"Tana, there you are!" Mrs. Kim rushed into the cavern and grabbed Tana's arm, pulling her toward the museum exit. "One of your classmates shattered an extremely intricate, expensive piece, so pardon my French, but we're getting the hell out of here."

Silence blanketed the school bus. The only sound was the quiet shuffling of bodies readjusting against the vinyl seats. After Mrs. Kim had bellowed herself hoarse about their destructive misconduct, nobody dared make so much as a peep.

Seated alone, Tana pulled her dogeared copy of *A Wrinkle In Time* from her backpack. After she was found on Torket, it had taken months for her to begin speaking in full sentences again, though she seemed to fully understand English. Her therapist postulated that she was suffering from trauma-induced muteness. A steady diet of books had been prescribed as a way to help hone and encourage her language skills. Even after her voice finally returned, the habit of getting lost within the pages of a paperback remained.

A Wrinkle In Time was one of her favorites. Mousy Meg, who not only went on amazing adventures but was also deeply admired by those around her, was the heroine she wished she could be.

As she flipped to the introduction of Mrs. Whatsit, the bus exited the highway, pulling into an oversize spot at a rest stop.

Mrs. Kim stood at the front of the bus. "I'm obligated to give you all a lunch and bathroom break," she growled. "But let me be very clear. If anyone causes any sort of trouble—and I mean anything—you will be in detention for the rest of the school year."

They filed out of the bus, each cluster of students finding a section of grass to claim as their own. Tana weaved through the groups, working her way to the back of the lot, where her lack of a social circle would be less conspicuous. No one paid her any mind, engrossed in their own hushed chatter and brown bag lunches.

She unzipped her backpack, pulling out the bag of food her mother had prepared. Home cooking all of their meals was a fairly new experiment for her mother, and neither Tana nor her father had the heart to say it was a near-total flop.

She pulled out a plastic baggie and winced. Fried hummus drops. A culinary adventure that produced bland, soft balls of mush. She looked longingly at her classmates' ham and cheese sandwiches and Lunchables.

With a sigh, she turned away from the other children, her gaze falling on the trees lining the grassy rest area. They dissolved into shadow a few hundred feet from where Tana stood, thick with overgrowth. Peeking through a gap in the branches, Tana could make out the white peak of Mount Rainier, beckoning to her and calling her into the maze of the woods. She swore she felt it tugging on the hem of her jacket, physically pulling her forward.

Tana glanced over her shoulder, searching for Mrs. Kim, who was sitting among the students, her eyes glazed over and her lunch untouched. If Tana was caught slipping away, punishment would surely be swift and furious. She'd be thrown into detention, but even worse would be her parents' disappointment. Though Tana's mostly B grades didn't warrant much enthusiasm, her polite, rule-following behavior was always noted on report cards and lauded by her family. Unbeknownst to them, this was more a reflection of her timidness than a respect for authority, a fearful stifling of her inner rebellion.

She thought of Meg from her book—courageous and always ready for adventure despite the dangers. She'd read this story so many times she could probably recite whole paragraphs from memory. Wasn't it time she finally pushed herself to follow Meg's example? And besides—she stifled a humorless laugh—it wasn't like anyone would notice she was gone anyway.

With a deep breath to steel her nerves, she took one last look at her classmates, then ducked into the trees.

Her heart hammered against her chest as the sounds of her classmates faded away. She was really doing this. Quiet, unassuming Tana was off on an adventure.

She weaved through the thicket, branches and vines tugging at her clothes. The view of Rainier was lost among the greenery, but she knew she was pointed in the right direction. She felt it, like a compass pointing her forward.

Each bend in her path gave life to flickers of imagination. She envisioned stumbling upon her own version of Mrs. Whatsit, ready to guide her to a magical new world—one without these miserable cretins that passed as her schoolmates. One where adults didn't walk into her or miss her during headcounts. One where she could finally be the heroine of her own story.

The ground began to rise, her thin legs straining to push her up the slope. Thickets and brambles gave way to patches of grass, and when she peered at the trees above, she saw growing swaths of blue sky. Sunlight streamed through the branches, illuminating the crest of the hill in a yellow glow. The ethereal vision was like a scene pulled from one of her fantasy stories.

Her pace quickened. A tiny twinge of hope flickered to life in her chest, the thought that maybe this was her storybook moment. An escape from everything that lay behind her. Though logically, she knew it was impossible, what if atop this hill lay a doorway to her own magical expedition?

She clutched at the tall grasses and sagebrush, pulling herself higher, the view of Rainier growing clearer and clearer, until at last, she rounded the final curve, stumbling onto the soft plateau of the hilltop.

Panting with the exertion of her climb, she closed her eyes, hoping—no, knowing—that the view would change when she opened them. The belief that her life was finally about to change was unshakeable. The force that had guided her to this spot was like a magnet propelling her closer. This wasn't a trick of her imagination. This was real.

And yet, when she cracked her eyes open, all she saw was the grassy knoll and Rainier's snowy peak. A beautiful sight, to be sure, but not life-altering.

Disappointment reared its ugly head, and she stamped it down, embarrassed at her own childish desires. She was twelve now, far too old to still believe in things like magic and portals to new worlds. While the other girls in her grade were focused on sleepovers and social status and boyfriends, Tana was chasing after a half-baked idea of adventure from some stupid kid's book. She consoled herself with the fact that at least none of her classmates were around to witness this humiliation.

She started to turn back the way she'd come when a shimmer on the horizon pulled her attention back to Rainier. Its peak flickered as though a wave of static cut across it. Tana blinked in surprise, wondering what the heck she'd just seen. Perhaps a trick of the sunlight? No, something was definitely moving up there. The snow and rock were shifting too slowly to be an avalanche or an eruption. The lumpy summit of Rainier was shrinking and morphing into a flat, smooth plateau.

"What the heck?" She rubbed her eyes, wondering if she was caught in a dream. The summit of Rainier was as familiar to her as her own backyard, and what she was staring at was most definitely another peak entirely. "Wake up, Tana," she whispered. When her bedroom didn't materialize before her eyes, that faint ember of hope once again ignited in her chest. It was actually happening. Something beyond the ordinary was taking place right before her eyes.

A scream cut through the air, and Tana jumped, the hair on her arms rising to attention. She spun on the spot, stumbling as she searched for the source. A second scream joined the first, higher in pitch, sharp as broken glass. It raised goosebumps on Tana's arms, the horrible sound settling in her chest, shredding it from the inside.

She raised her hands to her ears, trying to blot out the noise. Tears inexplicably leaked from the corners of her eyes, and her own scream merged with the others. "Stop it! Please, make it stop," she cried. The terrified wails felt like they were carving out her chest, leaving her hollow and vulnerable. It was unbearable. "Stop!"

And then suddenly, silence. All she heard was the rapid pounding of her own heartbeat. On shaky legs, she turned back to Rainier, now reverted to its normal shape. She wiped the wetness from her cheeks, amazed at the flood of emotion that had been released. She couldn't remember the last time she'd cried.

"I didn't imagine that," she whispered. Something incredible, something magical had happened. Both wonderful and horrible. Had she glimpsed another world? The thought was dizzying, and as scared as she'd been only moments ago, she yearned to be given another peek behind the curtain.

Down below, the rumble of a school bus roaring to life made her head snap up, all thoughts of fantasy worlds pushed aside.

"Oh crap."

So fast she was nearly flying, Tana raced down the side of the hill, branches grabbing at her hair as she tore past. She stumbled, her head flying over her feet, sending her pinwheeling down the slope. She crash-landed in a tangle of vines.

"Wait!" Her voice was garbled and frantic. Struggling to her feet, she tore the vines from her legs and charged through the forest. The sounds of her classmates were audible now, a flash of the yellow bus visible through the trees.

Bursting from the tree cover, she slowed to a power walk, yanking twigs and leaves from her hair as she joined the last few stragglers climbing aboard.

Mrs. Kim checked her name off a list as she trudged aboard, oblivious to the disheveled state of her student. "Tanaraq Walker. Ok, that'll do it." She turned to the driver. "Let's get this day over with."

Tana walked down the aisle, scanning for an empty seat. Being the last to board came with the penalty of limited choices. Several seats held only one student, but their occupant's "jock" or "popular" status stopped Tana from requesting a space. Chloe McMillan, head cheerleader, popped her sneakers on the seat as Tana moved past, blocking her access.

Finally, Tana spotted Bill Conley alone, likely due to the sharp odor that floated around him like a cloud. As she sidled up to his seat, he placed a hand on the bench.

"Bug off, Tana Banana."

At the sight of his smug, peanut-butter-smeared face, a surge of energy shot through her, fueled by the adrenaline still pumping through her veins. She grabbed his hand and flung it into his lap. "Move," she shouted.

Heads turned, a dozen onlookers eager for any kind of entertainment, but she didn't care. Cheeks flaming, Bill scooched toward the window, refusing to meet her eyes and instead glaring at the passing landscape. Tana dropped into the seat, letting the small victory settle over her like an elixir, strengthening her from the inside out. This burst of newfound confidence was intoxicating, and she leaned back to savor the moment.

Above Bill's head, the sight of Rainier's peak caught her eye. Something up there had been calling out to her. She was sure of it. The force guiding her up that hill had been as real as someone taking her by the hand. She thought of those horrible screams, the way they'd settled inside of her. Was she meant to help those people? Or had it been a warning to stay away from Rainier, or maybe that new mountain it had morphed into? Either way, it confirmed what she'd always hoped. There was something else out there, something beyond this bleak middle school hell.

She pulled *A Wrinkle In Time* from her backpack, its plain Jane heroine in full color on the cover. She may not have managed to escape to a new world today, but a warmth filled her chest with the knowledge that something greater awaited her. And one day, like Meg, she'd find her way.

Chapter Seventeen

The helicopter finally appeared overhead, a gleaming orange dragonfly, alighting on the snow just long enough to load Wyatt's body and confirm that none of them were friends or family before it took off again. The rescue team hadn't commented on his condition, but from their stony expressions, Tana guessed revival wasn't in the cards. The sudden pang of sadness caught her by surprise, especially for a man who had threatened to strand them on the mountain. In those final minutes, she'd felt a sense of kinship. She conceded the feelings could have been the rush of adrenaline or the thrill of finally holding someone's hand, though it was possibly something more. His loss gnawed at her.

While his death was sure to be mourned by his family, Tana knew all too well the harsh treatment his legacy was about to endure. From celebrity climbers to passing acquaintances she'd met on the trails, deaths were always met with a barrage of cheap insults typed below their online obituaries, from "natural selection at its finest" to "Darwin strikes again." She'd long ago accepted that her own fate would be met with such ridicule, no doubt from those who had never heard the siren song of adventure call their name. After her brief flicker of connection with Wyatt, she hated that he'd almost certainly be judged harshly by strangers who never knew him. The unfairness of it was maddening.

Brynn gestured at the steep slope before them. "Let's get back up there before Misty loses it. I'm sure she saw the helicopter. She'll be thinking it was you loaded on it, not Wyatt."

"Hang on," Tana said, turning back to the rocks. There was one more victim that needed to be checked on. Though every muscle ached, she forced herself to grip the slippery rocks and clamber on top of them. Slumped on the other side, so quiet she'd almost forgotten it existed, was the bear.

"Is it dead?" Calla asked, materializing beside her. "I figured it would have run off by now."

On Tana's other side, Brynn pointed at the bear's flanks, rising with each shuddering breath. "Still alive, barely."

Tana swung a leg over the top of the rocks, starting down to where the bear lay. She couldn't fully understand why she needed to see it, let alone vocalize it to the others, but was unable to extinguish the urge. They'd suffered a trauma together, and she had to know she wasn't the only survivor. With Wyatt gone, she needed to feel that connection, that someone else had made it through to the other side, even if it wasn't human.

"Tana," Calla hissed. "Get away from it." She held the can of mace aloft, ready to spring.

Tana waved her off, putting a finger to her lips for silence. The bear lay directly below her, so she maneuvered around its bulk, dropping to her haunches only a foot from its head.

The grizzly's eyes had glazed over, and a smear of blood ran across its snout. None of its limbs were bent at unnatural angles, but lying on such sharp, uncomfortable rocks suggested that it was unable to do otherwise.

"I wish there'd been a shadow person to help you too," she said quietly. A wave of helplessness washed over her. Another catastrophe, and nothing she could do to fix it. Life was one big series of blows, and all she could do was try to minimize the bruising after each one. It wasn't enough, passively floating along the waves, never grabbing the wheel to steer her own ship. No one should be that pathetic in their own life.

She choked up, the day's events finally catching up to her. "Your cub is waiting for you," she whispered, nodding toward the hill. "Way up there, all alone. Wondering if you've left her behind." A tear fell down her cheek, and she swiped it away. "Don't let her down, okay? Even if you think she's big enough to make it on her own, I promise you, she isn't. She still needs you."

"Tana."

Ignoring Calla's warning, Tana reached out her hand, pausing inches above the bear's head.

"Tana, don't you fucking dare."

She let her fingers fall, stroking the thick fur on its head. The bear stirred, its golden eyes finding hers.

"We need our parents. Please, don't let her down," Tana whispered.

Those golden eyes blinked, and Tana supposed that was all the response she was going to get. She gave the fur one last stroke, then stood, climbing back to the rocks where Brynn and Calla waited. While Brynn's face was open with admiration, Calla's was like a storm cloud.

"Do you have any idea how worried we were?" she asked, her voice a low growl. "Misty's crying her eyes out, someone is dead, and now that we've found you, you decide it'd be nice to go pet the damn bear. It's like you're trying to give me a fucking heart attack."

Tana bristled at the accusation. "Right, I decided to throw myself down the mountain just to give you a good scare," she shot back.

Calla let out a heavy sigh. "Look, I'm sorry. It's just...we thought you were dead and...I'm really having a hard time with this trip. I can handle a lot. I mean, duh, it's me." She let out a shaky laugh, the humor betrayed by a quiver in her lower lip. "But I'm feeling a little like Misty right about now." Turning to Brynn, she said, "Don't tell her I said that."

Brynn attempted to offer a wan smile. "She'd be happy to hear you've gone to the dark side. Responsible adulthood."

Tana's heart sank. Calla was a force of nature. In all the years she'd known her, not once had she given up on a climb, regardless of weather, injury, or fatigue. It was no accident that she'd chosen to climb Torket with Calla at the helm. She needed to reach the top, if only for her own sanity, and there was no one she trusted more to get her there. If Calla had finally hit her limit and bailed on the climb, Tana didn't think she'd have the will to continue, not if Torket kept throwing these deadly obstacles in her path. She wasn't skilled or brave enough to tackle the mountain alone, and she knew it.

"You're not actually thinking of giving up, are you?" The words came out more forceful than intended. The summit was calling to her, a palpable force drawing her closer. She needed to reach it, and she needed Calla by her side.

Calla's eyes met hers, their dark depths inscrutable. "Let's wait until we get back up to Misty, then we can talk. We have a hell of a walk up this damn hill to think it over."

Hours later, they rounded onto the plateau that held the Innuksuk Rocks, the same cluster where the bear had first appeared. Each woman tapped the stones with her ax in passing, a halfhearted celebration of the accomplishment. Camp Three was a short walk away, and the sight of an erected tent in the distance signaled the day's finish line. The smell of bacon wafted to them on the breeze, making Tana's mouth water. It felt like ages since she'd last eaten.

"Oh my God, you're alive!"

Misty jumped up from her spot at the stove and rushed over to them, pushing past Brynn and Calla to smother Tana in a back-breaking hug. She lingered several seconds, her arms like a vise, before pulling back to reveal red-rimmed, swollen eyes. "I didn't know what else to do after calling for rescue, so I set up camp and cooked dinner. Everything's laid out. Let me take a look at you, then we can set up your bed and let you rest."

Tana surveyed the campsite, the tent erected, and the orderly bowls of food laid out. Misty's extensive first aid kit was spread beside the kitchen dugout, each color-coded plastic baggie ready for action. In the face of danger, she'd gone into full-on coddling mode, showing love the only way she knew how: mothering. Tana bit her lip to keep her emotions from showing. The care Misty had taken was so touching she wasn't sure she'd be able to keep her eyes from spilling over. How could she keep dragging these people along on her pointless quest? If they wanted to go home, how dare she prolong their suffering when they obviously cared so much for her?

Misty pushed her into a seated position beside the stove and forced a piece of bacon into her hand, which Tana obediently shoved into her mouth. She nearly groaned out loud as the salt and fat washed over her tongue. Near-death experiences apparently had a way of turning food into a form of ecstasy. Calla snatched a piece of bacon but didn't sit beside them, choosing instead to walk the camp perimeter, seemingly lost in thought.

Misty dropped beside her and began examining her injuries, swabbing with an antiseptic wipe. "This one's deep," she commented, cleaning the gash on Tana's forehead. "Did you hit a rock?"

"Ice," Tana replied, shoveling more bacon into her mouth.

Brynn squatted down next to them. "Have you guys ever seen a bear—hell, any animal—that high?" she asked. "I know it's not completely unheard of. There was that famous leopard on top of Kilimanjaro. It's weird, though, right? Almost like it was coaxed up here?" She paused, waiting for the others to connect the dots, but Misty was digging through the medical supplies and Calla continued to walk the camp, her expression dark. "You know, by the spirits? What if all of these accidents are related? Maybe a warning system, like they want us to turn back? Or maybe the opposite. Maybe it's a test of our bravery?"

"Brynn?" Misty asked, her voice thick.

"Mm?"

"I love you, but can you please shut up for a minute?"

Since leaving the bear behind, Tana hadn't been able to shake the mother and cub from her thoughts. Her heart ached at seeing her own childhood mirrored in their fate. Was the cub running through the snow at that very moment, crying its heart out for a parent who had disappeared into thin air? If Brynn was right, and the spirits of the mountain were trying to send a message, why save Tana at all? If she'd been buried in the avalanche, that would've been more than enough to get the other three to call off the climb. She closed her eyes, trying to will the pieces into place. None of it made sense. It had to have been a coincidence, nothing more. Two parallel stories of orphaned children on the slopes of Torket.

"Your head's as good as I can get it," Misty said. "What else hurts?"

Tana pulled off her gloves to inspect the damage to her hands. "Christ." Her fingers were a mess of broken nail shards and bloody, bruised skin. Each fingertip was a mottled purple and blue. At Misty's horrified expression, she explained, "That's how I stopped myself. Using the rocks as anchors." She swallowed her mouthful of bacon. "Actually, it was one of those shadow people who told me what to do. As I was falling, I started to panic. I froze up, and they yelled at me to grab the rocks. At least, I think that's what they were saying. Without them, I would've freaked out the whole way down. I'd probably be dead."

Calla and Misty exchanged a glance before Calla went back to stalking around camp, her face screwed up in concentration. Or maybe it was an effort to keep her emotions in check. It was impossible to tell with her.

When nobody said anything, Tana asked, "What? You guys don't believe me?"

"Of course I believe you," Brynn said. "But how'd you understand—"

Misty shook her head. "It's not that we don't believe you," she interrupted. "It's been a long day, that's all. And frankly, when you think your best friend is dead..." She trailed off, her eyes again welling up. "I think we all need a stiff drink and a good cry." Her voice broke, and she finally let loose, dropping her head into her hands and sobbing. Brynn reached over and pulled her into a half hug, her own eyes red.

Calla dropped down beside them, pulling Tana into the huddle. At the sight of tears coursing down Calla's cheeks, something Tana had never witnessed, a dam broke inside of her, releasing a floodgate of pent-up emotions: the fear for her friends' lives and for her own, the pain at watching Wyatt, and likely, the bear, slip away, and the pain of putting her team through excruciating hardship, yet no closer to finding any answers. A sob erupted from deep within her, the force of it making her double over in pain.

Arms draped around each other, they let go and cried, all four of their heads drawn together. The stress and fear poured out, unabashed and unrepentant. Their hands clamped down on each other's backs, their trembling limbs clutching one another for dear life. They sobbed until the emotions they'd pent up inside had finally exorcised themselves. Face-to-face with her best friends, Tana swore she could physically feel the grip of anxiety and terror loosen its hold.

She looked into each puffy, runny-nosed face and felt her heart swell with love. Torket had tried to tear them apart but had only made them a stronger unit, unstoppable against whatever trials it threw at them. Even if they turned back now, she wouldn't be leaving empty-handed. She may have come here looking for her parents, but instead, she'd found her sisters.

Tana cleared her throat, wiping the wetness from her cheeks. "There's something I want to tell you all."

Chapter Eighteen

There was no reason for Tana to keep the truth hidden from them any longer. She'd wanted something for herself, a special keepsake of her family that was hers alone. But she realized there was no point in keeping a secret from the people who loved her like family. And she could no longer deny that there was something special about their bond.

Since her adoption, she'd been moving through the years with blinders on, deprived of love and sorrow, triumph and heartbreak, her senses dulled so that each day was a monotonous repeat of the last. But here, surrounded by Calla, Misty, and Brynn, the fogginess was lifting. She thought back to the small burst of joy she'd felt at seeing the night sky bedazzled with stars. Or the pang in her belly when lying beside Calla. And now, the cathartic outpouring of fear and love, an emotional display she would've found impossible only a week prior. The higher they climbed, the more pronounced the changes became, as though through their shared trauma, her teammates were removing the blindfold from Tana's eyes themselves.

She needed their support. She'd ached for it. She hadn't known how badly until now. Sharing her past was a way for her to cement their bond.

She stood and faced her teammates, their eyes still red and puffy. They sat in a semicircle around the stove, munching on the dinner Misty had prepared. Their faces turned to her expectantly.

"This is where my parents found me," she began. "Right here on Torket. I was six or seven. Nobody really knows. I came up here with my biological family, and we got separated. The memories are fuzzy, and I think at some point I was on the summit, but I'm not really sure what happened. All I know is my parents went missing and were never found. Twenty years later, I can only assume they're dead. I managed to walk down to the trail, where a couple—my adoptive parents—found me. A year later, they adopted me."

She paused. "I haven't been back since."

"Why didn't you tell us?" Misty asked. "We had no idea this place meant so much to you."

Tana shrugged. "Part of it was that there was nothing to really tell. No bodies were ever found. No missing persons reports filed. Back then, you didn't need a permit for Torket, so there's no record of their names anywhere. I have no idea if they were Native Alaskan, or a couple of hikers on vacation, or what."

"I doubt you're Native," Brynn said. "Not with that coloring." At Misty's beleaguered sigh, Brynn muttered, "Just sayin'."

"Why'd you want to come back?" Calla asked. "To try and dig up old memories?"

Misty raised an eyebrow. "You weren't planning to look for their bodies, were you?"

Again, Tana shrugged, palms open in confusion. "I honestly don't know what I was planning to do. The mountains have always felt like home to me. It was the only sport I ever really took to. I think all this time, wanting to be in the mountains was really me wanting to come back here, to Torket."

She paused, considering her words. "I dream about this place, about being here as a kid. Running through the snow, screaming for someone to help me. I know this is going to sound a little crazy, but it feels like the mountain was calling for me, telling me to come back. Like there was something it wanted to show me." At Brynn's raised eyebrow, Tana backtracked to safer waters. "I don't think there's anything physical to find, like a body or a jacket or something that belonged to them. I think maybe I came back to find some kind of—"

"Closure," Misty said with a soft smile.

Tana nodded, grateful for her understanding.

"Tanaraq, granddaughter of the tundra," Calla said. "I remember you telling us what it meant back in college. I gotta say, your parents picked a damn good name for you. Now it all makes sense." She smiled. "And now the prodigal granddaughter has returned."

"I'm really glad you shared that with us," Misty said. She reached over and gently squeezed Tana's hand. "I wish the mountain had been able to give you some memory of them. At least you were able to come back and see it. That's something."

Misty's words gave her pause. They sounded a little too close to quitting for Tana's liking. She treaded carefully. "I can't explain it, but I feel it in my gut. Whatever I came to find, it's at the summit," she said, trying to gauge their reactions. Her teammates shared a quick, worried glance, confirming what she already suspected. They were all planning to bail on the summit. "I know it sounds crazy—"

"Oh, not at all," Misty cut in, her voice dripping with sarcasm. Her flip in mood was alarming, a stark reminder of how desperately she wanted to get the hell out of here. She ticked off her fingers. "Brynn fell in a crevasse, you almost jumped off a cliff, Calla got nailed with a boulder, you were swept off in an avalanche, some random guy threatened to strand us here right before he died, a bear attacked us. What else? Oh, right. This all happened while being haunted by a pack of ghosts."

"Taqriaqsuit," Brynn corrected.

"So surely," Misty said, ignoring her, "soldiering on is the only reasonable thing to do, right?"

Crossing her arms over her chest, Tana tried to keep her voice steady. "I know how it must look."

Misty's eyes narrowed. "Do you?"

Tana pressed on, pretending not to have heard. "You know better than anyone that I'm not the kind to rush off and do something reckless. I want to be done with this as much as you. But I need to see it through. If I get up there, and there's nothing for me, then you can make me eat crow the rest of my life." She paused, her eyes sweeping the group. "If you want to turn back, I understand, and there's no hard feelings. But I'm going, even if it means alone."

Once the words were out of her mouth, their gravity pressed down on her. She really meant to continue on to the summit, even without any kind of support. That kind of bravery and resolve was usually reserved for people like Calla and Brynn, and it was a shock to hear the words tumble from her own lips. But the thought of coming this far, only to quit right before the end, was unfathomable. She had to keep trying.

Misty's mouth opened and closed, no words finding their way out. She turned to Calla. "Will you do something?" she hissed.

Calla was crouched beside her, head bowed in thought. With what appeared to be a tremendous amount of effort, she lifted her gaze from the snow up to Misty's enraged face. "Like what?"

"I don't know. Drag her off this thing? Make her listen to you!"

Calla's brow furrowed, her lips tightening to a hard line. "I'm torn about this whole thing, Tana," she said. "And that doesn't happen often." Her fingers twisted nervously. "I'll be honest with you. I'm actually pretty scared. Terrified, actually. I was sure you were dead today, and that's not something I ever want to feel again." Her gaze darted guiltily toward Misty before locking eyes with Tana. "That said, I'd never leave you behind. If you're going, so am I."

"I'm coming too," Brynn chimed in.

"The hell you are," Misty cried. "Tomorrow morning, you and I are heading back down. If you want the great outdoors, you can set up camp next to the truck. But we're getting the hell off this thing while we still can."

"Brynn, listen to her," Calla said quietly. "With everything that's happened, going down is the smart move. Tana and I will summit, then follow you two. Don't pull the ladder when you cross. We'll get it and meet you at the truck."

"You guys think because you're a few years older, you can boss me around?" Brynn argued. "I'm stronger than you"—she pointed at Misty—"more experienced than you"—she pointed at Tana—"and just as tough as you." She glared at Calla. "Don't bench me because things are getting hairy. I can handle myself."

"Oh really?" Misty shot back. "Remind me, who was it that fell in a crevasse? Who almost got smashed by rockfall? You think I want to call Mom and Dad to tell them you're dead?"

"Those weren't my fault! I'm not your child, Mist. I don't need you to protect me."

Tana's stomach twisted into a knot, each shout pulling it tighter. If she wasn't so selfish, so hell-bent on reaching the summit, they could be off the mountain by now, sipping hot rum at Calla's cabin. And for what? She was going to reach the top, have a look around at a view that was only marginally better than their current surroundings, and then turn around to walk back down. Her personal healing, if there was any, would be at the cost of their friendship and possibly their lives.

A bolt of anger tore through her midsection, a white-hot jolt of lightning that burnt away all doubt. Misty was the problem, not Tana. Soft, weak Misty, who used her overprotectiveness as a crutch, who didn't care one iota whether Tana found any sort of closure. She only wanted to get herself back to the safety of civilization and, of course, another bottle of wine.

As quickly as it had struck, the rage melted away, leaving Tana horrified that she could have felt such vitriol toward her friend. Sure, Misty was terrified and worried about her own life, but to think that she didn't care about the others was preposterous. She wanted to turn back out of care, not cowardice.

These new blips of emotion were worrying, a sign of screws shaking loose in her brain. She'd spent her life flitting from peak to peak, never once experiencing a fraction of these intense sensations. Was it possible that after decades in the mountains, she was finally succumbing to hypoxia, her brain splintering into pieces on the most meaningful climb of her life?

Calla's voice cut through her thoughts, a life preserver when she was starting to think she'd drown in them. "Please, for God's sake, Brynn, let it go. C'mon, Tana, let's finish setting up the tent and get some rest. We'll need our strength for tomorrow."

Tana obliged, relieved to let Calla take the lead. She tried to ignore Brynn's scathing glare and Misty's pinched, worried face. She'd wanted nothing more than to share her most precious secret, her origin story, as a way to seal their bond. Instead, it had only driven another wedge between them.

She swallowed down the guilt that threatened to bubble to the surface, grateful for her own small shred of resolve and for Calla's unyielding support. In twenty-four hours, if all went according to plan, they'd all be back on the ground, sharing a beer at some dive, laughing about how they'd cried and hugged and fought all in the span of two hours.

She just needed one more day to make everything right.

Chapter Nineteen

Beneath a canopy of pinned blankets, a circle of Barbie dolls sat patiently waiting for their turn to be primped, awarded a title, and sent into whatever storyline awaited them. A Lite-Brite filled the enclosed space with blue and purple light, turning Brynn's platinum blond pigtails into rainbow-hued tresses.

She picked up her favorite doll, a brunette with long, wavy hair on one side and a tight shave on the other. After Misty lectured her on ruining such a beautiful Barbie, she'd helped even out Brynn's clumsy razor strokes.

"Warrior Queen Daria," Brynn crowned her. A name based on the old cartoon Misty would sometimes let her watch when their parents were out shopping. She pressed a battle ax into the doll's curled fingers, a souvenir she'd stolen from the boy who pulled her pigtails at school. She placed Daria on her towering throne, a mess of pillows stacked nearly up to the blanket ceiling.

"And now," Brynn growled, "you will all bow before me—"

"Brynn Isabella Lansing, you get out here right now!"

Brynn's stomach dropped. What had begun as an order to clean her room had turned into a full play session, this new storyline replete with friendship, betrayal, and queens rising to glory. Not so much as a stray sock had been returned to its proper place.

She poked her head outside the blanket fort, and found herself staring directly into the enraged face of her mother.

"You think I like being the bad guy?" her mother asked. "You think I like yelling?"

Though Brynn knew enough to hold her tongue, it did seem as though her mother found at least a semblance of joy in her daily nagging.

"Either you clean up this pigsty in the next five minutes, or you're not coming today."

"I don't want to go anyway," Brynn grumbled. Who cared about a stupid mountain? Misty's Girl Scout troop was only one climb away from their mountaineering badge, and families were invited to attempt the summit alongside the girls. To Brynn, the idea of walking for four hours sounded like absolute misery, especially when it meant witnessing yet another one of Misty's grand overachievements: completing her hundredth Girl Scout badge.

"Fine," her mother spat. "Then you get to spend the day with Auntie Louise. She needs someone to help sort her stamp collection. Sounds like fun."

With an overdramatic sigh, Brynn crawled out of the fort and scooped an armful of loose K'NEX from the floor. Auntie Louise, technically her great-aunt, had a penchant for on-the-mouth kisses and two corgis that seemed to nip everyone's shins except for Auntie Louise. A clean room was a small price to pay to avoid her company.

Her mother watched from the doorway as Brynn sorted through the debris scattered across the carpet. "Ten minutes, missy, and then this room better look like something Martha Stewart would approve of." As Brynn tried to nonchalantly toss a handful of markers into the same bin as her blocks, her mother smacked the doorway in frustration. "Do it right, Brynn! C'mon, you're eight years old. You're not a baby anymore. You know better than that." She turned away, but not before Brynn heard her mutter, "Why can't you be more like your sister?"

The words sliced like a knife, causing Brynn to stop in her tracks, markers still in hand. Across the hallway, Misty sat in her own bedroom, backpack zipped and ready, her feet clad in her new hiking boots, engrossed in Animal Farm—a novel her parents were quick to point out was two levels higher than what her sixth-grade peers were reading. Her bedroom, from the neatly tucked bed to the pristine desktop, was like an excerpt from a catalog. Sensing Brynn's gaze, she lifted her eyes, a smirk playing over her lips, no doubt from their mother's words.

She stuck out her tongue and kept reading.

They pulled into the trailhead parking lot, a sea of minivans jockeying to claim one of the few remaining dirt spaces. Misty grabbed her backpack from the middle seat, her eyes landing on the doll propped against Brynn's leg.

"You're not going to bring that, right?" she asked. "You're too old for that stuff. It's embarrassing."

Brynn's cheeks burned at the slight, though she refused to give her sister the satisfaction of a defensive retort. She looked to her parents for support, but they were too busy zipping water and snacks into their backpacks to hear.

Or—Brynn's stomach dropped—they'd heard and quietly agreed with Misty.

At Brynn's stony expression, Misty sighed. "Whatever." She bounded from the car and raced to meet her friends, all of them wearing the same green Girl Scout T-shirt. One of the mothers corralled them all into a huddle to explain the rules for safely climbing a mountain, albeit a modest one.

Brynn trudged behind them, clutching Warrior Queen Daria in one hand as she joined the cluster of parents who were along for the adventure. So what if she wanted to bring Daria? Just because Misty had swapped dolls for a chemistry set when she was eight didn't mean Brynn had to as well, no matter how often her parents insisted on bringing it up. As if being the world's biggest dork was some kind of achievement.

As the Scout leader droned on and on about the buddy system and pacing themselves, Brynn scanned the surrounding wilderness, an endless swath of hunter-green ready to devour them. She imagined what obstacles lay between Daria and the mountain's peak. Dragons, probably. And surely an evil witch. If she could bravely defeat these villains along the way, her diamond-encrusted throne stood waiting at the top.

"All right, Girl Scouts, let's get that mountaineering badge. Hurrah!" the Scout leader shouted.

"Hurrah!" the girls chorused back.

Instantly, the mass of twelve-year-old girls stampeded down the trail.

"No running," the leader bellowed after them.

Brynn wandered along the trail, only peripherally aware of the parents hiking around her, shuffling into their gossip circles or jockeying to be one of the "athletic" parents at the front of the group. She held Daria over the passing rocks, pretending she was jumping from one to the next, always on the lookout for evildoers.

A sudden growth spurt the previous spring had given her long, coltish legs a new bounce, and she deftly weaved between groups of parents, their panting breaths evidence of far too many years since they'd climbed as much as a hill. She passed her father, who clutched his side as he walked, ending up directly behind her mother, chatting away with Mrs. Flynn and Mrs. Longwell, two mothers Brynn recognized from Misty's carpool group.

"I don't understand how they can be so different," Brynn's mother said. "Misty's all A-pluses, always has everything done on time. And then there's Brynn."

Brynn's head jerked up at her mother's laughter.

"Always making up stories, always leaving a disaster in her wake."

"They say the creative ones are messy," Mrs. Longwell said. "Something about left brain versus right brain."

Mrs. Flynn shook her head. "I think it's birth order. The first ones are always angels. Then, the second ones are off the walls. I think nature knows if we got the second one first, we'd never have another."

"Amen to that," Brynn's mother exclaimed.

At the women's laughter, the first hint of tears crept into Brynn's eyes.

Misty was the favorite. It was obvious, and she supposed she'd known it for a while. But to hear it said aloud—to hear them laughing at her, was so much worse.

She swiped at her eyes, clutched Daria to her chest, and plowed forward, her long legs propelling her until she was even with her mother, then several strides ahead.

"Honey, don't go too fast," her mother called.

Brynn ignored her, leaping from rock to rock, her head filled with an angry buzz, barely seeing the tree roots and boulders as she flew over them. Up ahead, her sister's hair swam into view, a bright red ponytail bobbing alongside her friends' brunette locks.

A fire lit in Brynn's belly, an inferno of envy and anger. How could her parents love Misty's boring grades but not care when Brynn wrote them a comic, turning her father into Mustache Man the Magnificent? So what if she'd left paint and construction paper littered across the dining room table?

She was close enough to hear her sister's voice now, a high-pitched laugh.

"Like, I don't know. Mikey is cute, but he's like, kind of annoying too, right?"

"What would you say if he asked you out?"

Brynn slammed her sister's arm as she strode past, cutting off their stupid, pointless conversation.

"What the hell, Brynn?" Misty shouted. To her friends, she laughed, the tone obviously fake to Brynn's ears, and Brynn knew she'd catch hell back home. "She's so dramatic."

The Scout leader was only a few yards ahead, trying in vain to keep an eye on all the groups of girls traveling at mismatched paces. As Brynn charged past, she called out, "Hey. Slow down. It's not a race."

Brynn continued on as if she hadn't heard, barreling toward a cluster of boulders strewn across the trail.

"Honey," the Scout leader yelled, "use the trail to the left. Don't try to go up the rocks. That's for the grown-ups."

Without a word, Brynn leaped onto the first rocks, never slowing her pace.

"Hey! Kid, I'm serious. Where are your parents?"

Still clutching Daria in one hand, Brynn reached for the second row of rocks, easily pulling herself up the face, her tennis shoes finding small cracks in the rock as holds. Her motions were fluid and instinctual—her scrawny eight-year-old limbs scrabbling up the granite with no sense of fear.

"Holy crap," the Scout leader murmured. She ran up the rocks, struggling to climb as quickly as Brynn. Finally, she pulled herself onto the same cluster of boulders. "Hey, hold up a sec, and I'll spot you," she said, her eyes shining. "You should always have a buddy on stuff like this. One wrong move and you could crack your head open, you understand?"

Brynn nodded, surprised at the lack of rebuke in the woman's tone.

"Let me take your doll." She pulled Daria from Brynn's hand and placed the toy in her backpack. "Okay, show me what you've got. Try to reach that hold right there." She pointed to a crack inches above Brynn's head.

Delighted by the attention, Brynn grabbed the crack, pulling herself up the rock.

"Now your foot, right here. Perfect."

As parents and Scouts rounded the curve to where they were climbing, the Scout leader motioned them toward the trail that bypassed the rocks, her attention still focused on Brynn. Misty's eyes bored into her sister, but she obediently took the side trail.

"She's a natural," the Scout leader called down to Brynn's mother as she appeared below them.

Swinging her leg over the next boulder, Brynn beamed at the Scout leader, who surfaced on top of the rocks a moment later.

"What's your name, kid?"

"Brynn."

"Brynn, I'm Debbie. You ever climbed a mountain before? Or gone rock climbing?"

Brynn shook her head.

"Natural talent, then. You've got a knack for it." Debbie pointed to the rocky crest a hundred feet above them. "That's the summit, the top of the mountain. There are a few more rocks to climb before we get there. We're going to take it nice and slow and stick to the buddy system. I'll give you some pointers along the way if you promise not to go too fast. Sound like a plan?"

Brynn nodded, her eyes shining.

Debbie turned and yelled to one of the moms. "Stacey, can you take the lead? Some of the girls ran up the trail. I'm going to stick with this one for a minute."

Stacey gave a quick thumbs up before jogging up the trail, weaving around the rock formations.

Debbie turned to Brynn. "All right, little miss thing, let's do this."

Together, they scrambled up the rocks, Debbie coaching Brynn on where to place her feet or how to relax certain muscles to conserve her climbing strength.

"Imagine doing this with snow and ice," Debbie panted, pulling herself up another pitch. "That's what it's like to climb the really big mountains. It's you against nature."

"Is it scary?" Brynn asked.

Debbie laughed. "Of course! Aren't all the best things in life?" She motioned to the last clump of boulders. Up above, a cluster of Scouts and parents who had used the dirt trail stood waiting, Misty and her parents among them. Brynn grinned at the sight of her sister's mouth twisted into a scowl—no doubt irritated that her big moment was being overshadowed.

"Last pitch to the summit," Debbie said. Nice and careful. Keep three points of contact."

She raised her hands, ready to catch Brynn if she slid, but Brynn scurried up the face with no trace of hesitation.

"On your right," Debbie coached. "There's a great rock to grab."

"You've got it, cutie," Stacey called down to her. "A couple more feet, and you've made it."

With one last heave, Brynn rolled onto the summit. Her arms stretched above her head in celebration. Seconds later, Debbie appeared by her side.

"You did it! Fantastic job, Brynn!" Her eyes found Brynn's mother in the crowd. "She's impressive, huh? You ought to get her into a climbing class. Imagine what she could do with some lessons." She pulled Daria from her backpack and handed it back to Brynn. "And if you're not in Scouts already, think about joining. We could use more kids like you." Debbie flashed Brynn a smile, then turned her attention to the girls who were fanning out to explore the summit.

Brynn looked out over the summit edge, reveling in her achievement. Debbie thought she was special, someone worth focusing her time and attention on. The notion warmed her from the inside, something neither her mother's look of surprise nor Misty's jealous glare could erase.

"Girls, gather around." Debbie's voice echoed across the summit, summoning the Scouts into a circle. "This is a really special day for everyone. Mountaineering is one of our toughest badges. It takes hard work, dedication, and months of serious training. I'm so proud of how much effort you and your parents have put into this, and you should all be extremely proud of yourselves." She pulled a handful of mountaineering badges from her backpack, handing out a brightly colored patch to each Scout. "And this is an especially important milestone for one of our girls who's gone above and beyond to earn her one-hundredth badge." She paused for dramatic effect, one last patch in her hand, while Misty stood beaming in anticipation. "Everyone give it up for Misty Lansing!"

As the parents and Scouts applauded, their dad even doing one of those embarrassingly loud two-fingered whistles, Misty and Brynn locked eyes. For half a second, Misty's blue-green eyes narrowed, her lips curving into a triumphant grin. Brynn may have stolen a shred of her glory, but in the end, it was Misty going home with all the spoils.

Brynn fought to hold her gaze, unwilling to show Misty how much this latest overshadowing hurt and how painful it was to feel the warmth of praise only to be shunted back into obscurity so quickly.

Misty blinked, turning her attention to the adults around her, her smile widening into the warm, effervescent look she reserved for accepting accolades.

Turning away from the crowd, Brynn hugged Daria to her chest, wishing she could absorb some of the warrior queen's strength. Nobody ever outshined Daria or left her feeling alone and forgotten.

The rock face stretched down before her, its height dizzying from the summit. She yearned to climb it again, to relive that delicious moment of stealing Misty's thunder. Emerging atop these boulders, for a brief moment, she'd been more than her sister's shadow.

She scanned the horizon for higher summits, her lips curving into a smile at the thought of conquering them, of earning the adulation of her parents, maybe even one of those obnoxious whistles from her dad. She relished the thought of Misty finally learning what it felt like to be second-best.

"Brynn, Warrior Queen of the Mountains," she whispered to Daria. No matter how difficult or arduous the journey, she promised herself that, one day, she'd make those rocky peaks her throne.

Chapter Twenty

At seventeen thousand feet, nighttime at Camp Three was bitterly cold. Though they'd erected their tents as close as possible to act as a windbreak, the gusts still bit through the nylon, chilling the air inside no matter how tightly the occupants snuggled together. Both Tana and Calla had pulled on every piece of clothing they'd packed, then pressed their sleeping bags together, spooning one another for warmth. Still, shivers racked their bodies, eating away at their precious calories. Neither woman had slept a wink since retiring to her bed.

"I'm going to have a six-pack from shaking," Calla said, her teeth chattering with every word. "Too bad we don't get much of a bikini season up in Alaska." She pulled one arm free from her bag and checked her watch. "It's one in the morning. Part of me wants to take another rest day tomorrow so we can get some shut-eye. But mostly, I want to get this over with."

Tana nodded, her beanie smacking Calla in the face. "Agreed. I don't want to keep you, or me, up here longer than we have to be." She paused, turning over the words she'd been holding onto all evening. "And thanks. For everything. Mostly for not giving up on me."

Calla laughed, her trembling body making the noise sound hysterical. "Anytime you want to ride off into danger, I'm your girl."

The sides of the tent rippled in a fresh gust of wind, the rat-tat-rat-tat-rat-tat of undulating nylon loud enough to ensure that sleep was impossible. With a groan, Calla buried her face inside her sleeping bag. "Though don't expect me to act happy about it."

Tana rolled onto her back and stared at the ceiling, letting her eyes adjust to the darkness. The rippling shadows looked like human faces, their mouths open and screaming. As a child, she'd seen faces in everything: the clouds, the plaster on her bedroom ceiling, the swirls and curlicues of her grandmother's wallpaper. She'd pretended they were visitors from one of her imaginative worlds dropping in to say hello. As an adult, she'd read that the brain's ability to see faces where there were none was actually a detriment. These people were more likely to believe in religion, psychics, magic, and all sorts of supernatural nonsense. It was a sign that their brains were searching for meaning where there was none.

The parallels to her current situation weren't lost on her, and she hoped that with Torket, there was actually some meaning to be found.

One of the faces opened its mouth and let out a low, anguished cry. Tana's eyes bulged, her throat constricting in terror.

"You hear that?" Calla asked. "They're back."

Tana let out her breath. Of course, the faces she imagined in the tent weren't talking. It was only the shadow people wandering around outside. The absurdity of how quickly she'd abandoned her atheism and embraced the supernatural made her wonder if she'd gone completely insane. When a parallel universe was just another mountain obstacle, life really had gone off the rails.

Footsteps joined the noise of the flapping nylon, blending into the sound, then jumping away, dancing on the gusts of wind. Both women sat up in their bags, listening to the footsteps simultaneously drift closer and farther away, circling the campsite.

"Why are they following us?" Calla asked. "If they're trying to hurt us, they must know it's impossible to cross over. The most they can do is scare us."

From the next tent over, Brynn's voice cut through the tent wall. "I've been writing about this. All kinds of theories. For all we know, they're trying to have a nice, calm climb too, and they're wondering why a group of four shadow ladies keeps showing up to haunt their trip."

Snatches of their whispers rode in on the wind, soft like rustling grass. Tana strained her ears, hoping to pick up more of their hidden language.

"I want to see them," she said, unzipping her sleeping bag, only to have Calla's hand clamp down on her arm like talons.

"Let's not push our luck. They haven't done anything to us yet, but we're putting a lot of trust in Brynn's half-baked internet searches."

"At least I'm trying," Brynn called back.

Tana shook her arm loose. "They saved my life in the avalanche. If they meant to kill us, why not let me fall?"

"Are you forgetting that's exactly what they did to Wyatt?" Calla asked. "You've seen horror movies before, right? Picking people off one by one, that's how this shit works."

"This isn't a horror movie."

"Could've fooled me," Calla retorted. Watching Tana pull on her boots, she let out an aggravated sigh before reaching for her own. "You're going to be the death of me." She hesitated, then reached into her bag and pulled out her handgun, tucking it into her coat pocket.

They slipped out into the night, flicking on their headlamps. Beside them, the sounds of Brynn rummaging through her belongings filtered through the tent walls. "Give me a minute. I'm coming too! Gotta record all of this. Maybe I can even snap a picture. Just need to find my notebook."

Tana and Calla fanned out, scanning the surrounding landscape for signs of life. Tana held her headlamp in one hand, peeking behind snowdrifts and boulders, desperate to catch a glimpse of their pursuers yet petrified to actually see one of them in the shadows. As her light swept the ground, every rock, every discoloration in the snow, every sparkling chunk of ice made her heart pound against her ribcage. The wind whispered as it blew past, making the hair on the back of her neck stand on end. She turned toward the trail and stopped cold, her heart dropping into her stomach.

A lone figure stood in the snow, its back to Tana, hair billowing around it in gusts.

Tana's scream caught in her throat. She backed away, her shaking hands fumbling with the headlamp, terrified that at any moment, this creature would turn around, all empty eye-sockets and bared fangs, and devour her whole.

"C-c-calla," she barely managed to croak.

The figure's head cocked at the sound. It angled its chin a fraction of an inch, exposing a pale profile through the tangled mass of hair. It turned toward the light with short, uncertain steps.

The blood drained from Tana's face as the creature's eyes met her own.

The cloud of hair gave way to a pale, ghostly face. The trembling light illuminated a pair of wide, ghoulish eyes, a slack mouth, a...Denver Career College hoodie?

"Misty?"

Tana nearly sank to her knees in relief. A strangled laugh gurgled out of her throat. "Holy crap, Mist, you scared the—" Her words were cut off at the sight of Misty's blank, unblinking eyes, the way she swayed on her feet, like a dandelion in the breeze, barely tethered to the ground. "Misty?" Tana repeated. "Can you hear me?"

Calla rushed to Tana's side, stopping short at Misty's catatonic appearance.

Brynn's voice emanated from her tent, echoing through camp. "Guys, Misty's not here. I think she went to the bathroom and didn't come back."

The tent's flap unzipped, and Brynn crawled out, notebook and pen in one gloved hand, iPhone in the other. "Is she out there with you?" Brynn hopped to her feet, following Tana's gaze to her sister. "Oh shit," Brynn whispered.

Calla reached out and grasped Misty's arm, giving her a rough shake. Misty's head bobbled back and forth, her gaze unfocused. A drop of saliva dripped from her open lips.

"It's the shadow people." The words left Tana's mouth before she could stop them. The memory of her ladder crossing came flooding back. How she'd been physically present in this world while her thoughts had been light years away, lost in a dream. They'd almost gotten her killed, and now, they'd come back for Misty. "They're possessing her! We need to get them out of her head." She turned to Calla for support.

Instead, Brynn rushed forward, one arm raised. She swung, her open hand connecting with Misty's face, the sharp crack of impact like a gunshot. Misty's face whipped to the side.

"God damn it, Misty," Brynn cried, her face contorted. "It's not the Taqriaqsuit," she said, her voice an uncharacteristic growl. "It's those fucking pills. She took another Ambien a few hours ago. I was writing in my journal, and she thought I didn't see."

Misty lifted a hand to her face. Her eyes had regained some of their focus, and she scanned their surroundings, brows furrowed. "What...where?" She looked down at her feet. "Where are my boots?"

Brynn stormed back to their tent and yanked the flap open. She grabbed Misty's boots and chucked them at her, ignoring Misty's cry as one connected with her shin. A moment later, Brynn emerged from the tent, holding several plastic baggies of assorted pills.

Misty's gaze sharpened as her brain managed to catch up with its surroundings. "Wait, Brynn, please don't—"

"Do you have any idea what it's like to be your sister?" Brynn demanded. "Watching as everyone fawns over every stupid little thing you do, and knowing I can never live up to it? And worse, knowing the whole time that you were cheating your way to the top?" She shook the fistful of bags so that the pills rattled.

"I tried so hard to beat you at anything. I worked my ass off to have one thing where I could say I was the best. And guess what, Mist: it worked. I'm a stronger climber than you, I went to a better school than you, I have a cooler job than you, and none of it matters! Mom and Dad still think of you as their little golden child because you popped out some grandkids."

Misty held on to Tana's shoulder for support, her expression anguished. "Brynn, that's not true. They love you so much."

Brynn scoffed. "That's what the favorite always says."

Misty softened her tone, her eyes fixed on the baggies in Brynn's hand. "I know you're upset right now. Can you please put those down so we can talk?"

A pained grimace stretched across Brynn's face. "This is all you care about," she said. "You're not listening to a word I'm saying. All that matters to you is making sure you have enough of a fix to keep up appearances. So nobody will ever suspect that below the surface, you're exactly like the rest of us: normal. I thought maybe when you slept through your second SAT test, you'd finally realize that all this shit you're doing to yourself isn't worth it. But it made you even more desperate. You traded being the perfect student for being the perfect mom, the perfect wife."

Misty stiffened. "The SAT test...how...how'd you know about that?" Her voice had gone ice cold, calculating. "I never told Mom and Dad about it. I was too embarrassed. I didn't tell anyone."

"Oh. Um..." Brynn dropped her gaze to the snow. "Small town, word got around..."

Seconds ticked by, the drugged haze around Misty dissipating. Fury radiated from her body. Her hands clenched into fists.

"It was you." A fire burned behind her eyes. "You swapped the pills."

"I don't know what you're talking—"

"Don't you dare lie to me," Misty seethed. "All this time, I thought I was crazy. That somehow I'd mixed up the meds, even when I knew—I knew—I hadn't. Everything was labeled perfectly. What'd you swap the Adderall with? Sleeping pills? Antihistamines?"

The seconds dragged out, and Brynn's gaze focused on the snow. Finally, she replied, "You were killing yourself, Mist. Was I supposed to watch you overdose just so you could get into college?"

"Don't you pretend like you did it out of the kindness of your heart—"

"I did," Brynn insisted. "Yeah, fine, I hated your guts, but I didn't want to watch you turn into a junkie either."

"What did you do?" Misty asked, her body thrumming with barely suppressed rage.

Brynn kicked at the ground, refusing to meet her sister's eyes. "Swapped it with one of Dad's oxies," she mumbled.

With an animal-like shriek, Misty rushed toward her sister, her fingers curved like claws. Calla darted forward, wrapping an arm around Misty's waist to hold her back.

"You ruined my life," Misty cried. She struggled against Calla's grip. "You stole everything from me. I was supposed to be a doctor. I could've gone into medical research, anything except a goddamn nurse."

Tana rushed forward to help Calla, folding Misty into a one-armed embrace. She rubbed Misty's back with her free hand, hoping to soothe away some of the anger.

Misty's voice trembled. "I jumped at that job in Boston because they were the only biotech company that would hire me. Big surprise: turns out nobody wants their medical talent from the Denver Career College." She tried to laugh, but the sound strangled in her throat. "You could've talked to me if you were worried, so don't give me that crap. Why'd you really do it?" she asked, her voice barely audible.

Brynn's eyes were bloodshot, but at the pain in Misty's voice, she had the decency to look her in the eye. "Fine," she said. "I couldn't stand for you to have another win, another victory for Mom and Dad to rub in my face and ask why I couldn't measure up."

A hysterical laugh bubbled out of Misty's throat. "So you decided to teach me a lesson? To make sure I peaked in high school and everything else was a slow descent into mediocrity?" A tear slipped from one eye and fell down her cheek. "Well, mission fucking accomplished. Because of you, I took that shit job and met Todd, and my self-esteem was so shot at that point I didn't think I deserved anyone better. And now I'm a stay-at-home mother to twins, and you know what I do on the weekends? I'm certainly not in a lab saving the world with my research. I'm on fucking playdates."

"Aw, c'mon, Misty," Tana tried to reassure her. "You love Todd and the kids."

Misty turned to her, and Tana was shocked at the pure, wretched misery etched into every line of her face.

"He's leaving me."

"Wait, what?"

"He's leaving me," Misty repeated. Her face crumpled in on itself as she began to cry in earnest. "He left his laptop open, he was in the shower, and I..." She struggled to catch her breath. "I saw all the messages between them. All the private jokes, all the dirty pictures, all the texts about getting it over with before the kids were old enough to be scarred by divorce."

Brynn cautiously approached them, placing a hand lightly on her sister's arm. "I'm sorry," she said. "You should've told me."

"So you could laugh in my face?" Misty spat, wrenching her arm away from her sister's touch. "So you could run to Mom and Dad and tell them one more thing I'd failed at? You want to believe that everything was easy for me. That I took a pill, and magically, my life was perfect. Maybe it makes you feel better about yourself. I don't know what childish bullshit goes through your head. But let me make one thing very clear: being the favorite was hell. All that pressure to perform and the disappointment if you slipped, even the tiniest bit. After that test, I daydreamed about jumping off the overpass near school. Thought about it every day for months. And that's a pressure that you'll never understand because I took it off your shoulders."

Calla and Tana exchanged a glance, eyebrows raised. As only-children, this was well beyond their area of expertise.

"I knew you were still jealous," Misty said. "It's obvious. The way you constantly brag about your climbs. And how you text everyone your Strava screenshots—as if anybody wants to look at those. But I never thought you were pathetic enough to sabotage your own sister to get ahead."

Brynn remained silent, her shoulders hunching over at the barrage of insults. In the dim light, she looked diminished, almost childlike.

Misty cleared her throat, trying to inject some dignity into her voice. "So that's my sad story, everyone. My marriage is falling apart, I resent my children, and my little sister torpedoed my entire career." She glared at Brynn. "The very least you can do is give me back my medicine."

"No." Brynn's face was pale, her eyes watery, but her voice was firm. "You were a nurse. You know exactly how bad these things are. And now you're popping them like candy." She tipped the baggies into her hand, emptying their contents. "I don't care how awful things are with Todd or the kids or how much you hate my guts right now. You're still my sister, and I'm not going to sit back and watch you turn into an addict." She turned and flung the pills.

"No," Misty shouted, but it was too late. The pills flickered in the glow from their headlamps before disappearing from sight. A small, mournful cry escaped her. "I needed those." She whimpered.

"They're a crutch," Brynn replied. At the sight of Misty's deflating figure, she sighed. "I know how angry you are right now. I was a shitty, jealous kid, and I overstepped—by a lot. But I'm not sorry for this." She held up the empty bags. "You're not alone, Misty. It probably feels like everything's falling apart, but you have me, and Tana, and Calla. Plus, let's be real, you could probably turn into a goddamn serial killer, and Mom and Dad would still rave about how perfectly you chose your victims."

When Misty didn't crack a smile, Brynn said, "Look, I'm sorry for what I did. I can't go back and fix it, but I can help you start fresh. I...I love you, Mist."

The words hung in the air, Misty making no indication that she acknowledged them. Tana tugged on her waist. "C'mere," she said, guiding Misty's feet to her boots. "You feel okay? Need some water? I can boil some coffee."

Misty waved her off. "I'm fine, just need a minute."

The slight tremble in her voice was heartbreaking, and Tana averted her eyes to give Misty a moment to collect herself.

While Misty fumbled over the laces, Tana looked up to see Calla nod at the empty bags in Brynn's hand and shoot her a quick thumbs up.

Tana retrieved a headlamp from Misty's tent, clicking it on so Misty could see her boots more clearly. "Hey," she said quietly. "Do you want to talk about everything? If you need some space, you can swap tents with Cal—"

A gust of wind cut across camp, voices riding on the waves, a reminder of why they were outside in the first place. The words encircled them, tightening like a noose. Footsteps raced around the camp perimeter. The four women instinctively pulled closer together, gazing into the surrounding darkness.

Brynn's words were breathless. Tana guessed from excitement as much as fear. "They're here."

Chapter Twenty-One

They stood in a circle, headlamps pointed out, letting the wind wash over them. A lone bright spot in a sea of black. The whispers intensified, growing into voices, the words foreign but clear.

"Anybody see them?" Brynn asked. Her phone's camera was open, ready to snap. Their lights fell only on empty snowbanks and patches of ice.

Tana closed her eyes, letting the words flow through her. Footsteps danced around them, making the others turn in place, searching for the source. Tana forced herself to hold still, listening to the words alone. If she tried to analyze them, they crumbled, broken and meaningless. If she let her mind relax instead, like staring into a 3D image, they began to take shape. Little by little, the syllables coalesced into something recognizable, not words necessarily, but feelings. Fragments of images and emotion.

"Keep going," she whispered.

"What?" Brynn asked, swiveling her phone toward a shadow, only to see it was Misty's arm.

"I think I can sort of understand them," Tana said. "It feels like they're pushing us forward. Like they want us to keep going."

Everyone stopped, turning to Tana.

"Keep going where?" Calla asked.

"What do you mean you can understand them?" Misty asked. Fear had erased the sorrow and anger from her voice. "What language are they speaking?"

Brynn trained her camera on Tana's face, tapping the screen to record a video. "Can you say that one more time?" she urged. "This is a huge breakthrough."

"It's not like that. I can't translate the words. It's like I can feel their emotions or something. Everyone, shut up," Tana replied, breaking free from their circle. As she walked toward the edge of the camp, the footsteps ceased, but the voices only grew stronger and more urgent. She turned her head from side to side, trying to catch the shadowy figures in the corner of her eye.

"Where do you want me to go?" she asked. "What do you want from us?"

"Careful," Brynn said quietly. "Remember they tried to lure you over a cliff? This might be a trap."

The shadows darted across Tana's vision. She tried to focus on one, but it dissolved under her direct gaze. The black silhouettes varied in size, some as small as children, others massive and hulking. They repeated a phrase, chanting it as a group, a chorus of voices urging her to understand.

"*Tiiq kachuk. Tiiq kachuk. Tiiq kachuk.*"

"What are they saying?" Brynn asked, her camera still rolling. Tana waved an irritated hand at her, urging her to stay quiet.

"*Tiiq kachuk. Tiiq kachuk.*" The tone was friendly and inviting. Urging her closer. An image of the summit flashed through her mind, gone as quickly as it arrived.

Tana called back. "I think they want to show me something. It feels...like they're telling us we're almost there. Just a little further."

"I think I can feel it too," Calla said. "Holy shit, it's like they're in my head."

Heart pounding against her ribs, Tana took one shuffling step toward the edge of camp, where a cluster of shadows stood waiting. "Were there any evil spirits in those myths you read about?" Tana asked Brynn, her voice shaking.

"Oh yeah, tons," Brynn said. "They have one, a seven-foot tall demon, that possesses humans. The jury's out on whether he's truly good or evil. There's a wolf god, I think an Anorak...no, Amarok? Anyway, that one's definitely a bad guy. It eats people when they go out alone at night."

Tana turned back, her eyes bulging. "What? Why didn't you bring that up earlier?"

"Those myths didn't mention shadows, so they didn't seem relevant."

"Getting eaten at nighttime feels pretty goddamn relevant," Misty said.

Trying to control her trembling limbs, Tana held her arms wide, hoping to indicate that she meant no harm. Her eyes shifted back and forth, never focusing on one spot so she could continue to keep the shadows in her line of sight.

"I'm here," she announced, having no idea if they could understand, let alone see her. She kept her pace slow, enunciating each word for clarity. "One of you saved me during the avalanche, and I wanted to say thank you. We also want to understand you. Do you need something from us? Are we upsetting you in some way?"

No answer.

"My friends and I aren't going to hurt you. We're trying to climb a mountain, probably the same as you. We're trying to reach the summit." For emphasis, she pointed behind her, where the summit sat in darkness. She paused, waiting for any kind of response, but the shadows had quieted. "Can you understand me?" she asked.

Silence met her words. Tana turned back to her friends, bewildered. Why bother to surround the camp and call Tana closer if they were going to disappear when confronted? She dropped her arms, disappointed.

"Hey, Mist, remember we used to try doing seances when we were kids?" Brynn asked, her tentative smile a clear attempt to break the ice between them. "And nothing ever showed up? That's what this feels like."

Misty ignored her. "What'd they say, Tana? Can you understand them?"

Tana shook her head. "It comes and goes, little flashes of what they're feeling. I figured they had something to show me, maybe something to do with the summit? But they're gone now. Calla, did you see any—"

"Tana, look out!"

At Calla's scream, Tana spun on the spot. A snow-white, bony hand reached from the shadows, its slender fingers grasping at Tana's loose strands of hair. The skin seemed made of ice and air, nearly translucent. Its wrist dissolved into blackness, the doorway to their spirit world.

Tana opened her mouth to cry out, but her throat was paralyzed, and only a weak croak emerged. Behind her, what felt like a million miles away, she heard Misty and Brynn scream.

The arm was next to emerge, its white skin extending up a sinewy forearm before dissolving into shadow. A series of bracelets, leather cord with pale, sun-bleached beads, encircled their wrist. Tana stumbled back, her boot catching on a tent stake, and she tumbled to the ground.

The hand curled into a fist as though gathering its strength, and with a scream of effort, the entire upper body emerged. Colorless as a corpse, with pale, dead eyes and white hair, it lunged forward, its gaze burning into Tana's. Tendrils of snow streamed off its body, dissolving and regathering as it moved. She sat, paralyzed, as it dropped to the ground and grasped her ankle in its bony clutches, ice-cold fingers digging into her bone. With a vicious yank, it pulled her toward the shadows.

"Help," she screamed, her voice a ragged shriek. She kicked with her free foot, but the demon didn't seem to notice. Its horrible face contorted as it pulled her back across the barrier.

"Tana, stay down!" Calla pulled the gun from her pocket and fired indiscriminately, several bullets striking the dark periphery before one finally made contact with flesh. It tore into the creature's shoulder, eliciting a howl of pain. A spray of blood, dingy and rust-colored, dripped down its chest, coloring the snow. Still it held on.

Misty and Brynn raced to stand with Calla, their arms full of rocks. "Leave her alone," Brynn screamed, winding up softball-style and whipping a stone at its face, leaving a shallow gash along its chin. Less accurate, Misty's throws were more of a distraction, pinging off the creature's shoulder and chest.

Despite their efforts, Tana was dragged, her loose foot disappearing into the darkness as she tried to kick at her captor's torso. Watching her boot dissolve into nothing made the blood drain from her face, and for a moment, spots flashed before her vision.

The creature was going to drag her into another world, just like her childhood fantasies. Only this was no Narnia or Land of Oz. This was a world overrun by ghastly, zombie-like apparitions. The phrase "be careful what you wish for" flitted through her head, a karmic joke at her expense.

An angry roar tore free from Calla's throat, drowned out by another blast from her gun. This shot hit the creature's abdomen, right on the line where the body met the shadow, causing a spurt of blood to splatter onto the snow. The monster let out a howl, and Tana, sensing her only opportunity to escape, slammed her free heel onto the knuckles grasping her ankle. The creature recoiled in pain, and she tore free.

Tana scuttled back to her friends on all fours, her entire body convulsing with adrenaline. Before her, the creature was retreating back into the shadows, cradling its wounds as it crossed the invisible barrier to the safety of its own world.

Misty dropped the rocks in her arms and crouched down beside Tana. "Are you all right?"

Tana nodded, not trusting herself to speak.

"I got it on video," Brynn shouted, tapping her phone excitedly. "It's not much, but you can make out its face and everything. Guys, we're going to be famous." She swiped through the footage. "Ooo, I even got when I hit it with the rock. This is amazing."

Misty examined Tana's ankle, prodding for broken bones where she'd been grabbed. "People will probably say it's faked," she muttered.

Calla, still holding the handgun aloft, inched toward the invisible barrier, her eyes shifting back and forth, searching for shadows. "I think they're gone," she said. She turned to glare at Tana. "Let's walk toward the monsters, huh? What's the worst that could happen?" She shook her head in disgust before turning back to the snow.

The others fell silent, listening. No voices, not even whispers, no footsteps in the snow. Their attackers obviously hadn't expected such resistance from the women, and it appeared that, for the time being, they had retreated to lick their wounds. Or if they were lucky, the shadow people had given up the chase altogether.

Calla crouched, her headlamp focused on a single spot of bloody snow. "Holy shit," she whispered, pawing at the powder for a better look.

Tana crawled forward to see the small, blood-spattered patch. Calla had carefully dug into the snow, pulling out a chunk of crumbly rock. She shook it into her hand, and Tana saw what she'd been digging for—the bullet, or the remains of it anyway.

Calla held it up to the light, whistling in awe.

"No freaking way," Brynn said, crouching for a closer look.

What Tana had assumed was a clean shot to the creature's midsection must have instead landed squarely on the border between worlds. Half had embedded itself inside his abdomen. The other half had continued its trajectory in this world, burrowing into the rocky ground. Held between two of Calla's fingers, split cleanly down the middle, was half a bullet.

Chapter Twenty-Two

Sleep was out of the question. Everyone's nerves were frayed to the breaking point, with Tana so shaken that she could barely hold the mug of cocoa Misty had prepared for her. Small sloshes kept spilling into her lap. She couldn't have drunk it anyway, not with her stomach twisted up in knots. The feel of its hand on her ankle, all hard bones and frozen skin, refused to dissipate, and she kept absentmindedly rubbing the spot where its fingers had made contact.

On the opposite end of the spectrum, Brynn was wired with pure excitement at this new development. As a failsafe, she transferred her video files to each of their phones in case anything happened to hers during the descent back to civilization. The shadows didn't show up on video, an issue Brynn was quick to dismiss, saying it only defended her Taqriaqsuit theory that the camera would be looking directly at them, rendering them invisible. But once the creature crossed the threshold, its ghostly figure was clearly visible. Each of them stared down at the footage, identical horrified looks spreading across their faces.

"It sort of looks human, if they'd been trapped in somebody's basement for ten years," Misty said. She pulled her coat tighter against the cold wind or perhaps the sudden chill emanating from the grisly images. "It's so white. Like looking at a corpse. Or a vampire."

"I think it must be some sort of hybrid creature," Brynn said, jotting something down in her notebook. "When it crossed to our side, did you notice that it wasn't quite solid? If it moved too quickly or if the wind picked up, it would fade a bit, like a snowdrift."

Calla shot her a look. "Hadn't noticed. Too busy keeping Tana from getting ripped to shreds."

"However," Brynn said, undeterred, "Calla was able to shoot it and actually draw blood, meaning that once it takes physical form, it's mortal. This is fascinating!"

Tana kept scrolling through the video, focusing on the creature's face, forcing herself to see past the pale skin and colorless eyes. With each new view, she became more convinced she wasn't looking at some sort of monster but, instead, a man.

His knitted brows and clenched teeth suggested he'd rather be doing anything except crossing into a foreign world to abduct a screaming woman with violent friends. Staring at his face, an inexplicable warmth spread through her chest.

She wondered if these specters of the mountain were even a separate species from themselves. What if they were simply the lost climbers trapped in a world of spirits and shadows? And when they crossed back to their home world, they regained their physical form, but with a new, ghostly color palette.

She was too embarrassed to speak the theory aloud, knowing how silly and desperate it would appear now that they knew of her parents' disappearance. Instead, she tucked the thought inside her heart like a talisman, a small comfort against the terror of the unknown.

"So much for not being able to cross over," Calla said. The gun was still in her hand—Tana was fairly sure she hadn't put it down this entire time. "I think it's safe to say we have no fucking clue what we're dealing with. But it sure as hell isn't a friendly parallel universe."

Brynn fixed her with an exasperated look. "We're working off of ancient myths, usually passed down orally. I think it's forgivable if they messed up a few of the details in a generations-long game of telephone."

Misty shook her head. "Hell of a detail to mess up. You'd think the 'Can this thing kill me?' question would be one they took a little more seriously."

Calla's finger tapped the trigger of the gun thoughtfully, causing Tana to edge away from her line of fire. "I don't think I've ever said this before," she mused. "But I can't wait to get the hell off this mountain."

Forcing herself to slug down her cocoa in one gulp, Tana nodded in agreement. "Then let's finish it. I can't stand to sit here any longer." The need to move, to work off the adrenaline and terror, was overwhelming. "The sun'll be up in a few hours, just in time for us to tap the summit. We can hit it, then turn around and catch up to Misty and Brynn easily before it gets dark."

"Fine by me," Calla said. She shot Misty a quick look, shaking her head at Misty's open mouth, no doubt about to issue another plea to come to their senses.

Tana caught the moment but said nothing. She'd already stated her case. What more could she say? She was grateful to Calla that another explanation, and likely, another fight, wouldn't be necessary.

Calla stowed the handgun back in her pocket and slipped on her summit pack, no larger than a child's school backpack, only big enough for her parka, some water and snacks, and their climbing gear. With no more camps to erect and no more heavy gear to haul, they'd be moving quickly over the final terrain.

While Tana pulled on her harness, Calla looped a thin roll of rope around her upper body. "Once we get to the summit rocks, we'll be setting up a line," she said. "If someone falls, they'll roll all the way back down to here before they stop. We're not taking any more chances. Not on this fucking mountain."

"No argument here." Tana clipped into their small, two-person rope team, the gravity of the impending climb already weighing on her.

Misty and Brynn stood, both looking forlorn, though for vastly different reasons. Misty pulled Tana into a tight hug. "I hope you find what you're looking for," she whispered. "If it turns out there's nothing up there, it's all right, you understand? You have so many people who love you. Get back quickly, okay?"

She released Tana and pulled Calla into the same bone-breaking embrace. "Take care of her," she instructed. "And yourself. Careful you don't shoot your own foot off."

Brynn's farewell was less heartfelt. "Make sure to focus on the details: anything they say, what they look like, how many you can see. Ugh, damn it, I really should be going with you. This is ridiculous. What kind of serious adventure author gets her details secondhand?"

Calla raised an eyebrow at Misty, an expression she immediately understood after more than a decade of friendship.

"No," Misty replied. "She's absolutely not going."

"It's not like it's any safer here," Calla reasoned. "This is where they grabbed Tana, remember?"

Misty folded her arms over her chest and glared at Calla. "Down here, we just have demons. Up there, you have demons and ice climbing. It's an easy choice. Trust me, if there was ever a time when I'd love to throw Brynn to the wolves, it's now. But the answer is no."

Calla gave Brynn an apologetic shrug. "Sorry, kid, I tried." To Misty, she said, "We're going to try and beat the weather that's coming in. Once you guys get packed, head down, all right? Don't wait for us. We should be down tonight or tomorrow morning at the latest. We'll be moving fast, and I saw plenty of spots where we could sit down and glissade to save time. If there's any trouble, I'll call you on the sat phone. There were a few bars of cell service at the trailhead. Got the keys?"

Misty held up the keyring, giving it a little jingle.

With a nervous sigh, Calla turned to Tana, both nodding that they were ready to begin. They pulled on their goggles, one last defense against the snow and high winds, and then faced the trail.

"All right," Calla said. "Wish us luck."

A steep yet technically easy slope greeted them immediately out of camp. It would take them most of the way to the summit. The final obstacle was a two-hundred-foot slab of ice and rock that would test their endurance and climbing skills. Even in the best of circumstances, Tana had been nervous about this section of their ascent. Now, she faced it with the grim determination of a gladiator stepping into battle. Failure was far more likely than she cared to admit, but turning back wasn't an option, not when they'd worked so hard to get here.

They moved in silence, each woman wrapped in the walls of fortitude she built around herself while climbing. "Embrace the suck" was a popular saying among the community, though it lacked nuance. The mountains were unforgiving, painful, exhausting, cold, and lonely. It wasn't enough to simply embrace the hardship without armoring yourself against it. Physical stamina could only push a person so far, and by itself, was never a strong enough motivator.

Some, like Misty, yearned for the camaraderie of a close team and the healing only nature could provide. Those young at heart like Brynn searched for adventure and excitement, each foray into the mountains their own private quest. Ego and glory, two of the strongest drugs known to man, fueled Calla and—though she'd hate to be grouped among them—many of the peak baggers she despised. Only one thing kept Tana from turning back from the piercing wind and unfathomably steep slope: her need for answers.

At eighteen thousand feet, the air was thin, and she fought to control her breathing, falling back on an old technique her parents had taught her. With every other step, she'd pretend to blow out a birthday candle, puckering her lips and letting out a long, hard whoosh of air. This forced her to suck in a lungful of air on the next step, keeping her in a steady rhythm.

Her stomach was queasy with knots, a common altitude symptom, though Tana was inclined to think it was due more to the harrowing experience of almost being abducted into a foreign world. As a gust of wind kicked up a confetti shower of snowflakes, she tried to calm herself, focusing on the beauty of the moment, the way the snow sparkled under her headlamp's glow. Darkness stretched around them, broken up only by their small circles of LED light and the thousands of stars above, bright enough to pierce through the wispy clouds. And far off in the distance...

"Calla, look!" Tana pointed.

Following her finger to the distant horizon, Calla turned. Her mouth dropped into a childish smile of wonder. "Been up here for years, and I've never seen it before," she said.

The green swirls of light were faint, but there was no mistaking them. They had caught the tail end of the aurora borealis.

Clicking off their lamps, they stood for a moment, basking in the neon glow. It felt foolish to admit it, especially after everything they'd been through, yet seeing the northern lights felt like a sign, some kind of promise that things were going to work out the way Tana needed them to.

As if reading her thoughts, Calla said, "Feels prophetic, huh? Like everything's falling into place. I'm not big on that hippie-dippie stuff, but I have a weirdly good feeling about us making it to the top."

Tana could have stared at the lights for hours, watching the swirls of color dance across the sky. How could something this magical exist in such a mundane world? A painful thought intruded on her reverie. Perhaps there had always been magic around her, and she'd been too blinded by her own indifference to see it. The others seemed to find joy and peace in their daily lives. It was only Tana who had trouble seeing the sunshine. Under the streaks of green light, she promised herself that if they made it back unscathed, she'd try harder to see the beauty in her days, no matter how bleak they appeared on the surface. The aurora was proof that wonderful things could always be found, provided you were looking.

Too soon, Calla's hand clapped her on the back. "Let's get moving," she said. "The wind's getting stronger."

Tana clicked on her headlamp to find that Calla was right. The amount of snow billowing around them had doubled since they'd stopped. And after standing still, the chill was starting to seep into her layers. Wyatt—rest his soul—may have had the right idea in trying to beat the weather.

A sudden flash of white in Tana's peripherals made her jump, sure that her would-be captor was making another appearance. At the sharp tug of the rope, Calla whirled around, gun already drawn, her mouth twisted into a snarl. Just as quickly, her aggression morphed into a chuckle. "Are they for real?" she asked, stowing her weapon.

It took Tana a second to realize what she was seeing: two headlamps cruising steadily in their direction. Misty and Brynn. Tana nearly laughed with relief. She hadn't noticed it until that moment, but their absence had been weighing on her, an oppressive stone in her belly. After staring down so much danger together, continuing on without them was like losing a limb. Sure, they could manage it, but it didn't feel right.

"Hurry up, slackers," Calla yelled. A stream of obscenities floated back up to her.

"Good thing we saw the aurora," Tana said. "They never would have caught up."

Calla nodded sagely. "See? Torket might be beating the snot out of us, but it still wants us to succeed. It's like an abusive parent."

Tana raised an eyebrow. "More secrets to tell?"

Calla laughed. "I promise, you know all my secrets now."

An unexpected bubble of emotion welled up inside of Tana. The love she held for these women made everything else, even her family ties, pale in comparison. As a team, they'd put everything on the line to push her toward her goal, wherever it might lead. And rising above the others was Calla, who'd bared her most painful secrets and pushed aside her own fears to protect them time and time again.

"Calla?"

"Mm?"

"I love you."

"Me too, dude."

Calla reached out her gloved hand and took Tana's, giving her a quick squeeze. The sensation sent shivers up Tana's arm, and she looked at her friend in shock. Butterflies were swirling in her stomach, and this time, there was no mistaking it for altitude sickness. She simultaneously wanted to drop Calla's hand in embarrassment and pull her close, never letting go. She'd known Calla for over ten years. Hell, she'd tried falling for her. How was this happening now?

"You okay?" Calla asked.

"Fine, just..." Tana tried to collect herself. Was her grip on Calla's hand too tight? Was she being awkward? Probably. She should let go. And yet, that unfamiliar fire inside her refused to relinquish its hold. She'd risked life and limb to stand here beside Calla, and she'd be damned if she wasn't going to enjoy the moment. She threaded her fingers through Calla's, her thumb caressing the top of Calla's gloved hand, silently begging her to understand. "I feel a little weird, that's all."

Calla glanced down at their intertwined hands, a slow smile spreading across her lips. "I think I know what you mean. It's like there's electricity in the air or something." She laughed, rubbing her other hand across the back of her neck, her eyes downcast—a move that Tana found adorable. With a nervous, little half-step, she scooted closer, their arms now pressed together, her chin practically resting on Tana's shoulder.

Tana felt the heat of Calla's body and smelled the faint whiff of her shampoo.

"A lot of things bubble to the surface when you're at altitude. Some mountains are supposed to be spiritual vortexes, like how Shasta is supposed to be a chakra point of the earth." Calla chuckled. "It's weird how a few days outside your comfort zone will have you spouting nonsense real quick, huh?"

They were dancing around the obvious, neither willing to be the first to admit their feelings. Tana opened her mouth to explain what she was feeling was far from nonsense. In fact, she'd never been surer of anything in her life. But the words caught in her throat. Brynn's face was now visible, her mouth open as she desperately sucked in air. Their private time was at an end.

"We...couldn't..." Brynn gasped, "let...you...have all...the fun." She stopped a few feet from Tana, bent over, her hands braced on her knees. "Running was definitely a bad idea," she wheezed.

Behind her, Misty was holding a stitch in her side. At their concerned looks, she waved them off, coughing into the crook of her elbow, a harsh, wet hack. "Against my better judgment, I apparently don't have it in me to abandon you," she said. "Also, this one"—she glared at her sister—"wouldn't shut up about her damn book."

Tana moved between them, pulling them both into a hug, marveling at how much love she felt for them both. Not romantically, like Calla, but still strong enough to be startling. Not for the first time, she wondered if the altitude was making her loopy. A warmth was spreading through her belly, a sense of contentment and joy that she'd only felt twinges of in the past. If her brain was misfiring from altitude, she certainly wasn't going to complain about such a delightful side effect.

"Thanks, both of you. This means the world to me."

"Don't mention it," Misty gasped. "Though it'd mean the world to me if we could get up and down this thing before the withdrawal symptoms kick in." She glared at Brynn.

"Oh shit," Tana said. "I completely forgot. Are you going to be okay—"

An irritated throat clearing pulled their attention to where Calla stood waiting, her gaze shifting to the light flurry of snowflakes falling from the sky. Above them, clouds had begun to materialize, partially obscuring the stars. The aurora borealis was shrouded, save for a single stream of weak, green light.

"Not to break up the party, but if we're doing this, we need to move. Otherwise, we'll be caught in a whiteout."

They fell into formation without a word, Brynn and Misty lining up behind Tana, mouths set and eyes shining with determination behind their snow goggles. Misty gestured at the trail ahead, her stiff motions betraying her nerves. "Lead the way."

Chapter Twenty-Three

With their heads bowed against the falling snow, the two rope teams advanced single file up the slope: Calla, Tana, Brynn, and Misty. Their steps fell in perfect rhythm—finally synched up after four days together, marching like soldiers heading off to war.

And with the finish line finally within reach, Tana was more than ready for battle.

Yet the higher they climbed, the more her grim determination became clouded by her churning, stormy emotions. Bursts of euphoria gave way to lovesick pangs, which melted into flashes of rage and sorrow. She wondered if she was losing her mind—if the thinning oxygen had caused a brain bleed, and before she died, she was going to experience every single emotion she'd been denied during her life.

She tried to concentrate on the climb itself, centering her thoughts on each breath or the simple task of putting one foot in front of the other without being blown over, but every new sensation robbed her of focus. The thought that she might be succumbing to HACE flitted through her mind as she imagined her brain swollen with fluid, pressing against her skull. A terrifying thought, but if that was how she went out, her heart bursting with emotion, surrounded by those she loved most, well, she could think of worse ways to go.

She continued up the slope, her head swimming with delights and despair, sound in her decision to keep moving as the minutes wore on and death still didn't come to claim her.

The sky was lightening, a reddish-orange haze dancing along the horizon, mixing with the thickening cloud cover. Silhouetted against the fiery palette was their final obstacle, two hundred feet of rock and ice, shooting nearly straight into the sky.

"In the reports I read, a ton of people turned back here," Brynn said. "There's no easy way up. You either know your shit, or you don't. There's no faking your way to the top."

Calla stopped, forcing the team to a halt. "Let's hope we know our shit then." She pulled off her backpack and rifled through it, extracting her ice screws. "We'll set up a line as we go. I'll lead, and you guys can follow one at a time." She scrunched her face up against the strong gusts. "Wish we had some better weather. This is tough enough without the wind."

Tana nodded. Setting up ropes was time-consuming as much as it was dangerous. On terrain this treacherous, with winds this high, the risk of Calla falling was more than she was comfortable with. At the thought of losing Calla to the mountain, another burst of fear and longing tore through her, making her double over in pain.

"You okay?" Misty asked. "You keep doing that. Jerking around or something. Do you have cramps?"

Tana shook her head. As a fresh wave of happiness washed over her, she almost joked that, no, she didn't have cramps—she was head over heels in love. Thankfully, she had just enough sanity left to tamp down that impulse. They had enough problems without adding her sudden irrationality to the mix. "I'm fine," she promised.

She turned away from Misty, trying to hide the stupidly wide grin that was spreading across her face, when her headlamp caught a glint of metal in the ice. She stepped forward, squinting at the apparatus, finally realizing what it was: an anchor. Stretching up from the anchor, what she'd first mistaken as a vein in the ice was actually a blue climbing rope.

"I think Wyatt left us another little surprise," she said.

The others followed her gaze, Calla shaking her head in disgust. "So much for 'Leave No Trace,'" she muttered. "Do people think because it's mountaineering gear, it doesn't count as pollution?"

"Are you seriously going to complain?" Misty asked. "Sure, he's a dick, but he's a dick that just made our lives a million times easier."

Brynn shushed her. "Don't speak ill of the dead," she whispered. She glanced over her shoulder dramatically. "Especially when we know there are spirits around. He might hear you."

Calla grimaced. "If Wyatt starts haunting us, I swear, I'm jumping off the edge. I can only take so much." She checked the anchor, tugging on the rope to test for sturdiness. It held fast against her pull. "Feels solid. I can't believe he left this though. Even if he doesn't care about littering, he left a ton of nice gear here."

"Maybe he's lazy," Misty said through gritted teeth. She rubbed a hand across her forehead, wincing at her own touch.

"Shit, Mist, you all right?" Calla asked. "Is it the altitude?"

There was no trace of mirth in Misty's bark of laughter. "Worse. It's a pack of do-gooder friends who've forced me to go cold turkey on my meds."

Brynn rounded on her sister. "This is exactly why you had to get off them. If you're getting sick, it means you were hooked on them."

The rest of her words were drowned out as Tana picked up the sound of voices in the wind. Maybe it was her emotions playing tricks on her, but they sounded playful, almost like laughter. She concentrated on the words themselves, closing her eyes to try to decipher meaning in their depths.

"You hear that?" Brynn asked. "I think the Taqriaqsuit are back."

"Can we please stop calling them that?" Misty pleaded. "We're obviously dealing with one of those demon things instead."

Tana opened her eyes. "I can feel them," she said. "The shadow people. They seem...happy? It's hard to be sure. I keep seeing flashes of Wyatt too."

Misty closed her eyes. "You're right," she said. It's like this pulse of joy." She opened her eyes and shivered. "This is so creepy. How can they do that?"

Brynn looked like Christmas had come early. She yanked out her phone, tapped the camera app, and started recording a video. "Can you tell what they're happy about? When you see Wyatt, are they happy that he left the rope? Or happy that he's dead?"

"Christ, Brynn," Misty spat. "Is that all you care about? Your stupid book?"

"I'm guessing they're happy he left the rope for us," Tana said. "They seem pretty intent on getting us to the top."

Calla scowled at the open space around them, presumably where the shadow people stood listening. "Whatever the fuck you are, you're sexist," she shouted. "We know how to set up a line, thank you very much."

"The fact that they want us up there makes me want to go anywhere except there," Misty said.

A flash of anger shot through Tana, so white-hot she clutched her stomach in pain. She tried to hold on to the fact that it was clearly an irrational mood swing, no more real than the euphoria she'd been experiencing mere minutes ago. But at the sight of Misty's hesitation, anger swallowed up the last of her dwindling patience. "Then get out of my way and let me do it," she said through gritted teeth. She pushed past her friends, pulling her ascender from her backpack.

"Whoa, easy, cowboy. What's gotten into you?" Calla gripped her arm and pulled her back from the ice. "We're going to take it slow and steady, like always. Follow my lead, okay?"

The last thing Tana wanted right now was to be protected or forced into second place—again. Her friends were always telling her to be more self-assured, to push herself, and to stop accepting mediocrity. And now that she finally felt the strength to do so, they were holding her back. It was maddening. These quick bursts of emotion, which seemed to grow stronger as they climbed, urged her forward, giving her more confidence than she'd ever known in her life, even if they made her feel like an unstable lunatic. Her blood began to boil as Calla deftly stepped in front of her, assessing the ice face.

Calla dropped her length of rope, leaving it in a neat pile with her ice screws. With Wyatt's setup already in place, they wouldn't be needing any of it on the way up. She pulled out her ascender, a handheld ratcheting device that she attached to both the line and her harness. As a safety, she tied a quick Prusik knot, looping one end around the line and clipping the other into her harness. If she happened to slip, one of these systems would save her life—assuming Wyatt's setup was secure.

The others attached their own ascenders, Misty eyeing Tana warily as she jerked and muttered under her breath, no longer in control of the rage coursing through her.

"Everyone set?" Calla asked. After three affirmative cries, she turned her attention back to the ice. "I'd rather not have all of us on the line at the same time, but if we take turns, we're going to get stuck in this storm." As if in response, an icy gust blew through their quartet, pinging snow crystals off their goggles and exposed cheeks.

"Give yourselves a little wiggle room, but try to keep close," Calla instructed, raising her voice over the wind. "With this weather, we might be a little sloppier than normal. If we knock something loose, we don't want enough space between us that it can build up speed. Got it?" At her teammates' nods, she turned back to the ice. She checked her knots, did a quick scope of the rock and ice above her, searching for holds, then lifted her ax. "Climb on," she muttered under her breath.

As she stepped onto the first hold, the sun peeked over the horizon, casting a yellow light over the slabs of ice, setting them aflame like a glowing, golden sandcastle. They watched as Calla ascended, her crampons digging into the ice, her long, lean muscles straining to reach the next hold. She chiseled the pick of her ax into an ice slab, creating a grip for herself as she pulled her body skyward, her left hand yanking the ascender along the rope with her.

When she was nearly ten feet above them, she yelled, "Okay, Tana, come on up."

Tana obliged, placing one foot on a bulge of ice and sliding her ascender as high as she could reach. The fiery colors reflecting off the ice made her feel dizzy, and she placed a hand against the pitch for support. What was she feeling now? Excitement? Anticipation? No, she remembered this feeling, a shred of memory from her long-forgotten childhood. This was wonder. The sense that magic was around every corner. It was overwhelming, so all-consuming she thought she might vomit. A giggle erupted from within, followed by the appearance of tears that pooled inside her goggles.

"You okay?" Brynn called up to her. "Need a boost?"

Tana shook her head, her face pointed at the ice hidden from their view. "Fine, just planning a route," she said, her voice thick. She swung her ax into the ice, using it to pull her up to the next holds, well out of Misty and Brynn's view. The last thing she wanted right now was to answer their questions, especially when she had no explanation for what was happening to her. All she wanted was to bask in this feeling forever. Was this what other people felt all the time? Was this normal? She didn't know and, frankly, didn't care. With a grin plastered on her face, she scrambled up the rocks and ice, clawing her way to the thick ledge where Calla stood.

An angry cry from below whizzed through her brain, slicing across her joyous mood. "Damn it, Tana, you need to call 'rock' if you're kicking shit loose." The words felt far away, unimportant. The only thing that mattered now was reaching the top, seemingly the source of all these amazing things she was experiencing.

Calla held up a hand as she approached. "Listen," she said.

Tana did, forcing herself to hold still though her body was thrumming with energy.

"*Ko ta chikoon. Ko ta chikoon. Ko ta chikoon.*"

The summit flashed through her mind, the colors vivid now, a pulsating urgency to the vision.

"They're telling us to keep going. The summit's only a little higher," she said, her cheeks widening into a delirious grin. She felt drunk with giddiness, her thoughts an incoherent mishmash of joy.

"Wonderful," Calla muttered. "There's nothing ominous about getting cheered on by the same people who tried to kill you." At the sight of Tana's dopey grin, Calla grabbed her face, pulling her close. She lifted Tana's goggles to peer into her eyes. "Hey, are you feeling all right? Did you take drugs or something before we started?"

Tana shook her head, trying to wipe the smile off her face, only succeeding in making herself look more deranged. "Nah. I'm just having a nice morning."

"Shit." Calla dug her crampons into the ice and leaned back against the rope, letting her ascender and Prusik hold her weight. "Misty, I think something's wrong with Tana. Get up here!"

At Misty's thumbs-up, Calla turned her attention back to Tana. "Let's have a seat, eh? Here." She patted a thick rock protruding from beneath the ice. "Sit with me, okay?" When Tana refused to comply, Calla grabbed her arm and dragged her into a seated position. "Let's take a breather until Misty can check you out."

Brynn reached their location a few minutes later, followed closely by Misty. "Sorry," Brynn said. "Normally, I'm faster. But someone"—she shot Tana a dirty look—"was kicking rocks the entire way up, so I held back."

Misty pushed past her sister, lifting her goggles onto her forehead to reveal a pale, clammy face. "How're you feeling?" She pressed her fingers to Tana's throat, feeling for a heartbeat. "You're a little over-excited," she said, counting the beats. "A rest is probably a good idea. Drink some water too." She clicked on her headlamp, shining it into Tana's eyes. "Oh wow. Calla, look."

"I know! I asked her if she was on drugs!"

"Tana, I need you to be very serious with me," Misty said. "Your pupils are about the size of quarters right now. As far as I know, that's not something altitude can do. Did you take something this morning before the climb?"

Tana shook her head. The happiness was beginning to morph, and another mood swing was coming to claim its place. She struggled to hold on to the feeling, suddenly terrified that she'd never again experience something this beautiful. Whatever magic had given her this precious gift, she prayed it wouldn't run dry.

But the last vestiges of joy were melting away. She swore she felt them physically dripping from her body, whisked away by the wind. In their place, rage poured into her veins, a pulsing red menace. The love and admiration she felt for her friends already felt like a distant memory. The voices were calling to her, cheering her toward the finish line, and these three idiots were only standing in her way with their questions and concerns. Everything she'd been deprived of her entire life—love, anger, sadness, euphoria, was waiting for her at the summit. She felt them growing stronger as they gained altitude, their energy nearly consuming her.

A burst of anger tore through her, snapping her neck to attention with the force of its surge.

"I'm fine," she spat. "I don't use drugs, you know that. And even if I did, you're the last person who has any right to lecture me about it." She stood, turning away from Misty's shocked face and looking impatiently at the pitches above. Glaring at Calla, she gestured to the ice. "You gonna get moving, or should someone more capable be leading this team?" At Calla's look of surprise, Tana's hands curled into fists. Why was everyone staring at her instead of moving? Couldn't they understand how important this was?

Words spewed from her tongue, the anger blinding her from the love she felt for these women. "You always need to be the leader," she screamed at Calla. "How fucked up are you inside that you can't let anyone else be in charge? No wonder nobody wants to marry you. You'd drive them insane. You're a control freak! You only let Brynn lead for a day because you knew she was starstruck, like one of those dumbshit teenagers running after a boy band. It's always about ego with you, isn't it? You loved being the hero, handing over the reins like some great, benevolent leader. You're pathetic."

She turned to Misty. "And don't even get me started on you," she snarled. "People think I'm basic? Look at you. Trapped in an unhappy marriage of your own making. Two kids that make you nuts. You gave up your nursing career to be a goddamn housewife, and now you drink wine and pop pills to make it through the day. You go climbing to try and find some sort of meaning in your life. It's hilarious that you claim to be a feminist because the movement would be ashamed of someone like you."

Eyes wide, Brynn looked between all three women, waiting for someone to explain what was happening.

"Tana, you're not yourself right now," Misty said, her voice shaky. "The altitude is affecting your brain. I'm going to give you a Dex, okay? And then I need you to descend with me. You're going to be fine, but we need to move quickly." Eyes red with the sting of Tana's insults, she nevertheless dutifully unzipped their first aid kit, pulling out a small bottle of pills. Peeling off her gloves, she extracted one tablet and held it out to Tana. Beside her, Brynn offered up her water bottle. "Tana, please, take this."

Tana glared at the small white pill. It signified the end. They were going to medicate her, drug her up, and drag her down to the safe, hollow purgatory she'd been living in for the past twenty years. Away from magic and danger, away from mystical creatures that possibly wanted to kidnap and eat her, and away from these incredible emotions that had been hidden from her for decades. Back to her comfortable, protected prison of a life. To willingly participate was unthinkable.

She swatted the pill from Misty's hand, catching the quick flash of white before it tumbled down the ice, lost in the falling snow.

"Over my dead body," she growled.

Calla shrugged, no trace of friendliness on her face. Tana's words had clearly struck a nerve. "Have it your way," she said. "I'll drag you down this goddamn mountain if I have to." As Tana's gaze rose to the ice above them, darting from hold to hold, Calla shook her head. "Don't even think about it. I'm all for an adventure, but when your brain starts to bleed, we call it a day." She raised her hands defensively, closing in on Tana. "I'm going to help you rappel down, all right? You've done this a million times, nice and easy." She reached onto Tana's harness, gripping the figure-8 descender clipped onto her side.

As she fumbled to open the carabiner, Tana saw her chance. It was now or never.

She slammed her knee into Calla's gut, delighting in her friend's groan of pain. All those years of being invisible, overshadowed by Calla's perfection, made her friend's face twisted in agony a welcome sight.

Calla dropped to the ground, clutching her stomach, her Prusik pulling taut as it held her from sliding over the edge. Hands fumbling with nerves, Tana unhooked her carabiner, freeing herself from both the Prusik and her ascender. She was no longer attached to the safety line. She was free.

Misty raised her hands instinctively against a blow, her eyes darting between Tana and Calla, unsure of who to focus on.

While she dithered, Brynn rushed forward, elbowing Tana into the ice. Tana's helmet smacked the glowing tower, sending an explosion of ice shards tumbling over them. "Are you fucking crazy?" she shouted, her face inches from Tana's.

Misty tugged on her sister's arm, yelling to be careful now that Tana was unhooked from the line, but Brynn either didn't hear or didn't care. Brynn's face was a mask of fury, and Tana smiled, knowing she'd hit a nerve when she'd compared her to a starstruck groupie.

"It makes sense that you'd idolize Calla," she said, her voice soft and syrupy. "One loser following another. Give it a few more years, and your whole perky Pollyanna routine will wear thin. And once people stop thinking you're cute, they'll replace you with a younger, prettier version. You'll be the washed-up, talentless hack, trying to get her book published, finally realizing you've been coasting on your looks the entire time." Tana had no idea where these thoughts were coming from, but it felt good— unbelievably satisfying—to say them out loud. To dismiss others the way she'd been dismissed her entire life. Shoved into the background, and for what? For being a little mousy-looking? For her bland personality and lack of emotions?

She laughed. That last one certainly wasn't an issue any longer.

She glared at Brynn, whose long, blond hair peeked out from beneath her helmet. She was so pretty, so charming and bubbly, she'd probably never understand what Tana had been through. All of them—Brynn, Calla, and Misty—were weak, coasting through life on the privilege of their good looks and outgoing personalities. Now that it was Tana's turn to shine, they wanted to pull her back, to force her to return to mediocrity. They could pretend she was their equal all they wanted, but she knew deep down that every group had its loser.

And she was so damn tired of the role.

She lifted her ax, scoping out the pitch above her. She had no doubts she could make it to the top, even without their help. Anger was giving way to resolve. Lava poured through her veins, fueling her determination to reach the summit and see for herself what the shadows had planned for her. Even the threat of death at their hands no longer frightened her. She kicked her boot onto a small outcropping of ice, digging in her crampons. This was it, the last stretch of her journey. Heat burned through her, urging her upward, when a hand clamped down on her arm, sucking the fire from her belly.

"Tana, listen to me, we have to go—"

Tana slammed her fist into Misty's chest, twisting her arm at the last second to give it more force. Misty dropped to her knees, the Prusik catching her from tumbling down the ice. She swung to where Calla still sat, clutching her gut.

With her ax raised, Tana glared at Brynn. "Anything you'd like to say?"

Mouth shut in a hard line, Brynn gave her head one quick shake, backing just out of range of an ax swing. Her eyes darted to where Misty lay, unmoving.

Biting back a bark of laughter, Tana turned back to the ice, kicked in her footing, and climbed.

Chapter Twenty-Four

Never before had climbing felt this natural. Tana's muscles stretched and strained, burning with the effort of pulling her skyward. The pain, raw and unfiltered, was a newly-discovered delicacy. She couldn't remember ever experiencing something this primal. Her senses thrummed, newly awakened, and even if she lived to a hundred, she felt she'd never get enough of them. The sky, a kaleidoscope of orange and purple, reflected off the ice in a dizzying display. The scent of her sweat overpowered the pure, snowy air. How had she never smelled herself before? The copper taste in her mouth, a sign of how much she'd exerted herself, was deliciously strange, like she'd drunk a mouthful of blood.

Her motions were fluid: swing the ax, test her weight, kick her feet, and pull. There was never a moment's hesitation, not even a hint of trepidation at the idea that she was untethered from the safety line. If anything, that perilous freedom made her all the surer that her footing was solid—because it had to be. The voices chanting around her grew in volume, urging her higher, and she knew that no matter what she discovered at the top, whether it be her family or her death at the hands of these creatures, it was meant to be.

The cries of her teammates echoed up to her. Misty was, as always, trying to coax her back to safety. Calla was less forgiving, shouting a mixture of profanity and threats. Her voice was the loudest, and even without looking, Tana had no doubt that she was racing as fast as she could to catch up. Even with Tana's newfound strength, she knew Calla would outpace her if she flagged even for a second, so she kept moving, not even stopping to assess the closing gap between them.

The shadows danced around her, the silhouettes of their bodies flitting across the edge of her vision. They shouted encouragement to her, and jeering insults to the rest of her team. Though they couldn't decipher the words, Tana assumed her friends must be terrified. The tone, harsh and unwelcoming, betrayed the creatures' hostility.

Tana lifted her ax, chiseling it into a gap between rock and ice above her head. Moving as fast as she was able, she lifted one boot, kicking into the next foothold. As she lifted her next foot, her carelessness finally caught up to her. The chunk of ice she'd trusted her weight to gave way with a sharp crack, the entire foothold breaking loose and tumbling to the ground below.

She screamed, both hands grasping her ax, her one lifeline, as her feet dangled in the open air. She glanced down at her boots, desperately searching for anything they could use as a step, and she saw Calla, Brynn, and Misty dodge the block of ice she'd dislodged.

Watching them scramble for cover, Tana's emotions took another deep dive, this time headfirst into terror. She could have easily killed them if they'd failed to duck in time. For that matter—she scrabbled at the ice with her boots until her front spikes found purchase—she could have killed herself. With her free hand, she grasped a sharp rock outcropping and heaved herself to the next ledge, a flat, level base where she could stop to breathe.

Her fears crashed over her, one after another, like waves in a storm. She was willingly putting herself and her friends in harm's way. Rushing into what was surely a trap of some kind, where hideous, pale monsters would rip her apart and gnaw on her bones. And her final words to the people she loved most had been intentionally hurtful. She could stop and apologize. She could end this entire nightmare right now by giving up and letting Calla catch her. But the thought of never reaching the summit, and whatever answers it held, scared her just as much, if not more.

She gripped her head in her hands, moaning into her palms. "I'm losing my fucking mind," she whispered. One more thing to be terrified of. Maybe her brain really was bleeding, or maybe after decades of robotic detachment, she'd finally snapped. Was this what a psychotic break felt like? A roller coaster of conflicting emotions with no basis in logic or reality?

Less than thirty feet separated Calla from Tana, a gap that was quickly closing. More than anything, Tana wanted to let her catch up, to let Calla hold her and say everything was going to be okay. An impossibility now, she knew. Either out of anger or protectiveness, Calla was going to force her back down to safety. And Tana couldn't allow that to happen.

She looked to the remaining pitches. They petered out nearly a hundred feet above, where, according to the photos online, the round plateau of the summit stood waiting. Her whole body trembling, Tana gripped the line with one hand, wishing she hadn't thrown off her safety gear. How could she have been so reckless?

The shadows tore past, their panicked sense of urgency flooding her brain, their words imploring her to hurry up before Calla could catch her.

Tana screamed back, "Maybe you could make yourselves useful and actually help me up this damn thing."

No response. Of course. Everyone was full of bright ideas until it came time to do the actual work. She was on her own.

As a safety precaution, she looped the fixed line around her arm so it could slide freely as she moved. If she fell, there was a chance it would crack the bone, but at least it would keep her from tumbling down the entire face. She planted her feet against the ice, gripped her ax tightly in her free hand, and continued to ascend.

"Tana, please, stop," Calla yelled. "We need to get you down to a lower altitude. You could die up here."

The concern in her voice almost gave Tana pause. The thought of Calla worrying about her safety caused another wave of love to crash inside her chest. She squashed it down, resisting the urge to fall for Calla's charms. She couldn't trust her emotions any longer. They'd gone haywire, threatening to derail the only thing that mattered anymore.

The strikes of her ax and crampons beat in time with her heart as she ascended. She refused to look down, no longer caring what lay behind her. It felt like another life, a distant dream fading from memory. Open sky stretched out above her, now a solid blanket of forbidding clouds. The summit plateau was one pitch away. She slammed her ax into a crust of ice, swearing under her breath as the entire piece tore away and tumbled down the slope. In the far corners of her mind, she heard Calla's scream, but it barely registered.

In frustration, she tossed her ax to the side—eliciting another shriek from Calla—and gripped the rope with both hands, planting her feet firmly into the ice. She pulled herself up the rope, one hand over the other, walking up the last ten feet of rock until she was standing upright. Wyatt's blue climbing rope ended at a thick, steel anchor screwed firmly into the ground. Tana dropped the rope, her mouth stretched into a delirious smile. The ground was almost perfectly flat, a fifty-foot circle that dropped off in every direction. Snow-filled gusts obscured the view, but in the distance, shrouded by clouds, she could just barely see Denali rising into the sky.

She had reached the summit.

Chapter Twenty-Five

Atop the summit, the storm churned around Tana, a cyclone of blinding white. Frigid gusts pelted her with shrapnel-like snow, pinging painfully off her already battle-scarred face. The oncoming clouds grew thicker with every passing second, obscuring the view of Denali, then the surrounding landscape, and finally, the sun. Shielding her view with one hand, she peered around the plateau, searching for anything that would indicate the shadow people had witnessed her victory.

"Hey," Tana yelled. "Where is everybody?"

The terrible thought that she'd climbed Torket for nothing crept into her head. Her brain was so scrambled. How could she be sure she hadn't fabricated the whole thing? What if she'd lost her mind completely and the shadow people were a figment of her imagination? These creatures, her friends, the climb itself...was any of it real? She wondered if maybe she was trapped in an asylum somewhere, drooling and ranting to herself about being chased by magical demons up a mountain.

She shook the thought away. "This is real," she said, sounding more confident than she felt. "This is all real. You're meant to be here." She wanted something, anything, to happen, even if it meant monsters materializing out of thin air to devour her. She slumped to her knees in exhaustion and disappointment, keeping her back turned away from the route, not wanting her friends—assuming they still were her friends—to see this pathetic conclusion.

The sound of boots crunching on snow signaled their arrival. Tana kept her head bowed in defeat, scared to meet their accusatory gazes. More footsteps followed. Two, four, ten people were walking the perimeter of the summit, and she raised her face, eyes wide with anticipation.

She heard their voices, the words muffled, ebbing and flowing with the wind.

"I'm here," Tana shouted, waving her arms for emphasis. "My name is Tanaraq Walker, and I'm looking for my family. Can you help me?" Her voice cracked as she fought to keep from crying in desperation. "Please?"

Flickers of their shadowy bodies roamed the perimeter, but if they heard her, they paid no mind.

She stumbled to her feet, hands held aloft, trying to feel them as their shadows darted past. "I can't go back without knowing what happened to them." Only the wind answered, wailing as it tore past. Tana finally lost all sense of control. A sob tore out of her throat, turning into a scream of frustration as it passed her lips. "Why won't you answer me?" she shrieked.

A shout of triumph pulled her attention to the other side of the summit. The footsteps were all racing to that one spot, their voices rising excitedly. There, almost perfectly camouflaged against the white sky, the falling snow seemed to coalesce into a solid form, a hand protruding from thin air, its skin milky white. It drifted in and out of focus with each gust, dissolving into powder before reforming.

Brynn's theories flashed through her mind. If there really were places where the barrier between worlds was thin, surely this was one. All these wonderful and horrible feelings inside her were a homing beacon, guiding her to this very spot, this link to her past. A place where not only the Taqriaqsuit could cross over, but maybe she could too.

Every ounce of her self-preservation begged to run away from that icy hand. But her desire to see the other side was overwhelming. She needed to know what lay beyond this world and if—as she so desperately wished—her parents were among the shadows, eagerly awaiting her return.

She ran, arms pumping as she sprinted toward the creature. The white, nightmarish fingers reached for her, beckoning her forward, as desperate to pull her in as she was to see the other side. She reached out, her fingers mirroring theirs, the gap between them shrinking quickly. With a few feet to go, Tana sucked in a deep breath and closed her eyes.

Without warning, she was slammed to the snow, and in that initial startled moment, she knew beyond a shadow of a doubt that she'd been tricked. It had all been a trap. They'd thrown her to the ground and were planning to tear her to shreds. When she opened her eyes, though, she found herself staring up at Calla's horrified face.

"Are you out of your fucking mind?" Calla roared. She pushed all of her weight onto Tana's upper body, pinning her solidly in place. "You know you almost knocked Brynn unconscious? You kicked a block of ice right into her face." Her ponytail had shaken loose when she tackled Tana, and her black hair flew in a tumultuous cloud beneath her helmet. To Tana, staring up at her dark features against the pure white sky, she looked otherworldly.

"Let me up," she shouted. "They're trying to show me something." When Calla refused to budge, Tana tried to inject some authority into her voice, a difficult feat while pinned to the ground and suffering from medical-grade mood swings. Even now, she couldn't tell if she was enraged with Calla or thrilled to be this close to her. "We've made it this far," she said, forcing her voice to remain steady. "If my brain's exploding, a few more minutes won't matter. Just let me see it. What if they know something about what happened to my parents?"

At this, Calla laughed an angry bark that cut through the wind. "No, Tana. You're not going to see the goddamn monsters. End of story."

"But my family—"

"Enough," Calla shouted. "Your family is gone, Tana. I'm sorry you didn't find what you were looking for, but I'm done putting everyone in danger—especially you—for a trip down memory lane. We're going home."

"Calla, please." She hated the position she found herself in, pressed flat to the ground and begging for mercy.

Calla sighed, the sharpness in her shoulders softening. "You really don't get it, do you?" she asked. "Fuck, Tana. All these trips, year after year, always making sure we found time for them. I love Misty, but I wasn't doing it to see her." Her eyes burned into Tana's, pleading with her to understand and not force her to say the words aloud. "I can't lose you."

Tana stared up at her, struck dumb as she processed what Calla was saying. All these years, all the phone calls that stretched into the wee hours, all the hugs, the jokes, the lingering glances, and cuddling in tents. A decade's worth of missed signals and lost opportunity. How could she have been that obtuse? She was so lost in her own fog that she'd never even noticed.

Calla's grip was like iron manacles on her wrists, a superhuman strength born not out of anger but years of unrequited love. The dark fury in her eyes wasn't a reaction to Tana's reckless foolishness but a guard against the terror of losing her altogether. Tana bit down on the inside of her cheek to keep the shock of this revelation from spilling out. Calla was willing to risk everything, including her own life, to save the woman she loved.

"Calla, I..." No. Words could never do it justice. Tana lifted her head from the ice, her muscles protesting against the force of Calla's weight, and caught one last sight of Calla's widening eyes as hers slipped shut. She tilted her chin, their helmets scraping together, her ice-cold lips brushing against Calla's, eliciting a surprised jerk that radiated through her captor's body.

The grip on Tana's wrists relaxed, the tension melting out of Calla's body as she returned the kiss. The frost thawed from their lips as they pressed together, and Tana felt a drunken dizziness wash over her. She arched her back, desperate to be even closer, free of these layers of metal and plastic and nylon while knowing no amount of closeness would ever be enough. She pulled her hand free of Calla's loosened grip and ran her fingers through that wild, untamed hair, wishing she could throw off her gloves and feel the thick strands between her fingers.

Their lips parted and reconnected, a sigh escaping from Calla as she wrapped her arms around Tana's body, folding her into a protective embrace. Tana wanted to drown in the moment. How beautiful it would be to let it wash over her and stay frozen in time: her first kiss, her first love, her first deep ache of wanting to give herself to someone fully.

After a hundred years, or maybe half a second, Calla pulled away. "Please," she begged, her voice barely a whisper. "Please, Tana, come down with me."

Tana hesitated. The warmth spreading through her was intoxicating, a remedy to a lifetime of loneliness. She ached to take Calla's hand and run away from this horrible place. The thought of escaping back to the cabin, warm and safe in each other's arms, was so tempting it was maddening.

And yet...she glanced at the opening to the spirit world, wisps of white indicating the Taqriaqsuit were still trying to break through. Retreat, as blessedly wonderful as it sounded, was out of the question. She'd come too far.

Calla followed her line of sight and shook her head. A sudden cold permeated the air between them. "God damn it, Tana," she sighed. "This isn't going to be fun for either of us, but I'm getting you back down alive." At the sound of clinking metal, she turned to see Brynn and Misty pulling themselves onto the summit. "I've got her, come help me!"

Tana's heart sank. She suspected Calla might have let her go if she'd been able to find the right words to tug on her heartstrings. But trying to convince Misty was a lost cause.

The two women rushed to Calla's side, immediately pressing their weight onto Tana's arms. A fresh streak of blood dripped down the side of Brynn's face. Misty's eyes were unfocused, her breathing labored.

"What should we do?" Brynn asked, refusing to make eye contact with Tana. "Can we call for a helicopter?"

"On it." With shaky hands, Misty removed the satellite phone from her pocket and tapped in a series of commands. "Oh no." She turned to the side, eyes squeezed shut and her throat working to keep its contents inside. She tossed the phone to Calla. "Deal with this. It's hitting me now. I think I'm going to be sick."

The smell of vomit permeated the crisp air as Misty retched into the snow. Brynn made an instinctual move to comfort her but pulled back, the guilt of inducing her sister's agony written across her face.

Muffled by her thick hair, Misty's voice drifted back to them. "Make sure there's room for two in that heli. I'm not climbing down this thing if I don't have to. Actually..." She groaned. "We're pretty high up. Can a helicopter even reach us?"

"There's no other option," Brynn said, eyeing her sister warily. "We have extra rope, and we could tie Tana up so she doesn't do something stupid. We'd still have to lower her down this thing though."

"Guys, I'm fine," Tana said, though no one acknowledged her. "Please, let me go. You're hurting me."

"We're hurting *you*?" Brynn snapped.

"Whatever we do, it needs to be quick." Calla jerked her head toward the corpse-like arms that were now scrabbling the barrier, trying to claw their way through, their fingers barely visible against the clouds. "I caught her right before she ran into that thing."

Misty turned to look, then screamed, spittle and vomit flying from her lips. She jerkily crawled backward, her eyes never leaving the floating arms. "Oh my God, Calla, get the damn gun! What're you waiting for?"

A grimace swept over Calla's face. "I left it in my pack."

"You did what?"

"I was chasing Tana! I had to move fast, so I left it behind."

"Uh, guys?" Brynn was staring open-mouthed at the arms, which had grown to include an entire upper body, including a pale, bug-eyed face fixated on them, the same figure who'd tried dragging Tana to the other side. As they watched, he struggled to pull himself further into their world, wrestling against unseen forces. With every gust of wind, his figure dematerialized, then reformed, as though he were part of the storm itself. "We need to get the hell off this thing—now."

Calla and Misty exchanged a glance, then simultaneously jumped to their feet, each holding one of Tana's arms. "Walk!" Calla ordered. The creature was yelling over his shoulder, calling out to unseen allies. Another of the Taqriaqsuit, this one female, drifted into focus beside him.

"Oh shit," Calla breathed. "Tana, fucking move!"

It was too late. Whatever last thread of barrier had lain in their way was broken, and a stream of sinewy, pale creatures burst forth, their ghastly figures merging with wind and snow. Their colorless eyes fixated on Tana.

They streamed around the women, frigid gusts following their every move, buffeting the four climbers with snow and sleet. Their words fused with the gale, an angry howl that lifted the hairs on the back of Tana's neck.

"Let's go," Misty shouted, grabbing Brynn's arm and tugging her toward their rappel line. They only managed to run a few feet before a blast of snow and ice knocked them sideways, sending them skidding toward the summit's steep drop-off.

Calla's grip on Tana's arm loosened, indecision flickering across her face. "Fuck," she spat. She released Tana and dove after Misty and Brynn, grasping at their coats to tug them away from the summit edge.

The creatures swarmed the three women, hands snatching at clothing and hair, yanking them sideways and knocking them across the snowy plateau. Tana swore she heard the faintest traces of laughter, barely audible over the wind.

She knew she ought to run and help her teammates but could only stand and watch, transfixed. Her brain implored her to jump into action, to listen to her friends and retreat before these unearthly beings ripped them all apart. But she'd fought tooth and nail to reach this point, to find some shred of resolution to her family's disappearance. Now that the moment was finally upon her, she couldn't stand to let it slip past.

She took one last look at her friends, their screams for help echoing across the summit. They had risked their lives for her again and again. Now she only asked that they do it one final time.

Tana scanned the ground for footprints, zeroing in on the spot where they all ended: the invisible barrier between worlds. She ran, her heart pumping against her ribs. No creature stopped her progress, though she felt their cold, blank eyes on her back. Terror and anxiety clawed at her insides, begging her to stop. She ignored them, her feet slamming the ice. A small cry passed her lips as she bolted across the barrier.

Mom and Dad, I'm here.

Then, a flash of light rendered her blind.

Chapter Twenty-Six

The world swam into focus: gold and copper flecks of light amid deep rose and violet. Tana raised her gloved hand against the rainbow-hued flashes. In her other, she clutched a jagged shard of rock, holding herself steady against gravity's pull.

To her seven-year-old eyes, the sight was impossibly magical, something pulled from one of the fantasy books her father read to her at night. Up above, the ice and rock gave way to the open sky, a sign that after nearly a week of climbing, the summit was finally within reach.

She curled her fingers around the rock and lifted her boot, searching for a passable foothold in the glowing ice. Spotting a small divot about knee high, she slammed her toes into the permafrost, kicking until her steel spikes were firmly embedded. A euphoric grin spread across her face as she pulled herself another foot closer to the summit, only to have her progress halted by a sharp tug on her waist.

"Hold up, kiddo!"

She turned to see her father, his mop of dark hair billowing out from beneath his helmet. A rope was looped around his torso, one end extending up to where she stood, terminating in a figure-8 knot clipped to her harness.

Behind him, the other end of the rope led to a hunched figure, a stream of curse words pouring from her lips. Her fingers played over the ice, searching for any surface jagged enough to grab. With a grunt, she swung her ax, its pick barely nicking the smooth ice before dislodging. "God damn it," she swore.

She lifted her face, her tired eyes searching for her husband and daughter. "Nate! Stop for a second, okay?" She planted her feet securely in the ice, one hand giving the rope a quick tug as if to reassure herself that she was, in fact, still attached to her husband.

"This isn't what we trained for," she yelled. "I don't think we should keep going. This is way too dangerous for Sierra."

Nate gestured up at their daughter. "Allie, she's fine. Look at her. We're almost at the top. Why would you want to turn back now?"

"She's seven years old! What were you thinking, picking this place?"

He let out an aggravated sigh. "Kids only a few years older than her are attempting Denali. Hell, teenagers have summited Everest. This is advanced, sure. But it's not completely out of left field. Sierra could be in the same league as those Everest kids one day."

Sierra gazed longingly at the smooth line where the ice met the sky, close enough that she could be there within a half hour if her mom would stop worrying. Why did she have to do this every time? Push her and support her all the way until things get exciting, then inevitably get nervous and backtrack on the whole plan.

"Allie, please." He started to descend to where his wife was planted, only to be halted by the rope attaching him to his daughter. "Shoot. Sierra, don't move a muscle, okay?"

She shot her father a quick thumbs up.

Nate uncoiled a loop of rope from his torso, giving himself enough slack to clamber down to his wife. "Honey, what's this really about? She's doing great up there. Don't take this away from her."

Allie sighed. "I know you want her to be your little climbing buddy. And she's really advanced, I get that. But I think sometimes you forget that she's still a child. This is dangerous. Like, CPS takes your kid away from you kind of dangerous. We didn't even set up a safety line, for God's sake. Just rush ahead, not a care in the world."

Up above, Sierra's feet itched to move, to kick into the ice and ascend into the rainbow sky. She dropped one hand to her waist, letting her fingers graze the carabiner anchoring her to her father.

"If we let her do this kind of thing when she's seven, what comes next?" Allie asked. "What's left for her to conquer? I can barely keep up with you two now."

Nate's face softened. "Honey. Shit. Is that what this is about?"

Sierra gripped the carabiner's lock, spinning it open.

"She's not going to outgrow you, Al. She needs you." Nate tried to pull her into a hug, found himself at an awkward angle on the ice, and settled for patting her arm. "One day, she's going to be a better climber than both of us, and that's a good thing. It means we did our jobs. And no matter how far she goes, you'll always be her mom."

Sierra unclipped her carabiner, placing it carefully onto the ice shelf. She chanced a quick glance back at her parents, both fully absorbed in one another. Neither looked her way.

Adrenaline surged through her body like electricity, sending shivers all the way to her fingers and toes. She was free. Untethered. With nothing to hold her back.

Or catch you if you fall.

The thought vanished as quickly as it arrived, a brief flicker of maturity that she wasn't yet ready to absorb. She grasped her miniature ax—a custom-ordered birthday present from her father—swung it into the frozen face and climbed.

Each kick into the ice, each pull from her growth-spurt elongated arms, flooded her body with sensory overload: the crack of the ice, the taste of copper on her tongue, the smell of the thin, clear air. How could she ever explain this to her friends back home in New Hampshire?

"Sierra!"

Her mother's panicked scream cracked through the air like a gunshot.

"Nate, grab her. She's not on the rope!"

Sierra gritted her teeth against the wave of frustration that followed in the wake of her mother's voice. She heard her parents' frantic kicks against the ice, their ridiculously overprotective instincts shifting into gear. Hadn't she proved herself? Countless hours at the climbing gym, followed by increasingly difficult winter ascents with her dad. When were they going to realize that she wasn't a baby anymore?

"Sierra, freeze! Not one more step, you hear me?"

A black cloud settled over her, extinguishing the joyous light that had briefly burst into a bonfire. She clambered onto the nearest ice shelf, taking a vicious pleasure in defying her father by slipping in that one extra step. With one hand resting on the ice for balance, she turned to face them, her mouth set in a defiant scowl. "I'm fine—"

As she turned, her crampon snagged on the opposite leg, the steel spikes catching her bootstrap. She gasped as her body pitched forward, her feet tangled together. The snow-covered ground, so distant a moment ago, seemed to rise up, ready to devour her upon impact.

A howl of terror tore out of her parents, the words unintelligible. Both stood with their hands raised instinctively, ready to snatch their daughter as she tumbled past.

Sierra's fingers slid on her weak handhold. A scream caught in her chest, unwilling to emerge into the world and confirm her terror. In a final last-ditch effort to stop her fall, Sierra swung her free arm, ax still held in her grasp, back toward the ice. The pick scraped along the blue surface, then finally caught.

For a second, there was absolute silence. Sierra stood on the edge of the small shelf, feet still tangled together, her tiny hand on the ax shaft the only thing keeping her anchored to the wall. At the sight of the ground far below, her knees trembled, and she felt along the wall for a hold with her free hand lest they completely buckle beneath her. She suddenly had to pee very badly. Searching out her parents with wide, terrified eyes, she managed to whisper, "I'm okay."

Allie let out a high-pitched whimper, a screech throttled in her throat. Her hands shook as she grabbed her husband's jacket and shoved him forward. "I told you. I told you. Get her. Go get her. Go!"

Sierra hated the high-pitched, robotic tone of her mother's voice, like a busted toy. Looking into her mother's pale, pinched face made her stomach twist with guilt. "Mom, I'm sorry. I'm fine now—"

"Get her," Allie screamed.

Nate snatched the slack rope and looped it around his torso.

Another pang stabbed Sierra's midsection when she saw that her father's hands were shaking as well. The enormity of her recklessness crashed over her, and she fought to hold back her tears. "Dad, I—" She paused, not knowing what to say to wipe the fear from her father's face.

"It's okay, honey. Hold still, all right?" His tone was stiff and clipped, his movements rushed and jerky.

All Sierra could do was nod and scoot to the back of the small ice ledge, carefully unsnagging her crampon. Retribution was sure to be swift and furious, but what scared her the most was the look on her father's face. His normal calm confidence was replaced with panic.

He kicked into the ice and swung his ax simultaneously, not bothering to maintain three points of contact. With his free hand, he scrabbled for any sort of handhold, not testing the ice for weakness before trusting his full weight to it. Allie followed his lead, so desperate to reach her daughter that she clambered onto steps before Nate had even left them. The short rope connecting them together bunched at Nate's feet.

Sierra watched them rapidly ascend. Twenty feet below her perch, then fifteen, then ten. Closer and closer to the moment when they'd clip her to the rope and force her back down the mountain, summit unclaimed. And she had no one to blame except herself.

"Almost there, honey," Nate called up to her, and Sierra was relieved to hear the warmth seep back into his voice. This close, the scent of campfire and burnt sage—a good luck ritual of her mother's—drifted off his heavy coat, a small comfort. His ax slammed the ice just below where she stood. With his free hand, he fished for the carabinered end of the rope Sierra had discarded. "Here you go, clip your—"

The sun seemed to dip behind the clouds, a shadow passing over him as the screech of metal on ice cut through his words. His pick, so carelessly embedded in the ice, wrenched free. He dropped Sierra's carabiner, desperately grasping for some sort of handhold, his fingers sliding over the smooth ice.

Sierra watched, horrified, as her father's arms pinwheeled, a slow-motion ballet pulling him into the open air. She stretched out her tiny, gloved hands, her fingers finding nothing but empty space.

His eyes widened, and the small flicker of joy at reuniting with his daughter extinguished, replaced by the cold realization that there was nothing he could do to save himself. His feet lifted free of the ice as he tumbled backward, crampons kicking up clouds of snow like confetti. The ax tumbled from his hands, a flash of orange sun glinting off the aluminum before it disappeared from view.

Nate reached for Allie, his one last chance at salvation. Their hands made contact as he sailed past, fingers desperately clawing at one another. But gravity refused to give up its hold easily. Nate crashed against the side of the ice wall, an explosion of rock and snow upon impact, before he was yanked free of Allie's grasp.

"No, no, no, Nate," she screamed as he plummeted out of reach.

"Mom, get down," Sierra yelled, her parents' constant self-arrest training managing to puncture the layers of terror and panic enshrouding her.

It was too late. What little slack remained in the rope had run out. Allie was jerked off her feet, her husband's weight an anchor, dragging her to the same fate that awaited him.

Allie reacted instinctively, swinging her ax at whatever solid ground she could find. The pick dragged along the ice's surface, never fully catching, barely slowing their descent as it tore through the upper crust. Allie swung her free hand up, her fingers latching onto a small, exposed rock ledge. She cried out as the inertia of her husband's fall pulled her body taut. Her fingers slipped on the rock, only the tips still engaged.

"I'm coming," Sierra yelled. "Hang on. I'll help you."

"Sierra."

"I can be down in a minute!"

"Sierra!"

Her mother's voice was firm, resigned. Sierra stared down at her, her vision blurring with the sudden onslaught of tears. She swiped a hand across her eyes.

"It's okay, baby." Allie's voice cracked. A shadow passed over her features, grief and loss settling in her warm eyes. "Everything's going to be okay."

And then she let go.

A ragged howl tore out of Sierra. She dropped to her knees, fingers clutching the ice shelf like talons, and peered over the edge, unable to make herself look away. Flashes of their coats—her father's blue and her mother's red—slammed down the side of the wall, crashing against outcroppings and tumbling over one another, a pinwheel hurtling toward its own demise.

Her father's body hit the ground first, the resulting boom echoing up the mountain so loud that Sierra recoiled in shock. Her mother's followed, the sound ricocheting through the crisp air.

A wake of shrapnel chased after them, a glitter of stone and ice, a morbid celebration of their grand descent.

Sierra stared down at them, from this height, no more than hazy patches of red and blue. "Please, God, please, please, please," she whispered. If she could only concentrate hard enough, she was sure she could will them to get back up. To brush themselves off and wave in her direction. To tell her they were a little bruised up—and that she was grounded forever—but that everything really was going to be okay.

The red coat began to move, and Sierra's heart leaped inside her chest. "Mom," she screamed, a joyous, nearly hysterical shriek.

But something was wrong. It wasn't the jerky movement of a person struggling to their feet. It was more of a gliding, alien and unsettling.

"Mom?"

The red coat slid along the ground, picking up speed as it neared the edge of what her dad had called the "safe zone." Beyond that narrow path lay a patchwork field littered with crevasses.

The reality of the situation sucked the air from Sierra's lungs. The world around her began to spin, her mind begging her to turn away, yet unable to force her to comply. There was no life left in those two splashes of color. Just gravity playing one last cruel trick on a scared little girl.

Her mother approached the crevasse, one last flash of bright red before she tipped inside, vanishing in the darkness. The rope pulled taut, jerking the blue coat to life. A high-pitched whine escaped from Sierra's throat at the sight of her father being pulled across the ice. This couldn't be real. Things like this didn't happen in real life.

The flash of blue was moving quickly, towed along by her mother's body. Sierra's thoughts began to crumble, the world around her becoming dreamlike, detached from reality. Her one last tether to the real world was her father's blue coat, now flying across the snow.

And then it dropped into the crevasse, disappearing from sight.

Sierra screamed.

The blood-chilling screech tore out of her, morphing into ragged sobs that shook her body. She beat her tiny fists against the ice, no longer caring if it gave way beneath her weight. What did it matter if she fell to her death? If she dropped like a stone and joined her parents in their deep, unmarked grave? She was Alice, alone and lost in Wonderland, only without a Cheshire Cat to guide her through this world where madness prevailed.

"I'm sorry," she cried, the words raw and sharp in the cold air. "Please, God, bring them back. I'll do anything! Please!"

No one emerged from the dark blue crevasse. Her family was gone.

Sierra crumpled in on herself, her arms blocking out the bright, accusatory sunshine. Blocking out the harsh truth that if only she'd behaved herself, her family would still be alive. They'd be standing on the peak at this very moment, celebrating. The truth was that this was entirely her fault. The anguish poured out of her, her body heaving against these horrible thoughts, blotting them from existence. She shrieked over and over again, each verbal outpouring a small exorcism of the horrors she'd just witnessed.

Get to the summit.

The sudden thought was a life raft among the turbulence, some last shred of sanity to cling to. As if in a dream, she pushed herself to her feet and kicked into the wall. She scanned for handholds, her foggy brain grasping onto this new goal. Maybe once she reached the top, everything would make sense. This confusing new world she found herself in would suddenly right itself.

The steady crunch of metal on ice was like a salve, soothing away her anxieties. One step after another, that's all that was required of her, and everything would be okay.

Everything's going to be okay. The words nagged at her.

With one final heave, she threw an arm over the final crest, her ax catching on the flat summit. She swung one leg onto the peak, then rolled the rest of her body onto the snowy plateau.

The summit stretched around her, a near-perfect circle. "Hello?" she asked, not sure who she hoped would answer.

Only the wind replied with an empty whistle.

Sierra dropped to the edge of the plateau, letting her feet dangle into the void. A numbness was spreading through her, a hollowing out of her inner self. She could almost feel it slipping away. Joy, anger, and sadness disappearing into dust, along with her ability to care about such things. The landscape around her, everything from the blue ice to the red boots on her feet, lost its saturation. The rosiness of exertion vanished from her cheeks, and the spark behind her eyes dimmed, leaving their normal chocolate brown a muddy gray.

She stared out at the frozen landscape, unseeing, as the light left her body.

Whispers rode in on the wind, words in an unfamiliar language swirling around the mountain's peak. Snatches of someone crying flickered in and out of focus, and Sierra briefly wondered what could make someone that sad before the thought dissolved from her mind.

She sat, unmoving, as the sun began its slow descent toward the horizon, draping the mountaintop and the small girl upon it in shadow.

Chapter Twenty-Seven

Another flash of white and Tana was catapulted back to the present, screaming gusts and blinding snow that knocked her to her knees. Even as shards of ice struck her body, these violent surroundings barely registered. It was all white noise, background music to the terrible truth she now understood: she had killed her parents.

"Tana!" Calla dropped beside her, one arm around Tana's shoulders for support. Her helmet was cracked, and a trickle of blood dripped down the side of her cheek.

"Sierra." Tana's voice was weak, barely audible over the storm. "My name is Sierra."

"What? Tana, listen to me. Brynn's setting up a line. We need to get off this thing now."

Tana shook her head. "I saw my parents, Cal. This whole time, the spirits just wanted me to know the truth." She swallowed, trying to maintain her composure. "They wanted to give me some kind of closure after all these years." The thought was a flicker of warmth in her chest. This vision, horrifying as it was, was a gift from these beings who inhabited the mountain, these Taqriaqsuit who had cried for her parents' death when she could not. It meant her decades-long search for answers was finally over.

A lock of her hair fluttered in the wind, and Tana caught it between her fingers, the dark brown hue foreign to her eyes. Even in the dim lighting, she saw the hint of auburn in her tresses, the same color as young Sierra's braid beneath her helmet.

She released her hair, letting her hand drop to her chest, where all those violent flashes of rage and ecstasy had churned minutes ago. The hurricane surging inside her had calmed, but not to the dull emptiness she'd accepted as normal over the years. No, this was different. Her senses were sharper, her brain more focused, her heart full. It was as though she'd been trapped in a cloudy aquarium her whole life and was now being released into pristine, tropical waters.

Her family wasn't the only thing she'd left behind that terrible day on Torket. Everything that made her whole—her drive, her curiosity, even her physical appearance—had been abandoned on the summit, waiting for the day when she'd come and retrieve them. After two decades of safekeeping, the Taqriaqsuit had given her back the ability to truly live. "Cal, they knew who I was this whole time. They wanted to save me."

Calla's hand was like a vice on her arm, dragging her to her feet. Her voice was tinged with steel. "That's definitely not what they're doing. Come on, walk."

Tana yanked loose from Calla's grip. "You're not listening to me! They're on our side. All they wanted was to show me what happened." How could Calla be so obtuse? Everything made sense now: her parents' disappearance, her monotone personality, even the vivid flashes of emotions as she neared the summit. They had given her the bitter medicine she needed to finally move on with her life.

"They almost dragged Misty over the edge," Calla bellowed. "They snapped our safety line. They don't care about you. They're playing with us. Can't you feel it?"

High-pitched laughter, cold and vicious, rode in on the wind. It reached a crescendo around them, raising the hairs on Tana's neck. The blood drained from her face at the sudden realization: she'd heard that sound before.

Alone and in shock, sitting atop the Torket summit while her essence—her spirit—drained from her body, Tana was sure that the creatures had been mourning alongside her. The wind had carried their cries to her ears, what she'd assumed were melancholy wailings at the tragic loss of two visitors to their home. But they hadn't been crying, and she knew that now.

They were laughing.

"But..." Her mind buzzed with confusion. "They wanted me to get to the summit. They saved me from the avalanche."

Misty's voice cut across her thoughts. Her figure was barely visible through the falling snow. "We're ready! Grab her, and let's go!"

Tana stood, frozen, even as Calla gripped her hand and pulled. Why would the Taqriaqsuit want to lead her to this point? None of it made any sense.

Laughter swirled around her, hateful glee tightening like a noose. Their anger pulsed through her in waves. She felt it prodding through her memories, pushing her to relive them, to remember.

She saw her father's face, framed by his dark curls, the lines around his eyes softening in relief at seeing his daughter unharmed. And then a shadow falling over him, so fast she hadn't noticed it before. A flicker of darkness settled onto his ax.

A second later, the pick wrenched free, and her father was flung backward to his grisly fate.

Tana's heart dropped into her stomach. "It was you," she whispered. Her parents' horrific fall, the unraveling of her entire life, none of it was an accident.

Brynn rushed over to them, her helmet gone, her blond hair a tangled bird's nest around her head. "What's the holdup?" she yelled. "We need to get down! The barrier is thin up here. They can cross too easily. If we get lower, I think we'll be safe."

No sooner had the words left her mouth than the white around them coalesced, a pale figure bursting from the snow, slamming its weight into Brynn's side. She crashed to the ground, pawing at the snow for purchase as she was dragged into the whiteout.

Calla dropped Tana's hand and raced into the blinding snow, screaming for Brynn to keep making noise so she could find her. Misty darted past, a flash of red hair among the white, calling out for her sister.

Tana stood rooted to the spot, completely overwhelmed. Her feet itched to chase after Brynn, but the sight of her parents, the knowledge of their murder...it was all too much. The ropes tethering her to reality were frayed. She swore she felt them snapping. Each new revelation was one broken thread closer to a breakdown.

A flash of turquoise cut through the mist. Brynn was tossed like a rag doll, her cries dragging Tana from her stupor. She forced her feet to move, only managing a couple of steps in Brynn's direction before she was hurtled to the ground, her face mashed into the ice so forcefully that she could no longer breathe. She sucked in a mouthful of snow, arms flailing at her attacker. Hands gripped the collar of her jacket, the rough, frozen fingers grazing her neck. She was lifted from the ground and tossed skyward, landing hard on her side. The air departed her lungs in a painful whoosh, leaving her gasping for breath, snow leaking between her lips.

These creatures seemed born of snow and cloud, crystalizing into humanlike shapes just long enough to grab the women and slam them to the ground before dissolving back into snowy mist and cackling laughter.

They're playing with us, Tana realized, like a cat tormenting its prey before it feeds. They hadn't brought her here to deliver closure. The entire climb had been one final taunting of a traumatized woman before finishing the job they'd started two decades ago.

An enraged shriek cut through the air. Tana turned at Calla's voice to see her friend emerging from the whiteout, kicking and twisting like an animal in a trap. The snow swirled around her. One ghostly white hand latched to her dark hair. A face swam in the white cloud, its hollow eyes narrowed, and its mouth twisted into a snarl. It dragged Calla across the summit, her kicks passing right through the snow and leaving the creature unscathed.

A hand clamped down on Tana's wrist. She gasped as she was yanked backward, her arm popping with the force of the pull. The world swam around her as the pain reverberated up her arm and through her body. A colorless face loomed over her, waxing and waning with each gust, a leering grin on its corpselike visage.

She looked to where it was dragging her: the edge of the summit plateau. Tana clawed at the fingers grasping her wrist, but upon her touch, they dissolved, reappearing after her hand passed through. "Calla," she cried, only to be thrown to the ground with such force that her head bounced off the ice. She groaned as flashes of colored light danced behind her eyes. The cries of her teammates echoed around the summit. Quick snatches of their bright parkas flitted past her blurry vision.

She struggled to lift herself from the ice, and as the world stopped spinning, she saw the summit edge was mere inches away. She crawled backward on all fours, trying to put some distance between herself and the precipitous drop, but the wind blasted her back into submission, a cage forged by nature itself.

To her right, she could make out Misty and Brynn. Like her, they seemed trapped on the summit ledge, their ropes and climbing gear out of reach.

"I'm sorry," Brynn cried. The anguish in her voice was clear even over the surrounding chaos. "I'm so sorry for everything, Mist."

Misty ignored her, focusing instead on the specter who blocked her way, pleading to be spared, if only for the sake of her children. Misty's weak cries were a bludgeon to Tana's heart. Misty should have been in a hospital, warm and safe as she recovered from her withdrawal symptoms. Instead, she was trapped on a mountaintop, her relationship with her sister severed, and her sons at risk of growing up motherless. And auntless, she reminded herself. All because of her selfish, relentless need to reach the summit. The weight of her guilt was unbearable.

Calla was held closest to Tana, a writhing, swearing, flash of color as she kicked and clawed at the invisible barrier. Every time she made contact, a ghostly figure would emerge, knocking her back to the ground—and dangerously close to the drop-off.

"Calla, stop fighting it!"

Calla paused, her chest heaving. "I'm not giving up on us," she growled. "And don't you dare either."

Her words were a knife in Tana's chest. It was Tana who had picked this mountain. Tana, who had pushed them to the summit. Tana, who had led them into this trap. And now, it was Tana who was letting them die without a fight.

She nodded, and Calla turned back to her captor, slamming her weight against its unrelenting restraints.

Tana took a deep breath and struggled to her feet. She closed her eyes, trying to feel the tenuous thread of emotions that sometimes linked her to these beings. *Please*, she thought. *Please let us go. You took my family. What else could you want from me?*

A howl of wind cut through her jacket, and her eyes snapped open. Before her stood a pale figure, hideous and ghostlike, though still undeniably human. His body was clearer now, more fully formed. She could make out the faint outline of a fur-lined coat and a hunting knife dangling at his hip. Snow swirled around him in an angry, thrashing vortex. Tana felt the rage pulsing through him—could taste the bloodlust.

Words flowed from his lips, foreign to her ears, but the hate in their depths was clear. It poured out of him in a river, and Tana caught flashes in her mind of other climbers stumbling onto the peak, their technicolor snow coats a harsh contrast to the natural beauty of the mountain. With each climber's elated face, the pain in his words intensified, building to an inferno of anguish.

This close, his emotions flowed easily, and beneath the rage, Tana sensed something more than blind hate. A protectiveness and a fear. A crowd of raucous climbers filled her thoughts. Their climbing gear was carelessly strewn about the summit. Rocks that had sat atop the mountain for millennia were casually kicked over the side. Ear-piercing laughter shattered the natural quiet while two colorful candy wrappers blew across the ground. One climber lowered his trousers to squat in the snow and relieve himself.

Tana's eyes shot open. "You're afraid," she whispered, her voice trembling. "You're afraid we'll destroy Torket like we did the others." She looked out into the sea of clouds where Denali lay hidden from view, no doubt covered with the throngs of climbers this creature despised. She took a deep breath, trying to bury her panic and sound reasonable. "I know you're protecting Torket. But you don't have to kill us. I promise we'll go back and tell everyone to stay away. They'll listen to us," she lied.

She hesitated, then reached out, grasping his hand in her own, hoping to appeal to some shred of his humanity—if he had any at all. Her fingers curled around actual flesh, not air, for a split second. It was enough for Tana to feel the smallest shred of mercy flowing through him. It settled on Brynn before flitting to Misty, then Calla, and finally, herself. Indecision flickered through him.

He wrenched his hand out of her grip, his nostrils flaring at her gall, and swung his fist so quickly that all she saw was a flash of white. It crashed against her face, knocking her sideways. She crumpled to the ground, inches from the summit edge.

Calla slammed against her snowy prison. "Leave her alone," she screamed.

"Please," Tana pleaded. Her ears rang with the force of impact. "You don't need to do this." With trembling fingers, she touched the side of her face where his fist had made contact. The skin was hard, crusted over with frostbite. She craned her neck, glancing at the edge of the summit. Would they toss her over? Let her fall to an icy death like her parents? Stab her first and let her bleed out? She was too exhausted to cry, yet ached for the release of tears.

And yet, she'd felt the Taqriaqsuit's doubt. If she could only find the right words to say, could she turn his reluctance to kill into their saving grace? She closed her eyes, prodding at his emotions, watching him cycle between the four women. Their faces flashed in succession: Tana, Calla, Misty, Brynn. Her eyes snapped open.

"Only one of us," she said, her voice breathless. Of course. The time-honored tradition of keeping a witness alive to tell the tale was the reason she'd been allowed to escape while her parents perished. She'd either be killed or live to see her friends plummet over the edge. Now the tears did pour down her cheeks, the unfairness of the situation finally too much to bear. Decades of unresolved trauma had turned her into a muted wisp of a person. And now that she finally knew the truth, now that she could finally rebuild her life—she glanced at Calla—and maybe even find love, it was all going to be snatched away along with the lives of her friends.

"You took everything from me," she shouted, pushing herself to her feet. She turned to her friends, still trapped on the summit edge. Who would he save? Who would be the lucky one to survive and share their story? Would it be her? Forced to descend this cursed mountain alone once again. She couldn't bear to suffer through that journey one more time.

"Take me," she whispered, quashing her survival instinct. "Let them go, and I'll be your warning to the world."

The mountain guardian only glared at her in response.

She looked out to Misty and Brynn, trying to hold on to the joy they had given her. Misty's love and nurturing, Brynn's zest for all life had to offer. Then she turned to Calla, her heart dropping at her flushed face and bright eyes. She would've given anything to run to her, to hold her and confess her torrent of feelings, to get lost in those dark eyes and never resurface.

Instead, she raised a hand in farewell.

"Tana, what are you doing?"

Tana backed toward the precipice, her heels overhanging the edge.

"Tana, stop!"

She raised her gaze to her captor's, her newly-chocolate eyes meeting his pale, soulless glare. Her heart hammered against her chest, but her voice was steady.

"My life for theirs."

For a moment, nothing. Then those dead eyes flashed in acknowledgment, the only hint that he might honor her sacrifice. It was far from concrete, but it was her friends' only hope, and she clung to it.

She opened her arms, leaned backward, and let gravity take her.

For a moment, she seemed to float on her back, suspended in the white sky. She felt a pulse of shock, whether her own or the Taqriaqsuit's, she didn't know and no longer cared. Her body tipped, leaning backward so that the horizon swam into view. A break in the clouds gifted her with one last look at Denali. A final goodbye before it was once again shrouded in mist.

She was falling headfirst now, the ice steps and spires flashing past. This must have been her parent's final view, these beautiful blurs of white and blue. The ground, a patchwork of dark blue crevasses crisscrossing through the snow, rushed toward her. She fought every urge to close her eyes against the oncoming impact. She'd lost too much of her life already. She wasn't about to lose a second more, not when she only had a few precious drops left.

She thought of all those wasted days, lost in a half-existence and all that time struggling to find some sort of meaning, some sort of magic to life. She thought of her parents—all four of them, and the love they had given her. She thought of Brynn, Misty, and Calla and their immeasurable gift of friendship.

A roar rose up in her throat, escaping into the howling wind. She screamed for love, for despair. For the gifts in life she'd been given—all the more precious for their scarcity—and for how cruelly they were ripped from her. She cried out with all her might, her voice growing ragged as the ground approached.

Closer, closer...

Until she was swallowed by shadow.

Chapter Twenty-Eight

Strands of copper, blond, and black were undulating like kelp fronds in the tide. Clouding her vision, obscuring their owners' pale, strained faces. Two pitch-black orbs swam into view, shining like obsidian, their edges blurred as if painted with watercolors.

Someone was screaming. The timbre dulled to a waterlogged warble. Panicked, jittery movement all around her, shapes blending together before fading to twilight. She accepted the darkness—the void—with gratitude, letting herself slide into its warm embrace.

Pain. A jolt of agony yanked her back into consciousness. An unbearable pressure collapsed her lungs, cracking her bones like glass as these horrible smears of color pushed and pulled her into whatever position seemingly pleased them.

Pressure on her arm, her hand. Fingers threaded between her own, each movement setting off a ripple of agony. Those black orbs, now close enough to take shape as eyes, peering. Questioning. Another scream, this one cut short by a roar from above.

A flash of orange cleaved through the white, the thrum of machinery deafening as it descended. Expanding until all she saw was its gleaming tangerine hue.

Indistinct figures poured from its interior. Swarming, touching, grabbing. Faces flitted in and out of view, mouths barking unintelligible commands. Hands lifting and contorting what remained of her physical self, each jostling movement a new form of torment. Waves of pain lapped at her consciousness, staining her vision with dark patches.

A drop in her stomach, a sense of weightlessness, of flight. A sharp prick in her arm, and then blessed, blessed, darkness.

Tana's eyes cracked open. Above, an expanse of sea foam green spread in all directions. The hideous color jogged a memory, though it refused to fully take shape. Was she at her parents' place? No, that couldn't be right. She remembered Calla's tear-streaked face beneath the green, leaning over her as she went in and out of consciousness. "They saved you. They saved you. They saved you." A broken record permeating her fuzzy memories.

"Calla?" she croaked.

Like magic, the face of her best friend—or were they something more now?—materialized, lined with worry. She appeared to have aged ten years since they'd left the cabin.

"You're awake," Calla breathed. "Do you need food? Water? Should I get a nurse? They've had you so drugged up, I..."

"Cal." Tana struggled to lift her upper body, but the jolt of pain was agonizing. She settled for raising a hand instead, surprised to see the warm, tawny tone of her skin, not the deathly pale she remembered. "Where am I?"

"We're in Anchorage, at the hospital. Your parents are on their way up. They went berserk when they heard that you'd gone back to Torket. You didn't tell them you were climbing it?"

Tana groaned. The last thing she wanted right now was to see her parents. She could picture her mother haranguing the staff, fussing over every aspect of her recovery, her father fighting back tears. And now that she'd had a vision of her biological parents, how could she ever explain a thing like that to her mom and dad? They'd think she'd lost her mind. "How long 'til they get here?"

"They'll be in by tonight."

Tana sighed. "Any chance the nurses can drug me into a coma?"

At this, Calla slipped her hand into Tana's, their fingers threading together. The warmth of her touch spread up Tana's arm, settling in her chest and loosening the knot of anxiety.

"Trust me. I get it. But once they heard what happened, there was no way in hell they were staying in Seattle. They want to do anything they can to help you out. I'll try to keep them calm and out of your hair. I promise."

Tana nodded her resignation, grateful to have Calla as a buffer. She tried to look down at her prone body, but her neck refused to bend to her will. The most she could see were the tips of her toes forming their own set of double peaks. Denali and Torket in blanket form. "How bad is it?" she asked, dreading the answer. "Am I going to be able to walk?" Calla paused, her eyes darting to the floor, and fear flooded Tana's body. Every nerve ending tingled with it. "Cal?" Her voice came out an octave too high.

Calla pulled her gaze from the ground as though it were a lead weight. "You'll walk again," she said, and the steely surety in her voice was like sliding into a hot bath. "You'll hike, you'll climb, you'll dance. All of it. But not for a while." She paused. "It's bad. It's…it's so incredibly bad." Her voice wavered, and her eyes shone. She swiped a hand across her cheek, refusing to be deterred. "I promise you, I'm not going to leave your side until you're back to your old self." She choked out a laugh. "And honestly, probably not then either."

The news settled over Tana like a shroud. She wiggled the toes she could see, grateful that they were at least moving. She tried to rotate her ankle next, wincing as fire tore up her shinbone. "How am I even still alive?" she groaned. "I watched my parents fall from the summit. I couldn't have landed more than a few feet from where they did. Why didn't I die?" At Calla's silence, she asked, "You believe me, right? I swear to you, it was real. I actually saw them—"

"I believe you," Calla interrupted. "We watched a bunch of ghosts pour out of the sky and toss us around like cat toys. You seeing your dead parents is the least crazy part of all that. I was just thinking about the second you went over." Her eyes were unfocused, remembering. Her grip on Tana's hand grew almost painfully tight. "It was horrible. Like it was in slow motion but so fast and sudden at the same time. I didn't know what to do. I couldn't tell you if I was crying or screaming or sitting there in shock."

Her words were a splash of cold water. Tana had been so focused on trying to save her friends that she hadn't spared a second to consider what she was leaving behind as a parting gift: the same traumatic aftermath that had blighted her own life. "I was trying to save your life," she whispered.

"As soon as you jumped, they let us go," Calla said, Tana's words appearing not to have registered. "I remember that. They looked like snow drifts, chasing you over the edge. When I finally got down to where you'd fallen…fuck." She pulled her shirt sleeve over her wrist and used that to wipe her eyes. "I thought there was no way you'd be alive. Your bones, oh my God, twisted in every direction. Some poking out." A sob clawed its way from her throat, and her face disappeared from view. A moment later, she reappeared, eyes red and puffy.

"You want to know how you survived? The spirits saved you, Tana. There's no other way. I don't know what changed. Why they went from attacking us to chasing you down the cliff. All I know is if they hadn't, you wouldn't be here."

The memory of her final moment on the summit drifted back. Her promise to protect the mountains. Her final offering in exchange for her friends' lives, and the acknowledgment in their captor's eyes. Had the Taqriaqsuit—those guardians of Torket—been moved by her self-sacrifice? Perhaps by the allure of someone on this side of the barrier helping to protect the mountain? Had they let her land hard enough to serve as a mangled warning to future climbers? A living, breathing testament to their power, rather than one more set of corpses? She'd never know. Yet if Calla was right, and her survival had been ensured by their hands, she knew she'd spend the rest of her life finding a way to honor their agreement.

"Misty did what she could to stop the bleeding, but she was an absolute mess at that point."

"Oh my God, Misty and Brynn." She jerked upright, only to have a wall of plaster force her back down. Casts, she realized. *Every inch of me is in a cast.* When the wave of pain subsided, she groaned at her own selfishness. Not once since waking up had she thought of her two teammates. "Are they okay? Are they here?"

"Easy, easy." Calla stood and straightened the blanket on Tana's bed. "They're fine. Well, they're physically fine. Brynn's pretty shaken up. She'll bounce back. Misty..." She sighed, blowing a stray lock of hair from her forehead. "Misty has a lot going on. The withdrawal knocked her flat for a couple of days. I'm not convinced she didn't start taking more pills just to get back on her feet. As soon as she stopped puking long enough to speak, she told Brynn she never wants to see her again. She also wants to leave Todd, but with everything going on, the thought of getting a divorce lawyer sent her into a spiral. She's all over the place, kind of manic. She's been in here, checking on you and ordering the nurses around. Pretty sure they're relieved she had to fly out today."

Tana nodded. She would've loved to see Misty, if only to smile and pretend that her bones didn't feel like jagged shards of glass. But sliding back into a routine with her children was probably exactly what Misty needed at the moment.

"How long have I been here?"

"It's been three days, four if you count the helicopter rescue. They think it'll be at least another week here, maybe two. You've got another surgery scheduled tomorrow. And then you'll need to go somewhere to rest and work on physical therapy."

Calla bit her lip, her eyes dropping to the floor. Her fingers played over the hospital blanket as if they yearned to hold Tana's broken body and somehow put the pieces back together. Despite the jolt of pain with every movement, Tana found herself wishing for Calla to abandon caution, climb into bed beside her, and pull her into her arms.

Instead, Calla grasped her hand, her fingers playing over the frostbitten skin at Tana's wrists. The sensation sent a shiver up Tana's spine. "I thought, maybe, only if you wanted, you could...come live with me? I've got plenty of space. The therapists would have room to work. It's out in nature, so it'd be relaxing. I'm growing a ton of food. You wouldn't have to eat any of that processed crap." The words spilled out in a rush. "I mean, if you wanted to get back to Seattle, I get it. Your whole life is there. But..." Her eyes bored into Tana's, a fire alighting in their depths. "I've been a coward. I should've told you years ago how I felt. God, all the way back in college. And after seeing you like that, thinking you were gone forever, I don't want to waste another second."

She took a deep breath. "I love you, Tana. Always have. Will you please, please, stay in Alaska with me?"

"Cal?"

"Yeah?"

"C'mere." The space between them was unbearable, even for another moment. Tana tugged on her hand, pulling Calla close enough to see the new spray of frost burn on her cheeks. She raised her chin, breathing in the scent of this wonderful, powerful woman who could have her pick of anyone and had chosen her.

She leaned forward, her lips playing over Calla's, delighting in their softness, in how she seemed both delicate and indomitable, a beautiful dichotomy. Their lips pressed together, years of unspoken affection swelling like a flash flood between them. Tana lifted her hand to Calla's face, tracing the sharp line of her jaw, the curve of her cheek, the soft baby hairs at her temple. An ache of longing burned through her midsection. At the sound of Calla's contented sigh, Tana nearly melted into the bed. There was nothing she wanted more than to wake up to her every day.

Tana pulled back, a brilliant smile stretching across her face.

"I'd love to."

Epilogue

A sunny, yellow 4Runner pulled into the Wonder Lake parking lot, kicking up puffs of dust on the unpaved surface as it slid into a spot. The driver, a young woman with dark hair, sat for a moment, her warm brown eyes fixed on the two peaks in the distance: Denali and Torket.

The car door opened, and she stepped out, her feet unsteady in new hiking boots. She gripped the car for balance, then started toward the small ranger station, a slight limp in her step. A bell tinkled as she stepped through the door.

"Oh, hey there." A heavyset woman appeared from the back room, a flannel button-down hiding most of her National Park Service T-shirt. A name tag on the flannel informed visitors that she went by Pam. "You lookin' to hike today?"

The woman nodded.

"Here you go." Pam grabbed a sheet of paper from a stack on the counter and pushed it toward her. "Fill out all your details so we can find you if things don't go as planned." She chuckled. "Don't let that scare you. We haven't had a bad accident here in a long time."

The woman raised an eyebrow at this but grabbed a pen from the counter and dutifully scribbled down her itinerary.

"What's your name, hon?"

"Sierra." Sierra Tanaraq Walker. Even after nearly two years, it still felt strange to say it aloud.

"You got plenty of water, Sierra? Enough snacks to get you out and back? A jacket in case the weather turns?"

Sierra nodded again, trying not to smile at the woman's motherly earnestness. Day hikers were the most likely suspects to need rescues, and she certainly looked a far cry from her backpacking prime.

"Let me get you a trail map. Sorry, I forgot to grab a bunch this morning, so I'll have to Xerox the station's copy. One second, all right?" Pam retreated to the back room, leaving Sierra alone in the visitor's section.

Sierra turned, taking in all the little ranger station had to offer. Cans of Coke and Sprite were lined up in a small refrigerator for two dollars apiece. Rows of Snickers and Milky Way sat in their cardboard displays, hoping to tempt a weary hiker. A shelf of maps and climbing books stood against the back wall, most of their covers faded by time and casual page flipping. But one book caught her eye, its colors still bright. A bold, blue spine with a familiar name etched in silver.

Sierra pulled it from the shelf, her stomach twisting into a knot as she scanned the cover. Although the artwork was stylized, almost cartoonish, she immediately recognized the flat, snowy summit. Torket.

Snow and Shadow, the silver text read, with Brynn Lansing typed below.

Misty had called to tell her it was being published, cautiously asking if she was okay with their story going public—as if Brynn would have put aside her chance at success to appease Sierra. Apparently, the book had been dedicated to Misty, but her terse, "I guess that was nice of her," left Tana wondering if their frayed relationship would ever fully recover.

A week later, two signed copies arrived in the mail, a gift that Sierra tossed aside the moment she realized what was inside the colorful wrapping: their shared nightmare, compressed into three hundred hardbound pages. The avalanche. Wyatt. Her parents' deaths. The terror of nearly losing her friends. And that final plunge that shattered her body into a thousand pieces. It was awful enough to revisit every night in her dreams.

Calla pored through the chapters, assuring Tana that everyone was portrayed in a positive light and that certain traumatic details had been smoothed over. Like, say, a friend throwing themselves to certain death after learning about her parents' murder.

At her psychiatrist's urging, Sierra had picked the book up on multiple occasions, trying to force herself to relive the journey up Torket, but she was never able to read past the first few pages.

She flipped through it now, landing on one of the last chapters, her eyes grazing the text.

...no longer shadows, but now men of flesh and bone. Ice ax in hand, I charged into the fight, swinging with every ounce of my soul. The ax clanged off teeth and claws, their screams of pain and fury fueling my rage. I no longer cared if I lived or died. All that mattered was saving the lives of my friends and making sure my young nephews grew up with their mother.

Despite herself, Sierra smiled. Of course Brynn would turn herself into the hero. Every good story needed a plucky protagonist, and Brynn fit the bill to a T. She closed the book and read the list of accolades on the back. When she reached the final one, she couldn't help but laugh. "I'll be damned."

In crisp white text, it read: *It's rare to find such a thrilling debut, but Lansing hits all the right notes.* It was signed by Bill Bryson.

"Here you go, honey." Pam reemerged and placed the map on the counter. She spotted the book in Sierra's hands. "Oh! That's a great little read—very spooky. It's not often we get a book about Torket, so I had to get a copy for the station. Everyone always wants to talk about Denali, you know? If you're local, we loan out the books. I can let you borrow it for a week or two."

Sierra smiled. "Thanks, but I have a copy waiting for me at home. It's about time I read it."

The scent of spruce and damp earth washed over Sierra as she stepped onto the trail. Every nerve in her body thrummed with fear, urging her to hightail it back to the parking lot and retreat to Calla's cabin. Hiking had been prescribed by her physical therapist as a way to restrengthen the muscles after surgery, and this particular location had been a suggestion from her psychiatrist.

Well...the suggestion had actually been a little nearer to Torket, but this was as close as Sierra dared go. Even two years after her fall, the memories of those horrible creatures were unnervingly clear. How powerless she and her friends had been in their grasp.

While Calla had offered to hike with her, both for moral support and for safety, Sierra insisted she come alone. Venturing back into the Alaskan woods was terrifying, and it had taken her months to finally build up the courage. This short hike was the first step in proving to herself she was no longer going to cower to her past.

And besides, heading back home to Calla's cabin after a day in the woods had a nice ring to it. Color flushed in her cheeks at the thought of Calla's arms wrapped protectively around her, the two of them snuggled under the comforter.

Permanently moving to Alaska was a bright spot among the painful years of recovery. True to her word, Calla had never left her side, tending to all of Tana's needs in those first few agonizing months of healing. In addition to her homesteading duties, she cooked all of Tana's meals, assisted her through the monotony of daily hygiene, and encouraged her to stick with her physical therapy when motivation flagged—all the tasks typically reserved for a long-term spouse. Despite her anxiety, a small smile tugged at Tana's lips at the thought that maybe someday, they'd reach that milestone. As their months together had stretched into years, Tana realized she had no desire to ever return to her life in Seattle. For the first time, she truly felt like she was home.

A neon green candy wrapper blew across the trail, and she dropped to one knee to grab it, wincing at the sharp ache. Five surgeries had given her back the ability to walk, but she'd live with pain for the rest of her life. She crumpled the wrapper and slipped it into her pocket.

A child's laughter pulled her attention ahead, where a family was hiking toward her, a puppy bounding along behind them. A young girl picked flowers as she walked, tossing the blossoms so that their petals fluttered around her. Behind her, a small boy dropped his plastic baggie of Goldfish crackers, the breeze whisking it into the grasses before his parents even noticed.

The sight, light and innocent, could easily be considered an idyllic moment. Time together as a family on the trails, with those little scamps up to their childish mischief. But inside, Sierra seethed. Her vision swam with red. Her family had died for those silly, careless sins, and she'd nearly given her life to atone for them.

The puppy ran to the side of the trail, squatted, and defecated among the wildflowers. To Sierra's relief, the father fished a baggie from his pocket and scooped the mess, twisting the top shut. Maybe there was still hope after all.

They were now close enough to hear their chatter. "You're really going to carry that back?" his wife asked, her mouth twisted into a grimace.

With a shrug, he tossed the full bag into the woods with a casual flick of the wrist.

Sierra dropped her head in defeat. The cycle would never end. People would continue to flood the land, destroying the very beauty they sought. The draw of the mountains was too strong. The pull of wild, untouched nature was a remedy to the modern world.

She pushed herself to her feet as the family passed by, the young boy giving her a shy wave, his fingers stained orange from the Goldfish.

Despite herself, Sierra waved back. He was only a child, no more guilty of malice than she was at that same age. She started to turn back to the trail but stopped short, her heart catching in her throat. The polite smile melted from her lips. She scanned the edges of the trail in a panic. Where had that Goldfish bag blown off to? And the dog poop baggie? "Oh God, no."

The boy stared at her, puzzled at her change in demeanor.

"Honey, come on, don't dawdle." The mother grabbed his hand, tugging him down the trail. She looked over her shoulder at Sierra. Her eyes were narrowed in distrust at the distressed, limping stranger.

A flash of orange caught Tana's eye, and she stepped off the trail to grab the packet of neon crackers, her first step toward fulfilling the promise she'd made two years ago on the summit of Torket. And if her instincts were correct, protecting these children from the same fate that had befallen her own childhood.

Perhaps it had been only a trick of the light, a passing cloud, or a glare in her sunglasses. But she swore, for just a second, that the sunlight had dimmed, a flicker of darkness falling over the trail.

And this happy, unsuspecting family, a single drop in the flood of destruction, had been marked by shadow.

About the Author

Heather Werner is a novelist and adventure writer. Whether she's scaling the Seven Summits, bicycling across continents, or giving a world-record haircut on the slopes of Mount Everest, she loves to find the small, intimate stories woven into the journey. Heather is a contributing writer for *Weekend Sherpa* and *Trail Sisters*, and although she currently lives in sunny Silicon Valley, her heart will always belong to the woods of New England.

Keep in touch with Heather:

Instagram: www.instagram.com/heath.er.wer.ner
Facebook: www.facebook.com/HeatherLindseyWerner
X: www.X.com/HeatherLWerner

Note to Readers

Thank you for reading a book from Launch Point Press. We have made every effort to edit this book. However, typos do slip in. If you find an error in the text, please email publisher@launchpointpress.com so the issue can be corrected.

We appreciate you as a reader and want to ensure you enjoy the reading process. We would like you to consider posting a review on your preferred media sites and/or your blog or website.

For more information on upcoming releases, author interviews, contests, giveaways, and more, please sign up for our newsletter, visit us at www.launchpointpress.com, and "Like" us on Facebook: Launch Point Press.

Bright Blessings